THE BROKEN PRINCE

DIRTY BLOOD
BOOK 5

PENELOPE BARSETTI

HARTWICK PUBLISHING

Hartwick Publishing

The Broken Prince

Copyright © 2023 by Penelope Barsetti

All rights reserved.

No part of this book may be reproduced in any form or by any electronic or mechanical means, including information storage and retrieval systems, without written permission from the author, except for the use of brief quotations in a book review.

CONTENTS

1. Harlow — 1
2. Harlow — 9
3. Huntley — 31
4. Ian — 45
5. Huntley — 55
6. Harlow — 73
7. Aurelias — 83
8. Harlow — 95
9. Aurelias — 107
10. Harlow — 125
11. Huntley — 141
12. Ivory — 157
13. Harlow — 163
14. Aurelias — 185
15. Ivory — 197
16. Aurelias — 207
17. Ian — 219
18. Aurelias — 253
19. Harlow — 269
20. Ian — 315
21. Harlow — 339
22. Huntley — 349
23. Harlow — 359
24. Huntley — 379
25. Ian — 395
26. Aurelias — 419

ONE

HARLOW

I returned to my father's office, ready to make any other argument to free Aurelias. My father was scribbling across a sheet of parchment, writing so quickly that his handwriting was probably illegible. When it came to communication and diplomacy, he always half-assed it because it wasn't his thing. He dropped the quill back into the ink jar. "What is it, sweetheart?"

"Sweetheart?" I stood at the desk. "Last time we spoke, you dismissed me like a guard."

He rolled up the scroll and dropped it into the tube.

"Basically called me a brat."

He sealed the tube and left it on the desk. "When you have a child of your own, you'll be more sympathetic to my plight."

"What a great apology."

He got to his feet and regarded me. "I've released the vampire."

My hostility waned as the truth sank in.

"I've specified the terms of his release—and he knows the consequences if he breaks them."

I hadn't actually expected him to do it. "Mother's good…"

He walked around the desk and prepared to leave, ignoring me.

"Why are you mad at me?"

He stopped, the scroll still tucked in his big hand. He took a breath before he turned to look at me. "I'm not angry with you."

"You didn't apologize."

His eyes shifted away momentarily. "Because I'm ashamed…"

My eyes softened.

"I'm ashamed of the way I lost my temper. The way I treated you. I thought I learned from my parents' mistakes, but I've repeated them."

"Father, nobody's perfect."

"But as King of Delacroix, King of Kingdoms, and your father, I need to be perfect."

"Those are ridiculous standards."

He looked at the scroll in his hand. "Perhaps."

I moved into his chest and hugged him, showing my forgiveness in a way he would understand.

His arms circled me, and he rested his chin on my head, his big palm rubbing my back. After he pressed a kiss to my temple, he stepped away. "I understand you've vouched for the vampire, but be smart, Harlow. He could be playing a very long game."

"If he were really our enemy, there're a lot of other games he could have played. Better games…" I wouldn't have known he was a vampire unless he'd announced it, and he could have used me and made me fall hopelessly in love with him to get what he

"I want Pyre," Mother said instantly. "I don't want him sent on a scouting mission."

Father gave a subtle nod.

"I want Storm too," Mother said. "But I know he'll protect you."

He stared at her, his eyes possessing endless depth, and said nothing.

"You won't go on this scouting mission yourself, right?" Mother asked. "You'll send other riders?"

He was still quiet. "I'm not sure."

"Why would you go yourself?" she asked.

"If you want something done right, do it yourself," he said simply.

She continued to stare, and her fiery expression suggested she had more to say but couldn't say it in front of us.

Father pretended not to notice her rage. "If the vampire breaks any of my conditions—kill him."

It was déjà vu.

We escorted Father to the field to say goodbye. He would fly Storm to HeartHolme, where he would remain for the foreseeable future. He was enormous in his battle armor, a walking executioner, a fighter who would terrify the most seasoned soldier. I didn't realize how safe my father made me feel until he wasn't there anymore.

He grabbed Atticus by the shoulder and squeezed. "Watch your mother's back."

My brother gripped Father's shoulder in return and nodded. "Always."

He brought their heads together quickly before he kissed him on the forehead. He turned to me next. "You need to be prepared for war at a moment's notice. No more sundresses. Wear your uniform and armor—and always carry your blade."

I nodded.

His eyes were pained as he spoke, like it hurt him to say these words, to tell his daughter to be on her guard instead of vowing to protect her. "You should be safe here."

I had no purpose at the moment, so I went to my favorite bar for a drink. Instead of wearing my dresses in the summer heat, I did as my father asked and wore my uniform and armor whenever I was outside the castle, the outfit identical to the one my mother wore. It was black and ugly and uncomfortable so I didn't care for it, but I would honor my father's wishes.

I sat on the stool, and without saying a word, the barmaiden brought me an ale.

"You know me so well, girl." I raised my tankard and took a drink.

She winked then walked off to serve another customer.

I took a drink, feeling the depression on my shoulders, never having appreciated the simplicity of my life until it was no longer simple. As I sat there, I felt a stare, one that punctured my skin with the sharpness of a knife.

My eyes shifted to meet my admirer—a gorgeous man with dark hair and dark eyes, his hand resting on the glass of scotch he drank like water. He was across the room, and it seemed like he'd been there long before I walked inside.

He raised his glass to me and took a drink.

I did the same.

Then he grabbed his drink and stalked to a table in the corner, moving as far away from me as possible, completely out of my line of sight.

Because he wanted to avoid me.

Because my father threatened to kill him if he spoke to me.

But my father wasn't here…

I grabbed my drink and joined him at the table where he sat alone in the corner, a booth that was unoccupied because it was a quiet night in the village. It'd been a hot day, and people chose to go to bed early to beat the heat the next morning.

He was dressed in all black, vitality returned to his face now that he'd eaten and bathed. His short black hair was combed back slightly, and the scruff on his jawline looked a few days old. He relaxed in the chair, one hand snaked around his glass. His arms were exposed in his shirt, thick and corded, powerful once again now that he'd been properly fed. "Are you trying to get me killed?"

"My father left."

He stared, his confident eyes guarded.

"And he said you couldn't come anywhere near me, but he said nothing about my coming near you."

A soft smile moved on to his lips, but it was gone a second later. "Where's he gone?"

"HeartHolme. He's going to investigate the east."

"I wish him the best." He took a drink of his scotch then returned it to the table.

"I'm nervous." I felt a constant gnawing in my stomach, a fear that a letter would be sent from HeartHolme, notifying us that my father would never return. It would be stained with my grandmother's tears. "I've heard the stories. How my parents fought so hard against oppression and injustice. How they defeated armies ten times larger than theirs. It's a thrilling story when you already know the ending. But now this ending is unwritten…and it's not so thrilling anymore."

He hardly blinked as he looked at me, his stare hard and intense, riptides of emotion underneath that even stare. "Men are always weak, their temptations their undoing in the end. They contract syphilis from one of their whores and die a premature death. They send their soldiers to win their battles and grow fat on the throne, so once they're required to lift their swords to save their own necks, they're too weak to do so. But your father is a mighty king with only a single weakness."

"What's his one weakness?"

He cocked his head slightly. "You."

My heart tightened into a fist.

"Which is why the Teeth told me to take you. Your father should have taken me on his mission. I could be much more help scouting the east than sitting here drinking my boredom away, but his weakness clouds his judgment."

"You turned on the Teeth. You should be afraid of them."

He gave a slight shrug. "They violated the terms of the deal. I don't feel bad about it."

"But what if you need them in the future?"

"If your father kills them all, that's a moot point."

"Aren't they your cousins?"

"Cousins many, *many* times removed."

"Then isn't that a betrayal?"

He took another drink. "You know how it is with family…you always forgive and forget."

"But if your vampires come to fight for us, that's hard to forgive."

He gave another shrug. "My father won't have a choice if he wants me alive. And since I'm his favorite, he definitely wants me alive."

"Your father has a favorite? That's barbaric."

"And you think your father doesn't?" he asked with a half smile.

"He doesn't."

"Right…"

"He has different relationships with me and Atticus—"

"You're his favorite, baby."

He hadn't called me that in a long time, and the second I heard it, I thought of memories I should forget.

"And I don't blame him."

"Atticus is an honorable man."

"But he's forgettable. You're like a bonfire in the middle of the snow. You burn white-hot, melt everything around you, make the witches come out and dance until they're ashes..."

"Witches?"

"You don't have witches here?"

"I—I don't know."

He swirled his glass, his eyes down on his movements. "What brings you here?"

"Same as you—a drink."

"I'm sure they have the finest wine at the castle."

"I've always been more of an ale kinda girl."

He gave a slight nod. "I can see that."

"Are you...looking for someone?" I asked the question without really thinking about it, and I wanted to cringe as I heard myself say it, because it came out with such insecurity.

"No. You?"

"No."

He stared. Took a drink. Stared some more.

A warning sounded in my heart, a reminder that I really didn't know him. "The Originals are dangerous, aren't they?"

His eyes left my face and scanned the bar like he would see someone he recognized—even though everyone was a complete stranger. "You ask a lot of questions."

"You're welcome to ask me anything you want."

His eyes shifted back to me. "A human princess isn't nearly as interesting as a vampire prince."

"I'm a lot more interesting than you give me credit for."

His eyes came back to me, and that soft smile returned. "How so?"

"I'm a descendant of a long line of kings and healers. As a result, I heal remarkably fast, faster than any normal human. I'm much less likely to die from blood loss than a soldier three times my size."

His eyes narrowed slightly—like I'd just proved my point. "Is this common among humans?"

"I've never heard of it in someone else. It's something my father and mother both possess."

"Are they related?"

"Maybe very distantly."

"There's a woman in my lands who's immune to the sickness that's claimed the lives of so many. We were unable to determine the reason for a very long time, assumed it was part of her makeup, but then discovered the source. Perhaps there's an explanation for your abilities—but you haven't uncovered it just yet."

"Maybe," I said. "But I suspect we never will."

"What else?" he asked. "What else is interesting about you?"

"My father has trained me in the sword since I could walk. I think I would be a worthy opponent if we sparred."

He smiled with his eyes. "You've only seen a hint of my abilities."

"Then perhaps you can teach me."

Now, the smile reached his lips. "I'm certain your father would want me nowhere near you with a sword."

"Not if you're making me stronger."

"The abilities I possess can't be taught. They're innate and integral."

"Because you're a vampire?"

"Yes."

"Were you born a vampire?"

He paused as he considered his answer. "Vampires can only be sired with the blood of humans and the venom of snakes. I was turned at the age I am now—and have remained preserved as if I were frozen in ice."

It took me a while to digest all of that. "And you wanted to be a vampire to have these abilities?"

"Yes. But what I truly desired was immortality."

Again, I had to digest that. "That means…you live forever?"

He gave a slight nod.

"Then—then how old are you?"

"Very old."

"Like…? A hundred?"

His eyes laughed. "Times that by fifteen."

I did the math in my head. "You're fifteen hundred years old?"

"Yes."

Necrosis was immortal, and the Teeth had prolonged life. But I'd never heard of another species having those abilities. "That means you don't have a soul..."

He took a drink. "No."

"Does that bother you?"

"Not in the slightest. And I don't have a heart either—but that has nothing to do with my being a vampire."

The man I'd shared those passionate nights with was truly a stranger. A man who'd had so many lovers in his lifetime and that gave him the experience to be incredible in bed. That was why he was so smart, so agile, so resourceful—because he'd had many lifetimes to practice.

This was a being I'd never heard of, as strong as Necrosis, but better hidden. If he hadn't told me what he was, it would have taken a long time to figure it out, and only if we'd had an intimate relationship. If he'd decided he wanted to kill me on that journey, my will and determination wouldn't have been enough to spare me. It would be like a helpless worm fighting the beak of a bird.

"You don't need to be scared of me."

"I'm not." I took a drink of the ale.

"Because I would never hurt you." His eyes were serious now, the knowing smile and amused gaze gone. "I just want to make that clear...in case I haven't already."

He could anticipate moves in battle, and sometimes it felt as if he knew exactly what I was thinking. It seemed too ridiculous to entertain, but now I started to believe the impossible was possible. "Do vampires have other abilities?"

He shifted forward, both elbows on the table. "We adopt the abilities of the snake that sires us. The Kingsnake Vampires can see in the dark, the Cobra Vampires can feel heartbeats, The Diamondbacks have unparalleled reflexes."

"And the Originals?"

He stared, his hand covering the top of his glass, as if he was considering telling me. "I like you, Harlow. But that's not enough to make me share all my secrets."

I felt him sidestep me, keeping his cards close to his chest like this was a poker match. "It sounds like you don't trust me."

"Can I ever trust the woman I abducted from her family?"

"You're free, aren't you?"

"Free? If I were free, I would be on the first ship departing this forsaken land."

"Even though we're on the brink of war?"

"It's not my war. And I have my own war to worry about."

"What's it like…where you're from?"

"Looking to move?" he asked playfully. "You're either hot or cold in this place. Nothing in between."

"I appreciate both. In HeartHolme, it's nice to have a fire burning in the stone fireplace while sleeping under a pile of blankets, the frost kissing the glass, your fingers cold because you can't stop reading your book uninterrupted. But the heat of Delacroix is lovely too, the flowers in full bloom, the harvest ripe, the sky the most beautiful blue. One isn't better than the other. They're just different."

changed it irrevocably. "You're scared of my father?" It was hard to believe, that a man who was superior in most ways feared a man who wasn't even here.

"No." His tone was chilled, like the insult doused his arousal.

"Then why?" I demanded, annoyed I wouldn't get my way but also embarrassed that I'd basically thrown myself at him and was rejected.

He came back to me, his eyes hard, pressing me against the wall. "Because I'm leaving these shores once the first opportunity arises. My home is a world away, and once I leave, I'll never return." He stepped back slightly. "Not to mention I'm a predator…and you're prey."

My eyes shifted back and forth between his in confusion. "Do you think I expect us to get married? To live happily ever after in Delacroix once the war is over? To pop out some vampire babies?"

Now his hard gaze turned cold in anger.

"I just want to fuck, Aurelias."

He looked away, looking toward the main street that was dimly lit. The lights at the inn were bright, right across from the bar where visitors got drunk before walking back to their rooms.

"As you're the best I've ever had, I'd rather screw you than a lesser substitute."

He still wouldn't look at me.

I remained against the stone wall, my sword at my hip, the metal of my armor concealing my flesh from his touch. I wanted a room with a bed, somewhere I could remove everything and feel those big hands squeeze me so hard it hurt.

He finally turned back to me. "No."

"*No?*" I knew he wanted me, felt the intensity of his kiss, the hardness of his dick against my body. "Gods… you're married."

His head cocked slightly, and his body noticeably tightened. "No."

"Then you have a woman—"

"When I'm in a committed relationship, I don't stick my dick in other people."

I noticed he said *when* rather than *if*. So there had been someone in his life at some point in time.

"I just don't want you, Harlow." As if that concluded the conversation, he turned away.

I felt the sting of an invisible palm against my cheek, the jerk of an unexpected force. It was a brutal rejection, the kind that would destroy anyone's confidence. But I snapped back instantly. "Really? Your dick is just hard like that all the time?" I asked incredulously. "Like a sword in your pants?"

He continued to walk away.

"You just kiss a woman like that? Grab her ass?"

He didn't turn back.

"You're full of shit, Aurelias. And you're a fucking coward for not owning up to it."

THREE
HUNTLEY

Storm landed in HeartHolme, and I dropped down to the ground.

"Rest." I rubbed his snout. "We have a big journey ahead of us."

He rubbed his head into my palm, his big eyes locked on mine.

I patted him and walked away, entering through the open gates of HeartHolme and into the city. It was still daylight, and the sunshine was enough to place some heat on the skin despite the chilly temperatures.

I approached the castle, needing to speak to my mother and brother and make arrangements for the forthcoming journey. Ivory and I had been separated in wartime before, but I'd never been separated from my children since they were born, and that was a horrible feeling. I should stay to protect them, but I had to protect my kingdom as well.

I entered my mother's chambers and was greeted with a hard embrace. Every time she saw me, she wore her emotion on her sleeve, made me feel loved and missed, and it always made me feel guilty because she never extended that affection to Ian, despite everything he'd accomplished, despite the fact that he'd sacrificed just as much as I had.

"Son." She pulled away and gently patted my cheek. "Harlow is well?"

"She's unharmed. Thankfully."

"We have much to discuss."

"We do. Let's call for Ian."

Mother addressed one of her guards to fetch him. When he was gone, she addressed me. "Before he joins us...there've been some issues."

My eyes narrowed.

"He's removed General Macabre as the head of the army, but he won't tell me why. He's also threatened to behead him if he comes anywhere near the castle or the barracks. His weapons have been stripped, and so has his armor. If he's betrayed HeartHolme, I imagine Ian would share that treason with me, but the fact that he's kept it a secret tells me it's a personal vendetta."

"General Macabre has served HeartHolme well. Fought in the battle against Necrosis."

"I know."

"Humiliation is a poor way to repay his service."

She nodded in agreement.

A moment later, Ian walked inside, dressed in his uniform and his armor. "How's Harlow?" He moved up to me and gripped me with a bear hug.

I squeezed him and patted him on the back. "She's okay. Not a scratch."

"What happened? How did she return?"

"It's a long story," I said. "We have a lot to catch up on..."

"Do you believe him?" Ian asked.

A part of me loathed the fact that I'd left Harlow when that vampire lurked around, but my duty required me to be elsewhere. I also knew that my wife would handle things while I was away. "Yes."

"It's not a ploy?" Mother asked. "A way to earn your trust?"

"If that's all he wanted, he could have gone about it in a better way." The vampire destroyed my life and my sanity when he'd taken my daughter. I would never forgive him for that, for causing the greatest agony of my life, even if I did believe he'd returned her to protect her. "He and Harlow had an...intimate relationship, so I suspect he cares for her. She's incredible, so it's impossible not to care for her."

Ian darted his gaze away, uncomfortable by the thought.

It made me even more uncomfortable.

"He's written a letter requesting his kin to sail to our lands and fight in the war in exchange for his freedom. I suspect they'll come. If what he says is true, he's the Prince of the Originals, so he's important."

Ian turned back to me. "Are you sure you didn't just invite a superior race to our lands so they can enslave us?"

"I haven't sent the letter," I said. "I need to see what we're up against first."

"That's a good move," Mother said. "Don't invite them unless it's absolutely necessary."

"If you have to, you'll kill the vampire?" Ian asked.

I knew my emotion clouded my judgment when it came to my prisoner. He anticipated every move I made, so he could have easily sliced that dagger across my jugular when we were locked in that cell. He could have bitten my daughter. He could have handed her over to the Teeth without a second thought. I was unfairly prejudiced against him, but it was hard not to be. "No."

"Then what will you do with him?" Mother asked.

"Tell him to fight for us for his freedom," I said. "I have my men keeping eyes on him right now. Told him to stay away from my daughter or I'll kill him. Hope he heeds that warning—because I meant it."

Mother watched me for a while, pity in her eyes. "And what if Harlow doesn't want to be separated?"

I wouldn't look at her.

"Being mortal enemies wasn't enough to keep you and Ivory apart."

I wanted to shut down this conversation, wanted to lash out and silence her, but she was my mother, and once I'd become a parent, I respected her even more. "Harlow is too smart to settle for someone like that."

"Like what?" Mother asked. "Superior in strength and agility?"

"He feeds off human blood. He's a monster."

Ian stayed out of the conversation, remaining quiet.

"He hasn't tried to feed off her, so he's not a monster to her—"

"This conversation is over." I rose to my feet and started to pace the room, my heart beating so hard it was like a drum against my ribs. I looked out the window to the cold world beyond, knowing I had more important matters than a possible suitor for my daughter. "I'll travel to the east on Storm to see what I discover in those lands. I'll take another dragon rider with me."

"And that rider will be me," Ian said.

"One of us needs to stay behind."

"And as King of Kingdoms, it should be you." Ian rose from the chair and regarded me. "I'm the one who should be risking my life."

"There's no one I trust more than myself." I didn't want to rely on someone else's efforts. I didn't want someone to give up and turn back when the task proved difficult.

"And there's no one I trust to protect you more than myself," Ian said. "So, we both go—and Mother will lead in our stead."

"My mind is sharp as ever," Mother said. "But I can't wield a blade as I did before."

I stared at my brother, preferring him to stay behind. "I need you to look after my family if I don't return."

"No one is going to watch your back like I will," Ian said. "We do this together." He stared me down.

I stared back.

His gaze was confident, like no argument would change his mind.

I finally gave a nod.

He gave a nod in return.

"But that means General Macabre needs to be reinstated." The second I said that, Ian's eyes twitched, doing his best to focus on my stare when he wanted to dart them elsewhere. "Why have you stripped him of his title?"

Ian stared for a long time before he answered. "Because he's a shitty general. I've found a replacement."

"What was his treason?" Mother asked. "He's faithfully served HeartHolme his entire adult life—"

"As the steward of HeartHolme, I decide who serves in our armies and who leads our armies. I don't need to justify my decision to anyone." He looked at me. "Not even you. I will have the replacement in position shortly." He walked off. "Let's prepare for the journey. We'll leave at nightfall—so we can travel undetected through the skies."

I entered his bedchambers, a sprawling section of the castle fit for a king more than a steward. It used to house his entire family, but now it was just him, and the space felt too large for a single man.

He stepped into the foyer, already wearing his heavy armor even though we wouldn't leave for hours. "What is it, Huntley?"

"I want to talk about General Macabre now that Mother isn't in the room." Crucial details were being omitted from the conversation, and it was imperative I knew the truth. "Because if General Macabre really has betrayed HeartHolme, he'll be put to death—by me. So tell me, do we have a traitor in our midst?"

Ian released a sigh, a long and slow one.

"Ian—"

"No." He continued to avoid my gaze.

"Then why have you dismissed him with dishonor?"

Ian dropped his shoulders and stepped away, slowly pacing as he carried the weight of his armor like it was suddenly heavy. "A personal matter, and I'd prefer it if you didn't pry—"

"I have to pry when your actions are unkingly. Now tell me what he's done."

"*He's fucking my wife.*" He turned back to me, his features more hostile than they'd ever been. The skin of his face was tugged off his bone, and his eyes were vicious like sharp swords on the battlefield.

It was a dreadful revelation, and it took a moment for me to process the horror of it.

"He walked up to me in the pub—and told me to leave her alone." He came back toward me, his shoulders tense like he would pull out his sword and stab me through the gut. "*My own fucking wife.*" He threw down his arm and let out a yell that shook the stone foundation of the castle. "Motherfucker. He's lucky all I did was remove him from service. I should have fucking killed him."

"Ian..." I wished I had something better to say, but I was empty.

"That's why I demoted him. That's why I've stripped him of his armor and weapons. That's why he'll live with dishonor among his own people—one, for crossing me, and two, for bedding someone else's wife." He started to pace again, his arms swinging like he needed someone to punch.

"Were you bothering her?"

"What?" He jerked back toward me.

"Why did he tell you to leave her alone?"

His eyes narrowed viciously. "What's that supposed to mean?"

"Ian—"

"I wasn't bothering her."

"Ian, I want to respect your privacy, but now that this involves the general of HeartHolme, I need to get involved. Was his warning warranted?"

The light left his eyes as he listened to the implied assumption. "Wow..."

"Ian, I'm just trying to get the full picture before I make my decision—"

"I wasn't bothering her—"

"Ian—"

"I went to her place because I was upset about Harlow, and one thing led to another, and we spent the night together." He came at me fast, getting right in my face. "That is no one's business but ours, but now I've betrayed her privacy because you wouldn't leave it alone." He threw his arms down and walked away again.

I gave a quiet sigh. "Protecting her privacy and being a gentleman are two different things. She clearly told him what happened, and that was why he confronted you. So, she's not the one asking you to leave her alone...he is."

Ian turned back to me, his gaze furious. "Now you understand why I'll make his life miserable as long as I live. Fucker shouldn't have fucked with me."

I moved to one of the armchairs and sat down, watching my brother stare out the window, his breathing elevated with rage. "Ian. I admit General Macabre shouldn't have come at you like that, but we're on the precipice of war and can't afford to lose any soldiers."

He slowly turned to look at me.

"If we replace him with someone else, it may impact communication throughout the army, and we simply can't afford that right now."

He slowly walked toward me, like I was about to be his next victim. "Of all people, I expected you to stand with me on this."

I got to my feet and met his gaze. "And in times of peace, you know I would—"

"I can be the general of HeartHolme. The general follows the orders of the steward, so nothing has really changed—"

"The general is down on the front lines while you're orchestrating events through the aerial sight of your dragon or from castle walls. You know you can't be everywhere at once. I'm sorry that this has happened, but we can't let it affect—"

"What if the situations were reversed?" he snapped. "What if General Macabre were fucking your wife?" He was obviously deranged to even suggest the idea and provoke my wrath.

"You know my duty is to my Kingdoms and my people. That must take precedence over my personal vendettas. You've known me longer than anyone, and you know I always put everyone else before myself. We can't afford to lose the general right now, but once the war is over, you can inflict your wrath then."

He breathed hard as he stared at me, like he might hit me in the head with the hilt of his sword.

"Have you spoken to Avice about this?"

His jaw clenched. "No."

"I think she deserves your wrath more than he does. In the eyes of the gods, you're still paired for eternity—"

"And she'll remind me how I betrayed those vows when I fucked someone else—"

"Then you're even," I said. "If she bedded you, there's hope. Forget General Macabre, and get your wife back."

"Would you forget the man screwing your wife?" he asked coldly.

"Don't forget someone else screwed her husband."

His eyes immediately narrowed.

"Imagine the rage she felt toward this nameless woman. The rage you feel right now. Focus on getting your wife back and nothing else."

FOUR
IAN

I'd thought I was broken when my wife left me, but now I was broken into even more pieces. I sat with Huntley at the table, looking at the details of a map created long ago with little information.

"We travel here." Huntley dragged his finger down the map. "We follow the river through the mountains. That way, we have it for reference on our return journey."

I stared at the parchment but didn't listen.

"Ian."

My eyes flicked up.

"Are you sure you can do this? Because I'm not about to risk my life with someone who can't focus."

I pulled back and straightened in the chair before I gave a nod. "I can do this."

"You're sure?" Huntley pierced my eyes with his. "Because our lives are on the line here."

I held his gaze, feeling inferior to my perfect brother, as usual. He always kept his strength, no matter the situation, even when his own daughter was taken. Someone else bedded my wife…and I lost my shit. "I can do this."

The guard stepped into the room. "Steward Ian, Avice wishes to speak with you."

My heart dropped, did a somersault, squeezed in pain…everything. My eyes shifted to Huntley.

Huntley gave a nod before he silently departed my chambers.

Fuck, I was nervous. She'd never come to me before—only the other way around. I fantasized about her asking me to take her back, to work on our marriage, but I knew she had a different agenda.

She walked in a moment later, wearing a long-sleeved dark blue dress with her dark hair secured in a tight braid. With a strong posture and a slender neck, she looked like a fucking goddess. Her eyes were lit with the flames of her soul, and when she walked up to me, I couldn't focus on anything else.

I rose to my feet to meet her, butterflies the size of dragons in my chest.

"Ian...I'm so sorry."

This conversation was already starting off a lot better than I'd expected.

"I never meant for you to find out like that."

I felt like shit again.

"Joseph never should have approached you."

"Approached me?" I asked incredulously. "He obviously told you a very different story from what actually happened."

Her hands came together at her stomach, like they always did when she was nervous.

"He threatened me to stay away from you—*my own wife*. The general of HeartHolme ordered me, steward of HeartHolme and second in line to the throne of the Kingdoms, to stay away from my own fucking wife. Should have beheaded him."

"When I told him what happened between us...he was upset."

I felt no sympathy.

"And he did something he shouldn't have done."

And it was done, and it couldn't be undone.

"But Ian, you can't strip him of his title."

"I can't?" I asked coldly. "Because I fucking did, Avice. Maybe he shouldn't have come at the damn steward of HeartHolme, brother of the King of Kingdoms. He can be replaced, but my blood and lineage can never be."

"I don't believe Huntley would support this—"

"Well, he's here, and he supports it just fine."

Her eyes flashed in disappointment. "Ian..."

Despite my fury and my hurt, I couldn't help but notice how damn beautiful she was.

"This is all my fault. I should have told you, but I didn't want to hurt you."

"This isn't your fault, and you shouldn't take responsibility for another man's stupidity. You're better than that, Avice. Macabre dug his grave—and now he can lie in it."

"You've never made a mistake, Ian? He acted rashly—"

"Are you kidding me right now?" I snapped. "I made a mistake. I acted rashly. Where's my sympathy? Where's my forgiveness?"

She stepped back, her eyes averted. "Not the same thing—"

"I found out my wife isn't just fucking someone, but she has a relationship with someone, in the worst possible way. That's worse if you ask me."

She turned away, clearly overwhelmed by my ferocity. "Ian—"

"How long has this been going on?"

She folded her arms over her chest.

"Avice."

"I don't want to talk about this—"

"Too bad." I walked up to her again. "Answer me."

"I—I don't know. A month…"

"And how did it happen?"

She still avoided my gaze. "What does it matter?"

"It matters because if the general moved in on the steward's wife, I have every right to behead him—"

"*Ian.*" Now her eyes were on me again.

"I'll fucking do it."

She stepped away.

I grabbed her arm and forced her back to me. "Avice—"

"Please don't do this to him—for me."

My fingers left her skin as I forced my hand to my side.

"Please…"

"You shouldn't have to right his wrongs, Avice."

"And he shouldn't lose his job for this."

"He can work in the fields or shovel manure—"

"Ian."

"The fact that I haven't killed him or exiled him from HeartHolme is enough mercy. You should be thanking me right now."

Her small hand covered her face, hid her little nose from view. She inhaled a deep breath, playing a game she couldn't win. "Ian...please." She looked up at me with those pleading eyes, eyes I used to stare into when we made love every night.

It tugged on my heartstrings, as always. "I'll return his title—"

"Thank you—"

"With two conditions."

Now her eyes were guarded once more.

"First, he must kneel and apologize."

Uncertainty flashed across her eyes, like she knew that would be a hard sell.

"And second, you end your relationship and work on our marriage with me."

"You can't be serious—"

"I'm dead serious, Avice."

"Our situation shouldn't have compromised his position in the first place—"

"And he shouldn't have fucked with me, Avice. He may be a general, but your husband is the fucking crown." I felt my voice rise again, felt the anger shake my limbs that she preferred someone of lesser title over the man who would be king if Huntley fell.

"I want to speak to Huntley."

I knew my brother's stance on the matter, but I knew his loyalty to me was stronger. "Guard, bring King Rolfe to my chambers."

He disappeared, and a moment later, Huntley entered, his eyes shifting back and forth between the two of us, trying to ascertain his role in this tense situation.

Avice stepped forward. "I demand you return General Macabre his title. Our situation shouldn't impact the position he's earned with dedication and sacrifice. Ian refuses to grant this request."

Huntley's eyes shifted to mine.

I stared at my brother hard, imploring him.

After a long stare, Huntley looked at Avice again.

"Ian says he'll only do as I ask if General Macabre apologizes—"

"That's something he should do, regardless," Huntley said. "Because his actions were dishonorable."

Avice flinched, not used to Huntley treating her like a peasant rather than a family member. "And he said I have to end my relationship with him and work on our marriage. But that's barbaric."

Huntley's eyes shifted to me again.

I inhaled a deep breath and begged with my eyes. Huntley was about justice and fairness, honesty and truth, about leading with integrity even when no one was watching. He'd inherited his sense of honor from our father, who ruled his people with the same moral compass. To agree to this was against everything Huntley stood for.

But family was more important than anything, even his honor…at least I hoped.

His stare was subtly angry, pissed off that I'd put him in this situation.

I gave him a slight nod and mouthed, "Please."

He lowered his gaze back to Avice. "General Macabre was barbaric when he spoke to Steward Rolfe with such disrespect, when he gloated about his relationship with you, a married woman, Stewardess Rolfe. It's an insult to the army of HeartHolme to have someone with such questionable character lead. If General Macabre wants his position reinstated, you must adhere to these terms."

Avice stepped away, clearly in shock that Huntley had issued such a ruthless ruling. Then she looked at me, as if she expected me to be surprised too. When neither of us spoke, she walked off and departed the bedchambers.

Huntley stared me down for minutes, waiting until he had complete certainty that she had left the castle. He stepped toward me, his eyes showing all the anger he didn't need to state verbally.

"Thank you."

"I betrayed my integrity for you."

"I know—"

"Get your wife back, Ian. And don't fuck it up this time."

FIVE
HUNTLEY

Elora finished securing the armor to the dragons, midnight black to blend into the darkness. "They have a matte finish, so they won't reflect the moonlight and give away your position."

"Thank you." I admired Storm in his black armor, the metal fitting him properly now that Elora had accommodated his bigger size. Ian would ride Cannon, a dragon that was deep purple, a dark color. He was a suitable replacement for Pyre, whom I had sent to Delacroix to protect my family and the Kingdoms. *Are you sure you want to do this?*

Storm turned his head to regard me with his large eyes. ***I'm the only dragon I trust to protect you.***

My hand rested on his cheek. *We'll protect each other*.

Ian joined us, dressed fully in his battle armor, his broadsword and bow and arrows across his back, his daggers on his belt. He donned his helmet when he came closer, the black plate protecting his entire head, except his eyes.

I walked up to him. "What did Avice say?"

"We haven't spoken."

I'd expected her to submit to the demands immediately, but she must have decided to discuss it with Macabre. "Can you do this?"

"Yes."

"This is life and death—"

"She's gone from my mind, Huntley." He gripped me by the arm. "We need to discover the threat to the east to protect our families and our people. I'm with you." After a hard stare, he released me.

That was enough to convince me.

Mother approached, the worry hidden from her features with the exception of her eyes. Like all mothers, she feared for the safety of her sons, even if one was a king and one was a steward, even if they were accompanied by dragons. "A true king serves his people, watches the border as they sleep in their warm beds, worries for their well-being as if they were his own children. You've done that—and your father would be proud."

"Thank you, Mother."

"Please return—both of you. No mother should ever outlive her sons."

"We will."

She embraced me with a warm hug before she did the same with Ian. "I love you both."

"We love you too," Ian said as he pulled away.

I moved to Elora. "Thank you for protecting our dragons."

"I did it to protect you." She hugged me before she released me, hugging Ian next.

We climbed onto the dragons, looked at one another, and then took off for the skies.

We flew close together above the clouds, knowing it would take several hours before we crossed the mountain range, and it was best not to expose our position to anyone down below. It was significantly colder above the cloud bank, all the heat from the earth trapped underneath.

The stars above were bright, so bright the light would have reflected off the armor of the dragons had Elora not given it a matte finish. It was so quiet and peaceful up here, only the sound of the dragons' flapping wings audible. It was easy to get lost in thought, to think about my family at home, to worry for them when I should be worried for myself right now.

I looked at my brother. "Let's descend."

He nodded in agreement, and the dragons dipped below the cloud bank, expecting to see nothing but darkness.

But we saw fire. Lots of fire.

"What is that?" Ian spoke loud enough for me to hear.

It was a ring of fire, though it was hard to gauge the size from this distance. It had to be enormous...half the size of HeartHolme. The center was black, but the ring of fire around it burned with the flames of a forge.

I stared, unsure what to make of it.

Ian turned to me. "What the fuck are we looking at?"

"I—I don't know." But whatever it was, it was bad. "We should land and wait until morning. It's impossible to discern details right now."

Ian stared at the ring of fire before he looked at me again. "We need to be careful, Huntley."

"I know."

We guided our dragons down, slowly approaching the earth where there was nothing but darkness. It wasn't until we came closer to the earth that we realized it was covered with snow. Starlight reflected off the white powder, and we were finally able to make out the landscape.

We remained quiet as we sat on our dragons, listening for any sounds, a snapping twig. I looked around, seeing trees in the distance, the mountains behind us. I waited, anticipating an attack even though I didn't detect one.

We stayed that way for nearly an hour, listening and waiting.

It seemed the coast was clear.

Ian spoke. "We'll have to travel on foot in daylight. Keep a low profile."

I nodded in agreement. "I can take the first watch."

"As if I could sleep right now…" He looked into the darkness even though there was nothing to see. "I have a bad feeling about this."

"Yes, I have the same feeling."

At dawn, we moved through the wild landscape, through the thick snow as we headed farther east away from the mountains. It was all trees and brush, like the tundra at the bottom of the cliffs, but with fewer pines.

We spent the day traveling, looking for signs of humans or trouble. We hardly said a word to each other, never left our dragons unless it was to relieve ourselves, and ate from our packs instead of hunting for game.

At the end of the daylight, we stopped in a field. The darkness descended, and we spotted fire.

"You see that over there?" Ian pointed far into the distance.

"Torches. A lot of them."

"We didn't see that the other night."

"Maybe the ring of fire was so bright, it masked everything else."

"We're getting close. The dragons may be too visible and too loud."

"I agree." Their size alone was noticeable, even at great distances.

"We'll need to leave the dragons behind and proceed on foot."

No.

I don't like it either.

I'm supposed to protect you.

You owe me nothing, Storm.

But I promised your mate I would guard you with my life.

Now I understood why he felt so obligated to look after me. *There's nothing I can do. I have to leave you behind. I can call for you if I need you.* "We'll call for them if we need a quick getaway."

"I'd prefer not to get caught."

"Perhaps I should go and you stay here alone."

"Forget it, Huntley. We do this together."

"Then we should move under the cover of darkness." I hadn't slept in a day, but the tension was so high I didn't feel an ounce of fatigue. "Take advantage of the poor visibility. Find a good position before morning."

Ian nodded in agreement. "Let's do it."

We hopped off our dragons and kept them hidden behind a dense group of pines then made our way on foot, moving through the snow at a much slower speed than we could traverse with our dragons.

Slowly, the torchlight became brighter and brighter as the leagues between us diminished. Once we were able to make out a stone structure, we kneeled behind brush and examined the fortress.

Guards were positioned along the wall, fully covered in armor, including their faces. There were archers as well, carrying crossbows instead of traditional bows. A black gate surrounded the territory, hiding our view of whatever they were guarding.

Ian was quiet beside me, and together, we both watched, the night fading and turning the sky a dark blue.

"The guards will switch at the end of the shift," Ian said. "That's when we make our move."

We had no idea if the guard change happened at daylight, but that was how we did it in the Kingdoms and HeartHolme. The day shift and the night shift. "Make our move to what?" I'd stared at the fortress a long time, and there was no indication of how to scale the wall without being caught.

"The fence is damaged there." Ian pointed. "You can see the soot now that daylight is coming. Looks like someone sent a volley of fire arrows against it at one point. Or something unleashed fire..."

"Like a dragon?"

"Maybe."

I stared at the weakened part of the wall, and once we got closer, we would be able to determine whether our blades could hack away the brittle pieces.

"They're rotating."

I looked up, seeing a surge in the number of guards, all chatting with one another. "Go."

We crossed the open area at a run, sprinting while no one kept watch at the most crucial time. We hit the gate and then withdrew our daggers to start cutting.

Ian sawed off a piece with ease. "It's badly damaged."

I stabbed my dagger inside and started to chip at the pieces.

Ian grabbed my wrist and steadied me.

I stilled, my eyes on him.

He nodded upward.

My gaze lifted, seeing the archer walking directly over us, oblivious to us beneath.

We went still and quiet and waited for him to pass before we started to carve at the warped wood again. We eventually made a hole big enough for us to crawl through, and then we were inside the fence, which was hollow. We could both stand fully upright.

Ian looked around and tested the beams with his hands. "This is cheap…"

"Come on." I took the lead, following the wall for several minutes until it ended. "It must connect to a mountain or rocks here."

"Should we break out into the other side?"

"That's the only way we'll learn anything." We took out our daggers again and started to carve through the wood, breaking the pieces as minimally as possible, trying to stay quiet because the sun was rising, and people would be stirring soon.

Once we made a big enough hole, we looked through to see the lands the gate sought to protect. Torches illuminated small huts that looked as if they were made out of grass and mud. There were pits everywhere, like they dug for minerals or stones in the dirt.

"It's nearly dawn."

"Let's wait here until nightfall."

Ian dropped his pack and took a seat, pulling out his canteen to have a drink.

I continued to stare into the unknown world, unsure what we were about to see once the sun came up. We sat there for about an hour until it was fully morning, and then people started to emerge from the small huts, clothed in the same attire, torn shirts and trousers. Silently, they all got to work in the pits.

Fully armored guards appeared and watched them silently, wearing armor unlike any I'd ever seen before. It was bright red, the plates covering every part of their body, even their shins. Their faces were concealed too, their mouths covered by the helmet, only an opening for their eyes so they could see. But I could not make out any eyes. The inside of the helmet was too dark.

"The ones in the pit are humans, but I'm not sure about these guys."

"They're tall."

"Really tall..."

One guard stood over each pit, looking into the depths without moving, not shifting their weight or fidgeting. They were as rigid as a plank of wood.

"The humans are prisoners to these guys," Ian said. "Whatever they are."

"What are they digging for?"

"Looks like we'll have to ask."

At nightfall, the prisoners went into their mud huts after a hard day's work, while the guards patrolled down the aisles, swords in their belts, crossbows across their backs. There were only a few of them, so Ian and I could take them out if it was absolutely necessary.

"I don't think this is a state or a village," Ian said. "I think it's just a prisoner's camp."

"I don't see anything else either."

"Let's go." Ian removed the piece of wood we'd used to block the hole and crawled out onto the grass.

I followed him.

The guard closest to us was headed the other way, so we moved to the first hut, a building so low that no one could stand upright inside it. It was more of an outdoor house for a dog than accommodations for a human.

It also didn't have a door, so we were able to poke our heads inside.

Everyone was side by side on the floor, sleeping shoulder to shoulder, in the same clothes they wore when they worked all day, caked in dried mud that had been there for who knew how long.

"You talk to them," I whispered. "I'll keep guard."

"You're better with words."

"But you're better with people. I usually scare them." I remained at the entrance, keeping an eye on the guard that was far in the distance.

Ian crawled inside and shook one man by the leg.

He woke up with a jerk and opened his mouth to scream.

"Shh!" Ian stifled the sound with his palm and forced him to quiet. "Make a sound, and I'll slit your throat."

I rolled my eyes because that was not the way to go about it.

Ian gently pulled his hand away.

The others were awake, backs against the wall, trying to get away from Ian as much as possible.

"I just have a few questions," he said. "Can you help me?"

"Help you?" the man whispered. "If the man catches me speaking to you, he'll kill me and everyone else—"

"Then tell me what I want to know quickly, and I'll disappear."

The man remained quiet, his eyes fearful.

Ian reached into his pocket and withdrew some dried meat. "This is yours if you talk."

The man's eyes darted down, and he must have been starving if a couple pieces of meat were that appetizing.

"What is this place?" Ian asked. "And be quick about it."

"A labor camp," he whispered.

"What are you digging for in the pits?"

"Crystals."

"Why?"

He shook his head. "We don't know why. We don't get to ask why."

"What are you from?"

"Palladium. It was our kingdom for generations...until it was destroyed in the great battle. All free men have since been enslaved. Some of us are in labor camps. Some of us serve the new lord. And others have gone rogue."

"Who is the new lord?"

"Typhon."

"Where is Typhon from?"

Now he turned quiet.

"Where is he from?" Ian repeated.

"Ring—ring of fire."

I glanced at the guard to make sure he was still elsewhere, but then turned back to the prisoner, unsure if I heard him correctly.

"What?" Ian asked, as confused as I was.

"The ring of fire," the man whispered. "Once it appeared, it never went away."

"What is the ring of fire?" Ian asked.

"No one knows."

"Have you seen Typhon in the flesh?"

He shook his head.

"Have you seen others like him?"

He nodded, his eyes down.

"He's not human?"

"No..."

"What is he?"

"A-a monster."

"What kind of monster? Does he have rows of teeth?" I asked. "Does he unhinge his jaw and push his teeth outward?"

Too frightened to even speak, he kept his eyes on the floor.

"Please... I need to know."

"He doesn't have lots of teeth..."

"Then tell me what they're like."

He was quiet for a long time, the other prisoners staring from their positions against the walls of the hut. His eyes finally lifted. "He's made of fire."

I could feel my arms prickle with bumps.

Ian hesitated, like he felt the same disturbance. "Made of fire?"

"His veins are red, and he smolders like hot embers," he whispered, as if one of the guards would overhear.

"A single touch…can melt the flesh off your bones. They're not human, they're not beast, they're…demons."

Ian stilled as he stared at the man. Even his breaths stopped.

I forgot to keep track of the guard around the camp, too absorbed in the horrible revelation we'd just uncovered. My breathing stopped too, because as a man who didn't scare easily…I was petrified.

Ian slowly turned to look at me.

Our eyes locked, and an entire conversation passed between us.

We needed to hurry back to HeartHolme…and send that letter.

SIX
HARLOW

I was dead asleep in my comfy bed when I felt the ground shake.

I jolted upright, and my eyes snapped open, my mind fully awake once it perceived danger. I gripped the edge of the bed as I breathed hard, the adrenaline flooding my blood instantaneous. I waited for it to repeat, but minutes passed, and nothing happened.

Did I dream it?

My breathing slowed as I moved to the edge of the bed, my feet touching the thick rug that was soft against my soles. My drapes were closed, but the morning sunlight still peeked through and stretched across the floor. The sound of singing birds was faint in the distance.

It seemed like it had never happened.

I moved to the windows and opened the curtains, expecting to see something besides the village and the fields ripe with berries and summer squash. But the grass was green, it was beautiful, and the world looked exactly the same.

But my heart hadn't slowed, like it still expected danger.

I continued to breathe. Continued to stare. But the warning in my heart wouldn't fade.

As my father had asked, I donned my uniform and armor, piecing together all the heavy plates to protect my arms and shoulders. I told myself if it wasn't a dream, then it was an earthquake, the very reason the cliffs had formed in the first place, but I continued to don my clothing in a rush.

I grabbed my weapons and departed my bedroom, noticing that the guards who were supposed to be positioned in the hallway weren't stationed where they should be. My throat was dry as I swallowed, and I headed down the hallway with my hand resting on the hilt of my sword—something I'd never done before.

The first thing I wanted to do was run to my father's study, but then I remembered he wasn't there.

I jogged down the hallway, took the stairs in a rush, and then made it to the entryway of the castle—which was also deserted. "Mother?" I raised my voice and felt it echo back at me.

I headed out the double doors and found her speaking with General Henry. She was dressed in her armor, and so was he. "Mother?" I moved right into their conversation. "What was that?"

She ignored me. "It was probably just an earthquake, but the fact that King Rolfe isn't here is too much of a coincidence. Prepare for war. Prepare the cannons. Prepare the archers. Prepare for everything."

General Henry nodded before he took off to fulfill his duty.

Mother turned on me.

"What's going on—"

"I need you to send letters to the other kingdoms. Call for aid." She said it so calmly, but her face was strained like a nightmare swirled inside her.

I remained rooted to the spot, paralyzed.

"Harlow, can you do that?"

"Yes—yes."

Her eyes softened as she looked at me. "It was probably just an earthquake, but I prefer to be paranoid like your father. Please send those letters immediately. Then I want you to take Pyre into the sky and keep a lookout."

"I'm not leaving you—"

"You aren't. You're providing aerial support."

"Pyre can do that on his own."

"Harlow—"

"No." I walked off and headed back into the castle to do as she asked, but then the ground shook again and I stumbled forward, almost cracking my cheekbone against the stone. Once I caught myself, I stayed still, the world vibrating so much that I couldn't stand up, no matter how hard I tried. I looked up at the castle above me—hoping that it wouldn't topple over on me.

The shaking finally stopped.

"Harlow." Mother was on top of me, pulling me to my feet. "Are you alright?"

"I'm fine." I straightened, still feeling slightly dizzy. "But I don't think that was an earthquake..."

The look on my mother's face said it all.

My heart dropped like a stone. "I'll send a letter to Father first—"

"He can't help us right now. We need to figure this out on our own."

"But they can send the dragons."

Mother gave a nod. "You're right."

"Queen Rolfe!" A guard ran up the hill. "They've broken through the gate. We can't stop them."

"Fuck. Who's *they*?"

She digested this information in a second of silence before she pulled her blade from the scabbard. "Take Pyre. Fly to HeartHolme and get the dragons."

"I'm not leaving you here, and neither will Pyre."

"He's on his way to you now."

"He needs to fight! Not flee—"

"Harlow."

We both turned when we heard the sound of men screaming…grown-ass men. A guard went flying up the hill, like he was lighter than a pebble. Footsteps were audible and sounded like a stampede, and then they came into view… Men…that didn't quite look like men. Their arms were exposed instead of covered in armor… and their veins glowed like liquid fire burned in their veins. They were slightly taller than most men, even taller than my father.

"What…what are they?" I pulled out my own blade, even though I had no chance to wield it against these opponents.

Her hand went to my shoulder without looking at me. "Run." She gave me a hard shove, pushing me harder than she ever had, like she hated me. Her guards surrounded her, taking their positions to protect their queen.

I couldn't run. All I could do was stare in sheer terror.

The one in the lead halted when he spotted my mother. The bones in his face were different from ours. They were much harder, much more square, like he had more bones than the average being. His skin was dark, the color of ash, and his eyes were dark but bright at the same time. He sneered as he looked at her

—like she'd been the object of this pursuit. "Queen Rolfe, I wish to have a word with your husband." His voice was deep, so deep it didn't sound human.

My mother said nothing.

I breathed so hard I was on the verge of blacking out. My father had trained me against men his size, but I had no chance against monsters like this. There was no outcome in which we survived this, in which my mother and I walked away from this alive.

She gripped her sword and took her defensive stance—as if she intended to fight him.

"No..."

My mother conjured courage out of thin air, faced monsters more terrifying than Necrosis with a spine stronger than the steel in her blade. "Looks like you'll have to deal with me instead."

The smile the monster wore widened, and his cheeks hollowed even more. He was surrounded by five of his own men, all far more powerful than any soldier in our military. Even if it were twenty to one, it was unlikely we would win. "With pleasure."

They all moved instantaneously, the monsters launching themselves at the guards already too terrified to hold their blades. It was a slaughter, heads chopped off, screams from men before blades were stabbed into their throats. It all happened in thirty seconds, probably less.

My mother was the last one standing.

The monster came down on her, swiping his blade with a speed I could barely watch, but my mother somehow kept up. She met his blade with her own, dodged the blade before it swiped through her neck, rolled out of the way before his bare fist struck her in the side of the head.

But then she lost her footing—and his hand gripped her by the neck.

"No!" I sprinted forward to save her, even though I had no idea what I would do once I got there.

She started to scream, scream in a way I'd never heard her before, and that was when I realized he was burning her flesh. Flames erupted from his hand, and he charred her skin as he continued to hold her—and he grinned.

"Motherfucker, let her go—"

I was knocked back so hard I rolled.

Aurelias threw his blade right into the monster's eye, and my mother dropped to the ground. She gasped as she grabbed her neck, which had turned bright red where her skin had burned away.

The monster screamed as he pulled the dagger from his pupil, throwing it straight at Aurelias's head.

He dodged out of the way, the dagger hitting the stone and bouncing away.

The monster let out a scream and directed his blade at my mother's stomach, ready to impale her right into the stone.

But Aurelias got there first and deflected his blade. "Run!"

I rushed to my mother and grabbed her by the arm, dragging her away as she struggled to breathe. "Mother, I can't carry you. Come on!"

She forced herself to her feet, using my weight to support her.

I used all my energy to keep her moving, and just when I couldn't go any farther, Pyre dropped out of the sky and released a mighty roar.

"I need you to take her."

Mother continued to struggle for breath, like her lungs gasped for air but nothing entered her chest. "She needs help. Take her to a healer in the closest kingdom. And fast...she can't breathe." I forced my mother to climb, forced her wrists around the reins.

But she reached for me and tried to pull me on top.

"I can't leave."

Despite the fact that life literally faded from her with every passing second, she looked like she was on the verge of tears. She shook her head.

I squeezed her hand, unsure if I would ever see her alive again. "I won't abandon my duty. I love you, Mama." I couldn't look at her a moment longer, couldn't accept the fact that this could be a final goodbye. I turned away from Pyre and turned back to Delacroix, which was already set ablaze from the battle. "Gods...have mercy."

SEVEN
AURELIAS

My blade met his, a clash of steel against steel, and I felt the strength that no human could reproduce. He was powerful enough to push me back, to make my boots slide across the stones.

He spun his blade then brought it down on me, and I only had time to dodge out of the way because I knew it was coming. I took the opening and sliced his bare skin, cutting deep into his arm, and instead of blood spouting out, it was liquid fire, orange tinged with yellow, glowing with its own internal illumination. "What the fuck..."

He came at me again, releasing a growl after I wounded him, and he picked up the pace, giving me a flurry of blows that would defeat even the best swordsman. But I blocked every hit because I anticipated it, and when one of his cronies snuck around behind me to fight with dishonor, I was able to anticipate that too.

But there was no way I could fight them all and survive.

A few of the soldiers had fled after the monsters had slaughtered their comrades in a few seconds. Now that the queen was gravely injured, the rest had lost their morale. The monsters had fought the soldiers of Delacroix in the field as the dragon circled above to burn them all, but I feared that had little lasting effect on monsters that seemed to be physical manifestations of flames themselves.

These guys were supposed to decapitate the king and queen, to hang their heads outside the castle walls before they burned the city to the ground or claimed it for themselves—and I was the only thing standing in their way.

Others jumped in, so it was me against five.

I couldn't win.

I could anticipate all their moves and block them, but I couldn't be everywhere at once. My energy would wane, and it would wane faster without human blood in my veins. But I kept moving, kept blocking, kept making my mark and pissing them off even more.

"He's not human," the one in charge said. "But he's not Teeth either."

I could barely keep up now, blocking and dodging, completely on the defensive because I didn't have the energy to land any blow. I only had the energy to survive.

Then one of them growled when an arrow appeared in its neck. It was an inconvenience but not a weakness, and he carried on. More arrows were fired, hitting them in their arms and backs, striking them where they failed to wear armor.

It started to slow them down, but it still wasn't enough.

The leader rushed me and came at me with a flurry of blows, anxious to end this battle that should have ceased long ago, but a rock hit him right in the face, and he staggered back.

"Attagirl." I threw my dagger in his face again, missing his other eye but still impaling him in the cheek.

He came back with a vengeance, leaving the dagger deep in his flesh as he rushed me, pulling out two short blades so I would have to deflect two blades while holding off all the other attacks. He spun and slammed his swords down with all his might, trying to break my will and stagger me.

Fuck, it was working.

He finally got a hit on me—and sent me flying across the stone.

I rolled and rolled until I finally came to a stop.

Harlow rushed to me, dropping down to help me.

I pushed to my feet quickly and shoved her hard. "Run." I barely lifted my blade quick enough to deflect the blow because I'd used that moment to push Harlow to safety. But I was out of energy, out of ability, and I felt the strength of the blow push me back again.

I owed these people nothing, owed this world even less, but I would meet my end at the hands of someone's enemy…all because I'd needed that damn venom. It was ironic, to die selflessly when I'd only lived selfishly.

I blocked the blade but didn't have the strength to push it back. The monster pushed it hard against me, ready to slice my throat.

"Noooooo!" Harlow threw another rock, but it wasn't enough to save me.

I closed my eyes, not wanting to see the monster gloat as he sliced that blade fully through my neck to the stone underneath. But then the pressure suddenly vanished, and the blade became weightless.

I opened my eyes and saw the blue sky above.

"Get off him, motherfucker." A man ran past, wearing armor that was black and red, and his black sword that had an engraved snake down the center impaled the monster right through the stomach.

I sat up, shocked by what I saw.

"Get your ass up and help us." A man in black and gold armor appeared, grabbing me by the arm and forcing me up. "You can't expect us to do everything."

My eyes widened as I stared at him, the shock so potent I couldn't speak. "Cobra?"

He winked. "Yours truly." He went after one of the monsters, taking him down with a couple of strikes.

There was a woman who wore the same armor as Cobra, and she held her own against the monsters, slicing and swiping, forcing the monsters apart.

Invigorated by a new sense of strength, I spun my sword around my wrist and moved for the leader, whom Kingsnake had engaged in a battle of fiery blows. "Step aside. This asshole is mine."

Kingsnake moved to one of the others, helping Cobra handle his two opponents.

I was pleased to see that smug grin was gone, that the victory had been wiped from his face like dust with a cloth. "Now that it's one-on-one, let's see how this goes." I made my strike, and he blocked it, and then we were locked in a heated battle with hits and counters, spinning in a circle as we gave it our all.

I didn't have to devote my energy to other opponents, so all my focus was on him, the monster that didn't have the energy to gloat. I knew what attacks were coming, so not only did I dodge them, but I sliced his arms and shoulders over and over, more of the liquid fire releasing with a plume of smoke.

"You look tired." I came at him harder, striking again and again, getting him good across the neck.

When he clenched his jaw, all the bones in his face jutted out even more, and he looked like he was made of rock and fire. He released a scream as he came at me, giving his all in the final push.

I blocked the hit, punched him square in the jaw even though it nearly broke my knuckles, and then stabbed him right through with the sword. I slammed my body forward with momentum, making a clean cut all the way through.

He toppled over, the fire leaking from his body and charring the stone underneath. I stared at his body, saw the way his eyes hardened as death took him. But the smoke wafting from his cuts persisted, like his heat source continued even though he was no longer alive.

I turned to help the others, but they didn't need my assistance.

The three of them took out the final one together, and another one dropped to the ground, smoking in the same way.

Kingsnake examined the unusual blood on his sword before he wiped it clean on the enemy's clothing.

Cobra grabbed the woman by the arm and asked if she was okay.

I stared at my brothers, unable to believe they were really there, right in front of me.

Kingsnake returned his blade to his scabbard as he approached me. He took off his helmet too, tossing it on the ground so his features were on display. The others did likewise, walking up to me, sweaty but unharmed.

When Kingsnake reached me, he gripped me by the shoulder.

I was still winded, so I breathed hard as I reciprocated the affection, gripping him in the same way.

Then he pulled me in for a hug.

I hugged him back, grasping him harder than I ever had. "You saved my ass."

He pulled away, a slight smile on his lips.

"You bet your ass we did." Cobra grasped me too, squeezing me hard. "You're welcome, by the way."

I turned to the woman, seeing her brown hair and green eyes, a woman I didn't recognize whatsoever. "Who are you?" She must be Cobra's new general for the Cobra Vampires.

"So, it's kinda a long story..." Cobra said. "But this is Clara...my wife."

My eyes widened as I stared at her, taking a moment before I looked at him again. "You got married. You?"

"Like I said, it's a long story," Cobra said. "Kingsnake and Larisa got married too. But we'll need to have that conversation after we have a more important conversation, which is...what the fuck is going on?" He threw his arms up. "You're fighting monsters for humans? Aurelias, have you lost your fucking mind? You *hate* humans."

"It's—it's a long story." I couldn't get into all the details now, not when Delacroix was still under attack and the queen might die.

"We have a lot to catch up on," Kingsnake said.

"Where is Larisa?" I asked.

"I asked her to stay back," Kingsnake said. "She's in the forest."

"Aurelias." Harlow rushed between Cobra and Clara and ran straight into my chest. "Are you okay?" Her arms wrapped around me, and she squeezed me hard.

My hands automatically caught her and brought her close. "I'm alright. What about you?" I pulled away, seeing the bruise around her left eye where she had struck the ground. Other than that, she was in good condition.

Her bottom lip started to tremble from oncoming tears, like there wasn't an audience of vampires just inches away watching our interaction. "You saved my mother..."

"Is she okay?"

"I sent her away with Pyre. She needed a healer..."

"You told me you inherited her healing abilities. Perhaps she'll heal herself."

"She—she can't breathe."

My heart clenched into a fist, thinking about my mother's final moments...when she was burned alive. "I'm sorry..." I could feel the turmoil inside her tiny body, the terror of losing the person she loved most. "You should have gone with her."

"I'm Queen of Delacroix now—so my duty is to protect our kingdom." Her heart broke as she said it, a physical crack right down the center.

Her people faced an enemy they couldn't defeat, and she didn't have the strategic experience to be victorious over such fearsome foes. She was alone, without her father for guidance, without her mother for courage.

All she had was me. "I'll help you."

"So will we," Kingsnake said.

Harlow turned away to look at Kingsnake, a foot taller than her, powerful in the armor that was similar to mine. She looked at the three of them in silence, and she probably realized exactly what they were without asking questions. "Thank you." She turned back to me. "I need to get to General Henry and assess the status of the battle." She stepped away, starting at a walk but moving to a run.

My brothers and Clara—my sister-in-law, apparently— watched her go before they turned back to me. Cobra smirked. Kingsnake stared with accusation. It was a long stare, packed with a lot of unspoken words.

Finally, Cobra addressed the tension. "So *that's* why you're fighting for humans."

EIGHT
HARLOW

Cannons fired. Arrows rained down below. Our army fought the monsters one-on-one in the field. So many people had already died on the battlefield, soldiers who weren't prepared for these kinds of deadly creatures. My brother was down there, and I feared he was one of those bodies.

Blade flew up above, blowing fire down on the monsters in the center of their ranks, but once he flew away, it was obvious the monsters weren't affected by the flames...because they were fire themselves.

I climbed to the top of the barracks and waved my arms frantically, trying to get Blade's attention. "Blade!" I jumped as high as possible, doing whatever I could to get him to look at me.

I finally got his attention, and he pivoted his body to stare.

I waved him to land nearby so I could climb up on his back. He flew into the village, away from the attackers, and I rushed over to climb up his armor and onto his saddle. "They're immune to fire, so your flames won't work. We need to do something else."

Blade launched into the sky, his wings so powerful that we were at the clouds instantly. ***Nothing is immune to my fire.***

"Well, these guys are. We need another plan."

I could face them on the battlefield.

"No. We can't risk anything happening to you." I tried to come up with a solution, but the stress of battle and my mother's condition made it impossible to think, when I just wanted to panic. But my mother didn't panic when she faced her opponents. And my father never panicked, even when he thought he'd lost me. "Come on, Harlow..." We continued to fly over the battlefield, and I tried to think of how I could help. "Boulders!"

What?

"Pick up big rocks and drop them on them. To the east."

Hold on. Blade flapped his wings hard, crossing leagues in seconds, and then swooped down to pick up a rock that had to be nearly as heavy as he was. He had to flap his wings hard to get off the ground, and the return journey wasn't nearly as fast.

"Don't just drop it. Roll it. Get as many of them as you can, but be careful not to hit our guys."

Blade swooped down and sped up, lining up his shot before his talons released the heavy rock.

It landed with a loud thud and rolled, crushing all the monsters in its path, knocking them back and breaking their limbs. A single boulder took out fifty of them at once. "Perfect! Again."

All the enemies were slain, their bodies smoking on the field like they'd been thrown on pyres. Our fallen were stacked to be burned later during the memorial. Once Blade landed, I was back on my feet, but I'd never felt so weak despite the victory.

Everyone else looked hopeless too. "Has Pyre said anything about my mother?"

He said he got her to a healer. Hasn't received news of her condition.

I nodded before I walked across the battlefield, seeing good men slain on the ground, next to the monsters that bled fire. Now that the threat had passed, I felt the fatigue in my body, felt my muscles scream from the exertion. My mind was broken too…and my heart was irreparable.

I found General Henry, who had survived the ordeal but was covered in blood from head to toe. "Have you seen Atticus?" I was afraid to ask the question, because I hadn't seen him anywhere, and knowing him, he would stop at nothing until he found me.

General Henry shook his head. "The last time I saw him was in battle, but I lost track of him."

I tried not to cry. Tried not to assume the worst. My father was gone. My mother might be dead. I couldn't afford to lose Atticus too.

I continued my search, moving across the field in the expectation of finding his dead body. Tears were in the backs of my eyes, but I refused to let them fall. Though, the more I fought them, the harder they burned.

Aurelias appeared before me. "Atticus is in the infirmary." He wasn't gentle with his words, didn't cushion them with affection or kindness.

"He's alive...?"

He nodded. "But he's badly hurt."

My eyes started to water with tears, hardly able to stand any longer. My family had been ripped apart by these...whatever they were. We may have won the war, but it felt like an empty victory... after the price we'd paid.

He came close, his hand sliding into my hair. "You are not alone, Harlow." He said the words I needed to hear most, as if he knew exactly how I felt, as if he could hear me speak the words even though they never left my lips. "I'm here with you."

My fingers grabbed on to his wrist, and I closed my eyes, tears streaking down my cheeks. "I've never been so scared in my life..."

"I know, baby." His thumbs wiped away the tears through his gloves. He guided me into his chest, letting me rest my face against his armor where I could cry in private, his arms hooked around me like steel bars of a cage. His chin rested on my head, and he cocooned me like the outside world was too harsh for my delicateness.

We stayed like that for a long time, and I sobbed, sobbed my heart out. My mother might have suffocated to death. My brother might succumb to his injuries. My father might return, and it'd just be the two of us…living with the ghosts of those we loved…or he might already be dead.

Aurelias held me with the patience of a saint, granting me the kind of affection we had never shared before. He was gentle. He was kind. He was supportive rather than ruthless and cold.

Once I'd had the time I needed, I pulled away, my eyes in pain from all the tears. I could feel their puffiness, feel the sting in my cheeks, feel the embarrassment for giving in to my grief in public when others were suffering just as much. I was surrounded by dead bodies that very moment, people who would be missed by those who loved them.

Aurelias kept his hands on me. "You alright?"

I nodded.

"I'll take you to Atticus." His hand grabbed mine, and he guided me with him, as if he knew I was a spirit that could just drift away into the sky if I weren't tethered to something strong. He guided me across the field, to the barracks, and then to the infirmary, a place I'd been before but had somehow forgotten the location of.

They took me to his room, and I stopped once I crossed the threshold, seeing him lying there on the bed, his body hidden under a blanket like he was cold despite the heat. It was almost sunset, and dark was coming soon, but the air was humid.

I slowly approached his bed, seeing how gray and sallow his skin was. "Atticus?"

He was knocked out cold, his breathing pained and ragged.

I lifted the blanket to look at his injuries—and I immediately wished I hadn't.

Gauze was around his midsection from a puncture of a blade. His armor hadn't been enough to protect him. His arm was wrapped in gauze too, like it'd been broken. I returned the blanket to his body, unable to look at it anymore.

The maiden came into the room. "Princess Harlow—"

"He needs medicine before that infection sets in."

"I've already given it to him, Your Highness." She stood over him, looking at the strong man who had become a corpse.

"We should move him to the castle...where it's cool."

"I'd rather not move him right now, Your Highness," she said. "I think it's best to wait until he's feeling better—"

"But it's warm out here—"

Aurelias gripped me by the shoulder. "Harlow, the maiden has done everything she can. We need to give Atticus time to fight this on his own."

I wanted to cry again.

He gripped my shoulder. "She's right," he said gently. "It would be a mistake to move him right now."

I nodded, my eyes still on Atticus.

"Let him rest. That's all you can do." He guided me out of the infirmary and back under the sky. The soldiers had lit the torches for extra light, the city illuminated in parts where it hadn't been destroyed.

I stared at the wreckage, unsure what to do or how to lead my people. I couldn't help my brother. I couldn't help my mother. I was powerless to do anything. I moved through the gate and up the hill, approaching the entrance to the castle, the site where my mother had nearly died on the spot. "I—I don't know what to do."

"Send a message to your father and inform him what happened."

"I meant about Delacroix. Did we win the war…or was that just a battle?" I turned to look at him, as if he would have the answer.

"Prepare for the worst and hope for the best."

"I want to see my mother, but I can't leave. With Atticus indisposed, there's no one else to lead."

His hand moved to my arm again. "There's nothing you can do for her right now."

"I don't want her to die alone—"

"She's not going to die."

"How—how do you know?"

"Because all those soldiers pissed their pants when they saw those guys, and your mother asked for their dance card. That woman is made of steel, and she has too much to live for. She'll pull through."

My eyes watered because the hope was so tantalizing. I wanted that more than anything.

"If there's another battle, it won't come now. We tend to the wounded, repair our fortifications, and rest. Go to your chambers and get some sleep. There's nothing else you can do right now."

I wasn't sure if I could close my eyes, not after everything that had happened, not when the horror still flashed across my mind. My father had trained me for war, but now that I'd seen it firsthand, I realized I wasn't prepared at all. It was too horrible. "Will you lie with me...?" I couldn't look him in the eye as I asked, as I exposed my vulnerability to a man who had hurt me with his rejection. But his affection was the only thing that had gotten me through the last hour.

I finally had the courage to meet his stare.

His dark eyes were focused and unflinching, like thoughts were swirling in a cloud in his mind. "I haven't seen my family in a long time. We have much to discuss."

"Oh, of course..." So many things had happened today that the sudden appearance of more vampires was forgettable. I felt foolish for asking, for leaning on Aurelias like he was more than an old lover who no longer wanted me.

"I can come afterward."

All the disappointment was eradicated instantly. "You don't have to climb this time...just walk in."

A subtle smile moved on to his lips before he stepped away.

I watched him go, his body powerful in his plates of armor, the man who saved my mother...and my kingdom.

NINE
AURELIAS

I sat at the head of the dining table, the surface covered with all the booze I could scrounge up. We had wine, ale, some of the harder stuff that my brothers and I preferred. There was one thing I knew they would prefer above all—but that wasn't on the menu.

Cobra sat with his arm over the back of Clara's chair, his eyes shifting to her from time to time. His dedication to monogamy was clear in how he regarded her.

The door opened, and Kingsnake returned, his wife and snake in tow.

I rose to my feet to look at Larisa, because the last time I'd seen her, she was a weak human who nearly died in the snow, her cheeks pale, her eyes dead.

But she stepped inside in armor identical to Kingsnake's, Fang around her shoulders even though he was too heavy for humans to lift, and her eyes now held the darkness the rest of us had. Unlike the others, she was an Original—as was I.

Her eyes moved to me, and a smile crept over both her lips and her eyes. "Aurelias."

"Sister."

She pulled me into a hug and squeezed me tight, her face at my chest. Fang slithered around my shoulders, wrapping us together like a string. "I'm so glad you're alright."

I released her. "You made the right decision." I looked her over, seeing an immortal being who would enjoy all the fruits of life while others faded in what felt like seconds. "I knew you would."

"Well, the decision was made for me." Her eyes glanced at Kingsnake. "But I wouldn't change it."

"Good." I gestured to the table for us to sit.

Fang slithered away, finding a comfortable spot on the couch next to a blanket where he could curl into a ball and rest.

We all sat together at the table again, and everyone helped themselves to the booze. Larisa and Clara opened a bottle of wine, while my brothers and I went straight for the stuff that burned.

When I left, my brothers were both single men, and now they were paired off, while I remained alone. "How's Father?" I already knew the answer, could picture his reaction when he'd realized I wouldn't be returning, but I still wanted the details.

Kingsnake took a drink before he answered. "Disappointed that I returned and you didn't. *Very* disappointed." He looked into his glass, like it was a sore subject he'd rather not elaborate on. "A lot has happened since we spoke. We defeated King Elrohir in battle, and then we formed a truce with the Ethereal, which was essential to winning the war against the Werewolf King."

"The Werewolf King?" I asked. "I wasn't gone *that* long."

"He staged a coup with the Kingdoms and took over," Kingsnake said. "We were too distracted with the Ethereal to notice."

"And a truce with the Ethereal? In what world would we ever regard them as allies rather than foes?" I'd hated the Ethereal since the beginning, never forgot the endless sieges, their obsession with eradicating us from the world.

"They betrayed their king in exchange for peace," Kingsnake said. "We took that offer."

I looked away from my brother, annoyed by the decision. "I doubt Father approved."

"He didn't," Kingsnake said. "Not one bit."

"And he was right for disapproving," I said bitterly. "For an immortal being who's experienced several lifetimes, your memory is poor..."

Kingsnake glanced at Cobra. A silent conversation happened between them.

I crossed my arms and sank into the chair. "Are you men or schoolchildren?"

Kingsnake swirled his glass before he released a sigh. "We discovered the reason behind the Ethereal's immortality, and while it was disgusting, most of their population was unaware of the practice. They destroyed their source of power, and some chose to join us in immortality, while others chose to embrace a mortal life."

My eyes shifted back to Clara and narrowed. "That's why I don't recognize you."

She gave a nod.

I looked at Cobra. "You married an Ethereal?"

"She's a Cobra Vampire, Aurelias," Cobra said coldly. "As you can perfectly see."

I turned back to Kingsnake. "Father didn't approve of this."

"We didn't give him a choice but to approve," Kingsnake said. "He's finally accepted the decision—and you need to accept it too."

A small smile moved to my lips, being ganged up on by my brothers like we were boys. "What happened to the Kingdoms?"

"Father is the King of the Kingdoms," Cobra said. "He's the king of vampires. He's the king of everything."

I gave a slow nod. "Now I understand why he's come around." That meant I was the Prince of the Kingdoms, that I would rule over the entire continent in the unlikely event of his death. That power would be transferred to me.

We sat in silence for a while as I took in all this information. Once I returned to my lands, life would be very different. "How's Viper?"

"He survived the battle," Kingsnake said. "I almost didn't."

I looked at him again.

"Father saved me..." He looked into his glass.

"Perhaps I'm not the favorite after all."

"No," Kingsnake said quickly. "You definitely are. But it's nice to know he still has some affection for the rest of us."

Silence hung heavy in the air, the world quiet after the battle that had shaken the foundation of Delacroix. The field was stacked with dead bodies, friends and foes, and the blood had stained the stones. Unless it was scrubbed, it would probably always be there. I admired the views this kingdom had to offer, the way the grass smelled in the heat, the way it functioned without a vampire ruler.

"I don't want to seem insensitive," Kingsnake said. "In light of the battle that's claimed so many lives…but we need to feed. It's been a long time since we had a proper meal. Can that be arranged?"

I released a heavy sigh, because feeding on the subjects was strictly prohibited by King Rolfe, a man who wouldn't hesitate to kill me if I gave him any reason to. "I've been subsisting off animal blood while I've been here. I suggest you do the same."

Kingsnake stared for a solid three seconds, in utter disbelief. "When was the last time you properly fed?"

"A couple months…"

Kingsnake stilled.

So did the others.

"You're lucky that thing didn't kill you," Kingsnake said. "Functioning on partial capacity…"

I refilled my glass and took a drink.

"Now it's your turn to catch us up," Cobra said. "What have you been doing these last few months? Besides ingesting animal blood."

I told them the story, kidnapping Harlow but then rescuing her instead, becoming a prisoner to her father until he finally released me once Harlow pleaded on my behalf. "He was only gone a few days before this shit happened."

"You think they're related?" Kingsnake asked.

"I'm not sure," I said. "It's one hell of a coincidence." King Rolfe might already be dead, but I didn't have the heart to tell Harlow that. He could have traveled to their lands, been taken, and they deployed this army to demolish his kingdom. The lead monster did ask for the king, but it could have been a taunt.

"Since you saved Delacroix, I think you're free to go," Kingsnake said. "You've earned your freedom."

"Let's leave tomorrow," Cobra said. "If there's no food here, we have no reason to stay. We'll return to the ship, where our volunteers are waiting, and feed on the return journey. I know you're hungry, Aurelias, but make sure you don't kill them."

Everything in my body hurt all at once, as if I'd been stabbed with a hundred blades. My expression didn't change, but I stared across the table at my brother, who was completely oblivious to the insult he'd just unleashed. I could feel it in his emotions—that it was completely unintentional.

But it fucking hurt.

"Cobra." Kingsnake didn't need to read emotions to pick up on my rage.

"What?" Cobra asked before he took a drink.

Kingsnake gave him a furious stare.

It took Cobra a few seconds to realize the problem, to remember the words that could provoke my drawn sword. "Fuck..." He looked away, clenching his eyes shut once the revelation hit him. "Aurelias, I didn't mean it like that—"

"It's fine."

"I'm sorry—"

"I don't accept your apology," I said calmly. "But it's fine."

The silence was heavier than it'd ever been. Seeing my brothers in the flesh was the greatest comfort, but now my heart felt empty.

"Since we can't feed, we can leave now," Kingsnake said. "Take advantage of the darkness." It was obvious he wanted to say something just to say something, to push past the tension Cobra had created.

"I'm not leaving." My arms were on the table, my palm on top of my glass.

Kingsnake turned to look at me.

Cobra exchanged a look with Clara.

I continued. "You guys can go, but I have to stay."

"But you don't have to stay," Kingsnake said. "We can leave right now, and no one will stop us—"

"Then let me rephrase my words," I said quietly. "I don't *want* to leave."

Kingsnake had never given me a look like that, like he didn't recognize his own flesh and blood. "The girl…"

I stared into my glass.

Cobra folded his arms over his chest. "But you hate humans…"

"Not this one," Larisa said.

"They don't have a chance against...whatever the fuck these things are." Not only was I the strongest kind of vampire, but I'd had lifetimes of experience with the blade, and even I had struggled to meet the might of their swords.

"And neither do you," Kingsnake said. "If we hadn't shown up, you'd be dead right now."

"He's right," Cobra said. "A single vampire isn't enough to make a difference."

"But an army of vampires might." I lifted my gaze as I took a drink. "I promised King Rolfe our army in exchange for my freedom."

"And that agreement is now void after you saved his queen and his daughter," Kingsnake snapped. "Delacroix would have a new king and all the humans would be dead right now if it weren't for you. You don't owe him a damn thing. The best way to protect the girl is to take her with us."

"I don't want to take her with me," I said. "And she wouldn't come anyway." She wouldn't leave her family or her people. She had the honor of kings, finding death preferable to dishonor.

Cobra stared. "You could turn her—"

"I will *never* turn her." I stared into my glass.

My brothers went quiet again.

"So let me get this straight," Cobra said. "You don't want to turn her, which means you don't want to be with her, but you're willing to sacrifice your life for her protection? Yeah...makes a lot of sense."

I lifted my gaze and stared him down. "When you return, ask Father to send the armies."

"Why?" Kingsnake asked. "He gets nothing out of it, so why would he agree?"

"Because I asked." And I had faith that my father would accommodate any and every request that I made.

"This isn't our war," Kingsnake said. "We just fought in a war. We're not sending our people to die for a cause that has nothing to do with them. Aurelias, do you realize what you're asking?"

Cobra jumped in. "You're asking your people to sacrifice themselves for *humans*."

"Whom you despise," Kingsnake added. "Whom Father despises."

I continued to stare into my glass. "They're good people."

"You returned his daughter, and he locked you up in a dungeon," Kingsnake snapped, growing heated. "He sounds like a maniac."

"He's only a maniac when it comes to his daughter," Aurelias said. "And I respect that."

"That's not enough reason, Aurelias," Kingsnake said.

"The queen is brave," I said quietly. "She has more spine than men twice her size."

"So?" Cobra said. "My wife is the most fearsome warrior I've ever seen."

"But she protected her daughter the way Mother would have protected us." My mother had had no skills outside the home. Her life was cooking, cleaning, and taking care of four rowdy boys. But she loved us so much that she would have done anything to protect us—like pick up a sword and fight.

Kingsnake went quiet again, his eyes glazing over with memory.

I pushed my glass aside. "I would never say this to her, but they have no chance against these monsters and the Teeth, not even with their army of dragons, not even when they're being led by a king like her father. If we leave them to their fate, they'll be conquered. They'll be killed or imprisoned. And Harlow… I know exactly what will happen to her." Because the Teeth had told me exactly what they were planning to do to her after I dropped her off, and it was enough to haunt my dreams every single night. "The world of men on this continent will be no more. It'll become a world of monsters—and there're enough monsters in this world already."

Kingsnake was quiet for a long time, soaking in my words. "Aurelias, you're not the empathic type. You don't care about others, especially humans, so this is solely about one person—the princess. And that would be fine…if you intended to make this woman your wife… But you said you won't turn her."

"Because I won't," I said simply. "And no, she won't be my wife."

"Then I don't understand," Kingsnake said. "I don't understand at all."

I considered my answer, trying to understand it myself. "It doesn't have to last forever for it to be worthwhile. It doesn't have to be forever for me to care. It can just be a moment—because a moment is reason enough."

No one said anything. No one even looked at me.

Finally, Kingsnake spoke. "Aurelias, she's been gone a long time—"

"*Don't.*"

"I'm just saying—"

"And I'd rather you not."

Kingsnake continued to stare at me. "I want you to be happy—"

"I'll never be happy, and I'm okay with that."

Kingsnake tried again. "You know what happened with Ellasara and me—"

"*Fuck you, Kingsnake.*" I stared at him, nostrils flared. "How is your ex-wife being a lying bitch comparable to what happened to me? A fucking insult..." I was tired of this conversation, tired of the direction it had taken. "You'll return home and ask Father to commit his armies to this cause. If he doesn't, I'll fight on my own, and I'll probably die. If he needs an incentive to come, the life of his son should be good enough."

I wasn't in the mood to see Harlow, to comfort her when my rage was compressed inside my lungs and about to burst. All I wanted to do was drink and be alone, to stare at the sky until the sun rose again. But the guilt was too much for me to abandon her, knowing she was probably wide awake, waiting for me to walk through the door and chase away her terror.

I walked straight into the castle because no one was there to stop me. Everyone worked into the night, tending to the wounded, cleaning up the fields, putting a broken Delacroix back together.

I figured out where her bedroom was in the castle based on its window placement. I took two levels of stairs, moved down several hallways, and then found her bedroom door. It was cracked, light streaming outside the room and into the hallway.

I poked my head inside and found her sitting against the headboard, her hair clean because she'd bathed, one side of her face discolored because the bruising slowly grew worse. Her gaze was out the open window, looking at the light of the pyres in the distance. Her eyes looked empty—like she'd lost everything.

I stepped inside, and the second she heard my boots, her head snapped in my direction. Her quiet mood quickly lit into a fire, her reaction to my presence warm and desperate. She straightened, the sheets covering her from the waist down, wearing her white nightgown. She didn't say a word, but her relief was paramount.

I stripped off my clothing, removing the armor that had been scuffed up in the battle, and left my sword at the foot of the bed where I'd gripped her by the chin and explored her as deep as I could. The sight of her in a nightgown should turn me on, along with the flashbacks from my previous visit, but I didn't feel anything since I knew how broken she was.

I undressed to my boxers then slid under the covers beside her.

She was on me instantly, her cheek using my shoulder as a pillow, her arm hooking around my torso like an anchor. She pulled the sheets to her shoulder and burrowed into me, like I was the only thing that could make the pain go away. "I started to worry you wouldn't come."

I rested my cheek against hers and circled my arm around her waist. Her leg was across my hips, so I gripped the outside of her thigh, feeling the warm skin I'd kissed and touched when I first met her. "I almost didn't..."

TEN
HARLOW

I stared down at my brother, who still hadn't woken up since he'd collapsed on the battlefield. "His color looks better..." He was still weak and decimated, looking small and helpless instead of the powerful soldier he'd trained to be. But I needed to focus on the positives... whatever I could find.

"Yes," the maiden said. "His breathing has become less labored too."

"How's the wound?"

"No sign of infection—so the medicine has worked."

I nodded. "I hope he wakes soon."

"I've seen soldiers in worse condition pull through," she said. "I think Atticus will make it."

I nodded, grateful for the encouragement. "Gods, I hope you're right." I stepped outside the infirmary, seeing Aurelias looking out over the fields, fully dressed in his armor and weapons like a killing machine. The bodies had been burned this morning in a memorial, and the enemy had been burned unceremoniously in a bonfire that still hadn't gone out. The stench was in the air, and the mark it would leave on the earth would be permanent.

I came to his side and pushed my mind to Pyre's. *Heard any news?*

No. I'll receive none—because no one tries to speak with a dragon.

I'd sent a messenger asking for an update that morning, but I hadn't received anything back yet. "Are they your brothers and sisters?"

Aurelias turned to look at me. "Brothers and their wives."

"How did they find you?"

"I didn't ask."

"They're vampires too?"

"Yes."

"Does that mean the others are coming?"

"They're going to return to my lands and ask the king for his forces."

These foes were different from Necrosis. They were invulnerable to fire...because they were fire. If their forces were significant, then we wouldn't stand a chance, not when our dragons were nearly worthless. "I can't speak for my father because he's not here, but... you don't owe us anything, Aurelias. You don't need to call for aid to earn your freedom. You already earned it when you saved my mother's life...and my life...and everyone's life."

His dark eyes the color of earth stared at me, his hard expression impossible to read unless he wanted it to be deciphered. With a force that rivaled lightning, he stared me down, almost the way he would regard an enemy on the battlefield. "I appreciate that."

My heart sank, knowing he would leave now that he wasn't required to stay. He would return with his family, back to the lands he called home, and leave us to our problems. "Do you need any supplies before you go?"

"The ship has everything they need."

"When are you leaving?" I'd thought I could manage a kingdom on my own because my father had selected me for the job, but now that I was alone, with my family members either gone or incapacitated, I was in way over my head. I would never admit that to another living soul, far too proud for that, but Aurelias made the burden easier to manage. Honestly, he was the one who should be in charge, not me since he'd saved Delacroix while I did nothing. I was inadequate for the job—and my father should have chosen someone else.

"I'm not."

My heart clenched so tightly I was forced to take a deep breath, the kind that he could see.

"They're leaving tonight."

"You—you aren't leaving?"

His eyes stayed transfixed on me. "No."

"Why…?" I swallowed, so relieved that he wasn't about to walk out of my life forever.

"Because you need me."

"You don't owe me anything, Aurelias—"

"I know I don't." He continued his stare, the kind that pierced me all the way through, that made me writhing hot and freezing cold at the same time. "I won't abandon you, baby."

When he called me baby, I felt myself turn to mush. "You said you would return to your lands…"

"And I will." His gaze hardened. "But not until this is done."

I felt the sting of disappointment, but it was muffled by his dedication and sacrifice, the way he stood beside me when everything else fell apart. Whatever this was wouldn't last forever, but I would appreciate every second of it. "I'm sorry for the way I treated you before… I said some shitty things."

"And I deserved every one of those shitty things. Don't apologize."

"No, you didn't," I whispered. "And I'm sorry for allowing my father—"

"I feel no resentment toward him. He's a good father."

My eyes closed, missing him more than I ever had. "He's the best…" I felt the tears burn behind my eyes, felt the heat sear the backs of my eyelids. "I wish he were here right now. I'm so grateful you're here because I couldn't do this alone." I said it out loud, admitted my weakness when no one should ever hear such a confession from a queen. "I don't have what it takes to do this. My father made a poor choice."

I felt his fingers move underneath my chin to force my gaze to meet his. Tears streaked down my cheeks.

"You could have fled on that dragon and abandoned your mother, but you stayed. Even though you felt helpless, you stayed. You did whatever you could to help, threw rocks at monsters, fired your arrows. Maybe it didn't win the battle, but you had the courage to stay, and that's what makes you the right choice."

My eyes dropped.

He tugged on my chin again. "Look at me when I speak to you."

My skin prickled with bumps.

"You were quick on your feet and used a dragon to drop boulders on the enemy. You took out batches of fifty of them at a time, saving the lives of the men who fought for you. *You stayed.*"

My heart raced at his intensity, at the way he stared at me, the way he spoke to me.

"I fought for you because I care for you. Because you made me care even when I tried so fucking hard not to. You're the reason Delacroix still stands this very moment—and no one else. I know how proud your father will be when he sees what you've done."

I sent the letter to HeartHolme before I exited the castle, dressed in my uniform and armor, unsettled by the way the guards and soldiers addressed me as Queen Rolfe...a name my mother had had my entire life.

Aurelias was there, taller than all the guards, so handsome he looked fake.

"I leave you in charge of Delacroix until my return." I was handing the keys to the kingdom to someone who wasn't even human, but I knew there were no better hands to hold them. "Unless Atticus wakes up...and I hope he does."

Aurelias gave a slight nod.

"I know I shouldn't leave right now, but—"

"Go to your mother," he said. "I will protect everything you hold dear."

"Thank you."

He gave another slight nod.

Blade squatted down so it would be easier to climb up the metal plates of his armor. I dropped into the saddle and gripped the reins, ropes that were attached to the armor, not for steering like a horse, but just to have something to hold on to as the dragon made unexpected dives and dodges. My legs were strapped in, just in case the dragon had to invert to avoid a cannon, and I wouldn't fall off. Now that war had marched on my doorstep, I realized my father was right to be prepared for everything…always.

Blade launched to the sky, and in just a second or two, Delacroix was a speck on the ground. The details of the cobblestones and the wooden beams of the structures were no longer visible. The warm air rushed past me and made my hair fly back as we made our way to Minora, the closest kingdom and the one that Pyre could reach the quickest. By dragon, it was a short flight, half an hour at the most, but for my mother, who had been unable to breathe, it had probably felt like a lifetime.

Pyre was visible from the sky, and Blade did a dive once he was near, knowing I loved the thrill. He pulled up just before the ground, swooping up and slowly lowering himself to the ground until his heavy body landed with a distinct thud.

"Thanks for the ride." I unstrapped myself and dropped down, giving him and Pyre a quick rub before I approached the kingdom. They were ready for battle, ready for what happened to Delacroix to come to them next, and they swung the gates open at my entry.

I entered the town and headed to the castle in the distance, walking fast down the main path that went straight through the buildings and served as the primary thoroughfare between the shops and homes.

I approached the castle a moment later, and Steward John was there to greet me. "Your Highness, how does Delacroix fare?"

"She's been beaten badly. We lost a lot of soldiers. But she'll recover, as she always does."

"And news on King Rolfe?"

I shook my head.

"Do you think there will be more?" He spoke quietly, as if he didn't want me to hear the question out of fear of the answer.

"We should hope for the best and expect the worst." Aurelias's face entered my mind, a man who pulled me close and pushed me away simultaneously. For a man who didn't want me, he was more loyal than the ones who did. "Let's discuss this later. I want to see my mother. How is she?"

Steward John guided me into the castle, into the cool darkness of the stone that was lit with crystal chandeliers and decorated with deep rugs and colorful portraits of the landscapes and the royal family. "The healer applied tonic to stop the swelling, and that seemed to calm the skin enough to open her airway. She can breathe, but she's still in great pain."

I closed my eyes in relief, grateful that she was alive.

"She said the burns traveled all the way through the skin, so it's hard for her to drink or eat."

Knowing my mother was miserable was too much to bear, so I focused on the fact that she was still alive—and that soothed my heart.

Steward John guided me down another hallway then gestured to one of the bedchambers. "I'll give you some privacy."

I turned to open the door.

"Your Highness?"

I looked at him again.

"Thank you for defending the Kingdoms. If Delacroix had fallen, Minora would have been next."

I didn't know how to accept the compliment. Aurelias had praised my dedication, but I still didn't know if I deserved it. All I could do was muster a nod before I stepped inside, immediately swallowed by the darkness of her bedchambers, the curtains drawn shut over all the windows. I closed the door as gently as possible then crept into the room, seeing her lying in bed with the covers to her chest, her eyes closed.

I approached the bed and looked down at her, seeing the horrible scars all along her neck and down to her collarbone. The top layers of her skin had been burned away, so there were still flaps where the outer layer of skin was visible. It was hard to look at, knowing the pain must be unbearable.

I was so glad Aurelias had killed that monster, but I wished I'd done it myself.

My hand moved to hers, and I cocooned her fingers in mine, just the way she did with me, and I forced myself not to cry, to cherish the fact that she'd survived instead.

My touch stirred her, and her eyes opened, finding mine instantly. It took her a second or two to recognize my face or to distinguish dream from reality, but then she sucked in a deep breath then grasped my hand like it was the hilt of a sword. "Honey..." Her eyes watered at the sight of me, her relief potent.

"I'm okay, Mama..."

She squeezed my fingers hard, the tears coming from her eyes. "My baby..."

I let her cry and felt my own eyes water.

"Atticus?" she asked, bracing for impact.

If he had been well enough, he would have been beside me, checking on her with his own eyes—and she knew that. "He was injured in battle...but the maiden said he should pull through."

She closed her eyes, her joy replaced by pain. "No..."

"He'll be okay, Mama." I didn't know what possessed me to say it, to make a promise I couldn't keep, but I guessed I just wanted to make her feel better when she was already crippled in pain. "He has Father's strength."

She squeezed my hand. "No word from your father?" She knew he would be the first person to see her if he were here, so if it was me instead of him, it meant he was still unavailable.

"I sent a letter to HeartHolme this morning. If he's there, he'll be here by tomorrow morning."

"Delacroix needs its king." She continued to squeeze my hand. "But good thing it had you…"

I couldn't take the credit, not when the soldiers had lost their lives to protect our gates, when our dragons had served us at their own expense. "Delacroix would have been taken without Aurelias."

"My life would have been taken as well." The memory seemed to return to her, the way the monster had gripped her by the throat and burned through her flesh and straight to the bone. "I regret the way your father treated him. You're fortunate that Aurelias's love for you is stronger than his resentment toward your father."

"It wasn't love." I said it immediately, knowing there was an invisible boundary Aurelias had placed between us. I couldn't see it, but I could always feel it, always sense his distance, no matter how close we were.

Her eyes locked on mine. "There are only two reasons a man risks his life—for duty or for love. And we know he has no duty to protect a kingdom he doesn't call home. He showed you his cards, Harlow. He's lost the match."

My eyes shifted away.

"I hope he survived the battle."

"He did. His brothers came searching for him, and they helped in the battle as well."

"More vampires are in Delacroix?"

"Yes. But if they're loyal to Aurelias, I don't fear them." Aurelias would never allow them to be a threat after he'd risked his life for our kingdom. "Are you able to move? I'm sure you'll be more comfortable at home."

"It hurts to move, but I want to be there when your father gets home."

I nodded.

"Without my healing abilities, I would have suffocated to death." She supported her body with her arms and shifted herself upright, her back against the headboard. She closed her eyes briefly, wincing at the pain, but then she took a breath. "Pyre must be so worried about me… I've been asleep this whole time."

"Let me help you get out of bed." I took her arms and supported her as she got her feet on the floor. "You think you can ride Pyre home?"

"I know he'll get me there safely."

ELEVEN
HUNTLEY

We discussed venturing deeper into unknown territory to investigate further but decided it wasn't worth the risk, not when we were still undetected. The slave may rat us out in the morning. Ian bribed him with all the food in his pack, but he might turn on us the second we were gone.

We returned to the dragons hidden far into the distance, and we finally took our first true breath now that we were away from the enemy.

Ian helped himself to the saddle and pulled out the food he had stowed inside since his supply was depleted. He took a few bites, his eyes on the mountains as they reflected the dying light. "What are they mining for?"

"Crystals and gems for jewelry. Without the costs of labor, easy money."

"But do you think demons care about jewelry?"

I stared at him, a prickle in my heart.

"What if it's for something else?"

"Such as?"

"I don't know…"

Now the discomfort in my heart intensified.

"Made of fire…what the fuck?"

I stared at my brother, knowing he was just as scared as I was.

"The ring of fire…is that where they come from?"

"It would be unwise to check."

"If we could find the survivors of Palladium, they could probably tell us everything."

"We'll never find them in a land we don't know, Ian. We need to leave."

"We know what they are, but that's it."

"It'll have to be enough," I said. "The Kingdoms need us both. If we die out here, no one will know what's coming. No one will know Rancor's allies."

Ian looked across the barren landscape, his breath escaping as vapor. We hadn't slept in several days, only taking short power naps while the other kept watch. Water was low, and we couldn't afford to search for more and be spotted. "I think we need to keep going. Fly farther east under the cover of darkness. See what else is out there."

"We know what we need to know."

"We know we're dealing with fire demons that probably crawled out of the fucking ring of fire. How do you defeat fire, Huntley? Our dragons will be useless against that. When you add fire to fire, you just have more fire."

"I know you're scared—"

"*Scared?*" he asked incredulously. "I'm fucking terrified, Huntley. I'm terrified that I won't be able to protect my wife and daughter from whatever-the-fuck these things are. They're at least a foot taller than us, and that's saying something because we're already fucking tall. Yes, we know what they are, but that doesn't help us defeat them."

"As true as that all is, I'm uncomfortable leaving the Kingdoms a moment longer than necessary. Last time I left, Harlow was taken, and if I had been in Delacroix, that never would have happened under my watch. It'll take the Teeth a long while to move through the mountains to reach the other side, so we have time."

"But we're already here, Huntley."

The light was fading further. The mountains were almost invisible. "Dread is swollen in my heart…"

Ian's expression hardened.

"It's just a feeling, but it's heavy."

"What do you mean?"

My eyes stayed on the mountains. "I'm afraid something will happen to Delacroix while I'm away. It's a fear without reason, but it feels very real to me."

"That's anxiety, Huntley."

My eyes shifted back to him.

"You've never had it before, have you?"

I continued my stare.

"I didn't have it either…until Avice left me. Yours probably started because of Harlow."

Now I avoided his look, ashamed of my weakness.

"I'm anxious to return too. But it also feels pointless because I couldn't defend HeartHolme against this enemy even if I were there. We would both be useless, Huntley."

"You're making a lot of assumptions."

"They're demons, Huntley. *Demons*."

There had been a human civilization here that had fallen to their dominance, and I feared the Kingdoms would be next. "I understand that, Ian. But if we're caught, they'll know we're on to them. They could launch an attack sooner than they would otherwise."

"I think it makes sense for me to stay behind…and you to return home."

"No."

"Huntley—"

"Forget it, Ian. I will not leave my brother out here alone."

"It makes the most sense—"

"*I said, forget it.*"

His eyes contained his annoyance, the kind that wanted to burst into an explosion.

"We're going to return to HeartHolme. We'll decide what to do then."

Ian said nothing, but his anger was so strong it was heavy in the air.

"Come on." I moved to Storm, ready to climb up and fly away now that the darkness had descended.

"Whatever you say...*Your Majesty.*"

We returned to HeartHolme, the long journey taking us the entire night. By the time we arrived, it was dawn, the sunlight slowly stretching across the earth and casting long shadows. I was relieved that it was exactly as we'd left it, that nothing had transpired in my absence. I hoped the same was true for Delacroix.

But once we came closer, I realized something was different.

More guards were along the walls, at least ten times the usual number.

I looked at Ian as he sat upon his dragon.

He felt my stare and looked back at me. "I see it too..."

"Hurry, Storm."

Despite the long journey, he picked up speed and descended on HeartHolme, landing much harder than usual because speed was more important than safety. I removed my bindings and dropped down, not waiting for Ian as I jogged to the main gate.

The door swung open for me, a slow creak because the stone slabs were so heavy, and I moved through the crack between the doors, Ian catching up to me. Once we were inside, we saw all the soldiers, fully armed to the teeth.

A soldier passed in front of me, and I grabbed him by the arm and yanked him toward me. "Why is HeartHolme armed for war?"

He didn't look me directly in the eye, as if he feared me. "Delacroix was attacked, Your Majesty."

My fingers loosened on his arm, and the world suddenly became blurry. An invisible poison entered my veins and paralyzed my thoughts and my movements. It was too horrible to confront, the realization that I'd left my family when they needed me…again.

"Huntley!" Mother appeared at the top of the hill, the terror in her face confirming the truth.

Ian released a heavy breath. "Fuck…"

We both ran up to her, getting to the top of the rise that led to the city. I didn't say a word as I faced her, not knowing where to start, what to ask. "Mother…" It was all I could get out, too scared to ask if Delacroix had survived the attack…if my family had survived.

"I just got this letter from Harlow." She unrolled the parchment and held it out to me.

With shaky hands, I kept it open while Ian read over my shoulder. In a hurried scribble was my daughter's message.

Father,

Delacroix was attacked by foes I can only describe as monsters. A fissure opened in the surface of the earth, and at first, I assumed it was just an earthquake, but we suspect that's where they came from.

We were the victors in the battle, but barely, and only because we were lucky. Many lives were lost…

I'm unharmed, but Mother is really hurt… Pyre took her to Minora to see their healer, getting her away from the battle because she was in no position to fight or lead. Atticus is injured as well and hasn't woken.

Please return as soon as you receive this.

"*Fuuuuuccccccckkkkkkk.*" I crumpled the parchment in my closed fist and dropped to my knees. "*Fuck. Fuck. Fuck.*" I slammed my hands into my chest plate over and over, hurting my hands and bruising my chest in the process. "*By the fucking gods!*"

Mother was silent as she stood there, having no words of comfort for such a tragedy.

Ian said nothing either, his face paler than the snow.

Still shaking with anger, I got to my feet, my eyes wet with furious tears. I said nothing to my family before I returned the way I came, all the soldiers still as statues while they listened to my tantrum. It was dead silent, my boots against the earth the only sound—along with the pounding in my temples.

Ian came to my side and walked beside me.

"*No.*" I grabbed him by the shoulder and shoved him back so hard he almost toppled over. "Your job is to protect HeartHolme. Protect your family better than I protected mine."

Storm was tired from our journey and hadn't eaten either, but once I told him what had happened, he raced across the continent with the speed of the wind, just as attached to my family as he was to his own brother.

We arrived in Delacroix an hour before sunset, the field charred in places where the pyres had been. The gate was missing because it'd been removed from its hinges entirely. The castle remained, but the wall around it was broken in places.

Storm landed with a hard thud, and then I was on the ground, running as fast as my legs could carry me, exhaustion and hunger too weak to dampen my determination. I ran past the guards into the city, running to the entrance of the castle so fast my legs burned.

Harlow wasn't there to greet me. Instead, it was *him*.

The man who had destroyed my life.

His eyes locked on mine as he stood in midnight-black armor, his broadsword slung over his shoulder, his cloak hanging down his back and getting caught in the slight breeze. He was there when I should have been, and now my wife and son could be dead.

I pulled my sword out of the scabbard and approached him, desperate to swipe his head clean from his shoulders. "The second I leave, Delacroix is attacked…and you just happen to be here."

He didn't pull his blade out of the scabbard, choosing to keep his arms by his sides. "I fought for Delacroix with the same dedication I would fight for my own people." He was calm in my fire, not the least bit intimidated by my intentions.

"Where's Harlow?"

"She's in Minora to visit her mother."

My girls weren't here, and that killed me. "Then Atticus has recovered?"

"No."

"Then who's in charge?"

His eyes hardened, like he didn't want to answer.

"You motherfucker." I rushed him, striking him down like he was the enemy at my gate.

He blocked the sword with his vambrace then dodged my next attack. All he did was evade, didn't even pull out his own sword to fight me.

I hit him with a flurry of blows, only getting him on the shoulder once. "How." I kept going, determined to chop this fucker into pieces. "Do." I slammed my sword down where his should be, but he was gone again. "You." Pissed off, I struck my sword as quick as I could, not focusing on strength or form, just desperation to hit my target. *"Keep doing that?"*

At that moment, Pyre passed directly overhead and circled, preparing to land.

I stepped back as I looked at the dragon, my heart in my throat because I knew who was on his back.

He landed as gently as he could and immediately flattened onto his belly to bring his body as close to the earth as possible.

Harlow sat behind her mother, supporting her around the waist as she gripped the reins.

"Baby." I rushed forward and grabbed my wife, stilling when I saw her neck...that it was burned.

Her eyes met mine, and they lit up with an unspoken joy. "Huntley..."

I got her into my arms and helped her to the ground before I cradled her into me, hugging her like I never had before. My lips kissed her forehead, and I felt my eyes moisten when I pictured the sight of her neck, the damage she would carry for the rest of her life.

Because I hadn't been there.

"I'm so sorry..."

"It's okay, Huntley," she said into my chest. "It's okay..."

Harlow walked over, her eyes damp at the sight of us.

I didn't want to release my wife, but I needed my daughter, so I pulled her into us, hugging both of my girls at the same time. The tears burned hotter as they fell down my cheeks, all my grief and relief coming together as one. "I'm so sorry..." It was all I could say, all I could get out. "I'm so fucking sorry."

"It's okay." Ivory pulled away, her hands cupping my face. "We're okay."

My daughter had a bruise on the side of her face, and even that was too much for me.

"We're okay, Father," Harlow said. "The maiden said Atticus should pull through…"

"Delacroix survived," Ivory said. "As did all of us. That's all that matters." She swiped my tears with her thumbs, her eyes watering in pain because I was in pain, seeing her like this. "It's alright."

I'd left my family…and I would never forgive myself.

I turned away from them and looked at the vampire I had foolishly released, and I pulled out my blade again.

"Father," Harlow said. "What are you doing?"

"What I should have done in the first place." I came at him again.

Like last time, the vampire refused to draw his sword, choosing to evade my attacks instead.

"*Father!*"

"Huntley, stop this!"

I ignored both of them, intent on killing this bloodsucking bastard.

"*Huntley, he saved me,*" Ivory said. "I would be dead right now if it weren't for him."

I stopped in my tracks and looked at my wife incredulously.

Ivory slowly approached me. "One of those monsters had me by the throat, and he was going to kill me...but Aurelias put himself between us so I could run. He saved my life. He saved our daughter. He saved Delacroix."

My heart shook my ribs with every beat, the anger so deep it couldn't be controlled. Now I was indebted to the man I hated—and that made me hate myself more. I turned my gaze to look at him, his stare neither smug nor arrogant, just calm. I should have been the one to protect my wife and daughter—but I was gone. I was gone...and he took my place.

I returned my sword to my scabbard and severed the tense eye contact between us. "Where's my son?"

"The infirmary," Harlow answered.

With my cheeks wet with my tears and the rage bottled inside my chest, I walked off and headed to the barracks.

TWELVE
IVORY

I walked into the room and found Huntley at Atticus's bedside. He sat in a chair against the side of the bed, his hand resting on our son's bicep, his eyes wet from the tears he had already shed and the ones that were on the horizon.

My son was tall and strong like his father, just as proud but not nearly as stubborn. His skin was tanned from all the time he spent outdoors serving his kingdom, but that beautiful skin had faded to the color of milk. His breathing was labored, like every breath cost too much energy for his broken body.

Huntley didn't look at me, his eyes distant as he stared at our boy.

My hand went to Atticus's, cold to the touch despite the warmth of the day.

My husband still didn't look at me—as if he didn't notice I was there.

The pain in my neck was unbearable. Heat seared my flesh as if the flames were still there, burning deeper and deeper. It was hard to look in the mirror, to see the horrible scars I would carry for the rest of my life. But I was still here...still breathing...and that made the suffering tolerable.

"You should rest, baby." His voice was quiet, broken. "I'll stay with him until he wakes."

The guard brought me a chair, and I took a seat.

Huntley wouldn't meet my look. "I spoke to the maiden outside. She said the infection was defeated and his wounds are healing nicely. It sounds like he'll be okay... His body is just tired."

Huntley didn't move.

"Delacroix needs its king, Huntley."

A dark chuckle escaped his lips. "Look elsewhere—because there's no king here."

I closed my eyes in pain. "This isn't your fault—"

"I traveled to their lands to discover what they are, but what use is that when they were here murdering my family?" He spoke quietly, like if he raised his voice, it would wake our son, who was utterly indisposed.

"Our family lives."

He dropped his voice even more, bringing it to a whisper. "I can't even look at you..." He closed his eyes, breathed hard, and when he opened them again, new tears appeared.

My eyes watered at his pain. "I'm alive, Huntley—"

"And forever maimed. You think that would have happened if I were here? You had to lead our people into a battle, had to defend our daughter, when I should have been the one standing guard while you fled."

"You know I wouldn't have fled—"

"Taking care of our children is not a surrender. It's a duty." He finally looked at me, his eyes vicious. "And you would have done it."

Now I was the one to look away. "These monsters... they're unlike anything I've ever seen. I think the only reason Aurelias survived is because he's not human. They killed our best soldiers in less than thirty seconds—"

"They're lesser men than me—*and so is that vampire.*"

I looked at him again, seeing his eyes on our son. "That vampire is the reason I'm sitting next to you."

He ignored me.

"You could have at least thanked him—"

"Thanked him for doing what I should have done? Thanked him for protecting my family when it should have been me? I'd rather die, Ivory. I'm not thanking the man who took my daughter—"

"He *loves* your daughter."

He inhaled a deep breath, a painful one.

"And I think the feeling is mutual…"

He continued to look away, continued to pretend I didn't say what he didn't want to hear.

"You weren't here because you were serving your kingdom the best you knew how at the time. None of this is your fault—and I can speak for all of us when I say we don't blame you. There's nothing to forgive, but please forgive yourself."

He breathed harder, his eyes watering.

"Let it go."

More tears fell down his cheeks. "When my father was slain, it was just us. My mother was raped…she was powerless…and we struggled to survive a world so fucking cruel. I vowed that would never happen to my family, that my wife would never know such struggles… And I failed. My kingdom was attacked in my absence, and my family suffered."

I reached my hand out to his arm, letting my fingers rest against his armor even though he couldn't feel my touch. "Your mother wasn't powerless. She became the greatest queen I've ever known and raised two powerful sons who took back what's rightfully theirs—and she'll probably outlive us both."

I hoped that would pull a smile at his lips, but it did nothing.

"And your wife and children are not powerless either. Your daughter saved my life and got me to safety. She rode our dragon through the sky and demolished our foes from the air. Your son led his men in battle and won. We may carry scars for the rest of our lives—*but we are not powerless.*"

He took several breaths before he slowly turned to look at me. He stared for a while, his beautiful eyes shining with his tears. Then he moved his hand to mine, grabbing it and placing it on our son's arm, where he could feel us both. "I love you…more than I can say."

I cupped his cheek, my thumb brushing away the tear that fell. "I know you do…"

THIRTEEN
HARLOW

I walked to Aurelias's home, the cottage he'd taken from someone else, and helped myself inside. I expected him to be alone, but he stood there with his vampire kin, all of them speaking close together like they were about to conclude their conversation.

"Sorry." My eyes went to Aurelias, who looked at me with his arms folded over his chest. "Hope I didn't interrupt anything."

Aurelias gave me a slight nod, inviting me to come inside.

Now I was very aware of the fact that I was in a room with several vampires, distant relations of the Teeth, beings that could tear me apart and drain every drop of my blood. But with Aurelias there, I knew I was invincible.

I walked up to the man in black-and-red armor. "We didn't really meet before. I'm Harlow." I extended my hand to shake his.

He gave a slight smile before he took it. "Kingsnake." He turned to the brunette beside him, a beautiful woman in matching armor. "This is my wife, Larisa. Don't fear the snake around her shoulders. He's harmless."

I shook her hand then smiled at the snake. "He's cute."

The snake stuck out his tongue as he looked at me with his yellow eyes.

Larisa grinned. "He likes you."

"And this is my brother Cobra." Kingsnake indicated to the man in gold-and-black armor. "And his wife, Clara."

I shook hands with them both. "Thank you for your help in the battle. And for saving Aurelias."

Cobra smiled. "What are brothers for?"

"And sisters," Larisa said.

"His sacrifice cured the humans," Kingsnake said. "The least we can do is check on him."

Aurelias listened to all of this with a hard expression, contrasting against them in his midnight-black armor with the golden snake in the middle of his chest. He was clearly the odd man out in the family. "They were just leaving."

"Oh..." I felt out of place, intruding on a private moment. "I see."

"I've asked them to relay my need for aid to my father," Aurelias said. "We'll see what happens."

If it didn't happen, I suspected we would all be dead. But why should the vampires care what happened to us? My father wouldn't come to their aid if the situations were reversed.

Larisa moved to Aurelias, drawing near and sharing quiet words no one else could hear.

Kingsnake came closer to me. "Can I give you some advice?"

My eyes moved to him, seeing features similar to his brother, handsome and strong.

"Think of Aurelias as a boulder. The kind your dragon dropped from the sky. And you're a tiny little hammer." He pinched his forefinger and thumb together, leaving a small space between them. "It'll take a lifetime to chisel your way to the center, but if you do, there's a block of gold waiting for you."

I wondered what Aurelias had said about me to make his brother say that, but I would never know. "I've encountered the hardness you've described…"

Aurelias finished his goodbye with Larisa, and then the vampires moved to the door to depart.

"We'll send word soon," Cobra said. "Don't die in the meantime."

One by one, they walked out, and once they were gone, the cottage felt freezing cold in the heat of summer.

I turned to Aurelias. "You don't have to stay—"

"I've made my choice."

I came closer, seeing him stare at the door as if he expected them to return. "You seem close."

"We aren't that close," he said. "But family is family."

"Larisa isn't family, and you two do seem close."

He turned his head to regard me. "She's the first human to ever impress me."

I tried not to be jealous, because her beauty was breathtaking and she provoked a wave of affection in his eyes. She had some invisible power over him, and while Aurelias wasn't mine, I felt territorial.

"And you're the second."

My body always behaved strangely when I was alone with him, when I was the recipient of that intensity. My body was hot and cold at the same time, and the ache in my chest hurt so much it actually felt good. My lungs were full of breath, but I still felt breathless. "I'm sorry for my father's behavior—"

"Stop doing that."

"What?"

"Apologizing for someone else's behavior," he said. "You aren't responsible for his actions or his emotions. And as I said before, I don't take it personally. His feelings are perfectly understandable."

I stared into his dark-colored eyes, eyes that were rich in intensity, deep in magnitude. "You talk about people like you know what they're thinking."

His eyes remained on mine, his expression so hard that my little hammer would never break through. "How's your brother?"

I didn't want him to change the subject, not when I wanted an answer to my suspicion, but I couldn't get his mountain to move to my demands. I had to be patient...as his brother suggested. "I'm not sure. My parents are still with him. They'll probably remain at his side until he wakes up."

"I'm sure he'll pull through."

"I hope so." We hadn't stood together in this cottage in a long time. The last time I was there, I'd slept on the couch, a blanket pulled over my naked body, and when I tried to sneak out, I discovered his true intentions. It was hard to believe we were in that same house again—and I didn't want to kill him.

I wanted to be on that couch again, his hips between my soft thighs, succumbing to the heat that had never died out between us. The flames had been extinguished, but the coals remained red and hot. Now the fire returned, a slow burn that would eventually turn into an inferno—whether we gave in or not. "Aurelias—"

"I meant what I said before." Now his gaze was elsewhere, looking at the cold fireplace. "When this is over, you'll never see me again. There's only one way this ends."

"Why do you keep saying that?" I stared at the side of his face, stared at the shadow on his jawline. "You speak of the end when there hasn't even been a beginning—"

"Because expectations need to be managed." His eyes were on me again, hostile. "They're ironclad, Harlow. Irrevocable. Permanent. If I survive, I will leave these shores, and you'll marry someone suitable. No matter how intense this becomes, no matter how right it may feel...it's temporary."

"You're afraid to hurt me..."

All he did was stare.

"Aurelias, I'm the kind of person that lives in the moment. I don't think ahead, nor do I think about the past. I live in the moment, and now I'll live in the moment even more, knowing tomorrow is not guaranteed. So don't worry about me. You aren't responsible for my feelings—and I'm entitled to feel exactly how I want to feel when I want to feel it."

His breathing escalated, only slightly, his eyes a wildfire of intensity.

"I've wanted you for a long time, and I'm tired of waiting."

I'd barely finished the sentence when his lips were on me, his powerful mouth taking mine with brute force. His hand slipped into my hair, and instead of cupping the back of my head, he fisted the strands like reins to a horse. Once he had my mouth, the pressure eased, and his full lips caressed mine as he wrapped my hair around his fist, getting it all in his grasp.

My hands planted on his arms then his chest, but the armor protected his skin from my touch. Cold to my fingertips and hard as steel, the metal wasn't the material I wanted to explore, but my fingers did trace the snake in the center of his chest, feeling the inlay of gold.

I expected to end up on my back in the corner of the couch like last time, but my feet left the floor as he scooped me into his arms and brought me to his chest. I was heavier in my armor and uniform, but he still carried me like I weighed no more than a pile of feathers.

He took me upstairs, to a part of the cottage I'd never been to, and then I was placed on the unmade bed, where he slept every night. He removed one boot and then the other before he unlocked the pieces of my armor, taking them apart like he knew exactly how they worked even though he was a stranger in this world. When he was down to the clothes, he rushed to get those off as well, pulling off my pants and my underwear at the same time, exposing my wet sex for him to take.

I propped myself on my elbows and watched him undress himself, watched him work every single piece of his armor to loosen it and expose his clothing underneath. It was a strip show, all the powerful pieces dropping away to reveal the powerful man underneath. His sword was placed against the foot of the bed. His daggers on the floor in their sheathes. He removed his tunic and bared all the hard muscles that I longed to touch, his chest that was as hard as the steel plate he wore to protect it, the abs that looked like rivers between mountains.

I wanted to come at the sight of him.

He paused before he removed his bottoms, watching me stare in anticipation, eager to see what I'd already seen before. He loosened the drawstring then dropped his bottoms, revealing the hard cock whose acquaintance I'd already made in several ways.

I couldn't believe it was finally happening. Those lonely nights with my fingers were about to be replaced by the real thing, the man who made all other men obsolete.

His arm curled around the small of my back, and he scooted me up, bringing my head to his pillow.

My hands finally got to touch him, to palm his hard core, to feel the strength of his muscular arms and shoulders. I was already breathless, so anxious to feel him in every way imaginable.

He slipped between my thighs and widened my legs, his arms hooking behind my knees to fold me underneath him. My hands were on his chest, fingers pressing deep into the muscles that turned me on like crazy. I breathed harder and harder, anxious to feel him fill me to complete satisfaction.

He released a knee to guide himself to my glistening sex, and he moaned the second he felt my arousal soak his tip. He pushed inside, gliding through my slickness, and then returned his arm to my knee as he inserted himself as far as he could go.

"Oh fuck..." My head rolled back because it was better than I remembered, the best dick I'd ever had. My eyes watered without a climax, just because I longed for this every time I looked at him. "Aurelias..." One hand snaked up his neck, and I cupped his cheek, reunited with the man who could make my spine shudder.

He started to thrust, his lips above mine, his core tight as he engaged his entire body to push inside me over and over.

I panted as I enjoyed it, feeling the climax in the distance. The burn had been between my legs anytime I looked at him, and now that I finally had him, my body was engulfed with flames. He didn't have to do anything to make me come. He could stay completely motionless, and I would still come around his dick.

He gave a moan against my lips. "Baby..."

My nails sliced into his skin. "I love being your baby."

He started to move faster, his dick a little harder, like that turned him on. "Fuck." His eyes looked into mine, dark with restraint, doing the best he could to finish last.

"I'm about to come..."

He rocked harder, grinding his hips hard against my clit.

"Yes...." I gripped him as the fire burned, as it numbed every sensation in my body to heighten the pleasure. My lips felt his in a partial kiss before the moans started, before my hips bucked on their own, before the tears started to squeeze past my closed eyelids. "Aurelias."

He moved faster now, fucking me hard enough to tap his headboard against the wall.

I finished, stars in my eyes, my hands on his hard body. "Slow down..." I grabbed his ass and set the pace, making him slide through me nice and slow. "Feel how wet you make your baby..."

He closed his eyes and groaned against me, his breathing deep and labored, his skin blotched with redness from his arousal.

"Come inside me." I spoke into his ear, my hand deep in his hair. "Then make me come again..."

Another groan came from his closed lips as he continued his slow thrusts. His breaths turned shaky as his dick hardened inside me. Then he inhaled a deep breath as he released, moaning like a hungry bear, dumping all his seed inside me with forceful pumps.

"Yes..." I whispered in his ear as he came, feeling the weight of his release. "I love feeling you inside me."

When he finished, his eyes moved to mine, more intense than they'd ever been. His dick remained hard inside me, like that was the warm-up we both needed after an eternity of abstinence. He released my knees so my thighs could grip his torso, my ankles locked together against the top of his ass.

He fucked me hard, fucked me until the headboard marked the wall, fucked me until I screamed his name. "Aurelias!"

I'd fallen asleep.

When I opened my eyes, the sheets were to my shoulders, and white candles brought the room a faint glow. Aurelias was beside me, glorious in his nakedness, the sheets bunched at his waist. His eyes were open and focused on the ceiling, his hand resting on his hard stomach.

I wanted this quiet moment to last forever, to look at him beside me, a living statue of one of our guards, and forget about all the horrible things that happened over the last few days. I looked out the window behind him, seeing the pitch-black of the night. I knew I needed to return to the castle before my parents worried about my whereabouts, but I wanted to stay like this...forever.

He turned his head my way, as if he knew I was awake even though I hadn't moved. His dark eyes locked on mine, and he stared, as if he experienced the same serenity that pumped through my veins. That invisible barrier was no longer between us, and I was ecstatic to feel my emotions to their full intensity rather than masking them and pretending they didn't exist.

He turned toward me and came close, his arm moving around my waist, his smell surrounding me. He dipped his head and caught my lips with his for a kiss before he lay on the pillow beside me.

My fingers reached to feel the stubble against his jaw, to stroke the coarse hair on his handsome face. This man made me wet every time I looked at him, and if I didn't have somewhere else to be, I would be on top of him right now. "I should go home..."

He didn't ask me to stay, probably knowing that was best. "I'll walk you."

"I think it's best if I'm seen alone at this time of night."

"As you wish, Princess."

I grinned. "I prefer 'baby.'"

"Alright." His palm flattened against my back, and he drew me close, pressing a hard kiss to my lips, an invitation to stay in that warm bed with him deep between my legs. "Baby." When he pulled away, he did the sexiest thing, a subtle rub of his nose against mine. He left the bed and moved for his clothes, buck naked and powerful.

I stared at his muscular back that looked like it was carved with little daggers before I left the warm sheets and donned the clothes and armor I'd worn here. I fixed my hair with my fingertips so it wouldn't be obvious that I'd been fucked incessantly the last few hours.

He pulled on his boxers and walked me downstairs, through the dark cottage, and to the front door.

He opened the door, like he didn't care if anyone was outside who could spot him in his nakedness. "I'll see you in the morning."

"Goodnight." I rose on my tiptoes and kissed him, but my hand reached for his crotch and gave him a gentle squeeze.

He grinned against my lips. "Goodnight."

I walked out and headed home, unable to suppress the smile on my face, the heat in my cheeks, the relief between my legs. When he'd denied me in the alleyway, it had hurt far more than I cared to admit. At first, I thought it was just the sting of rejection, but when the pain lingered, I knew it was more than that.

It was the pain of wanting someone so deeply…and not having them.

I walked back to the castle, following the light of the torches, and I entered the place I'd called home my whole life. The guards had returned to their positions around the castle, but none of them looked at me or questioned me, so my parents hadn't asked them to alert them to my presence.

They were probably still with Atticus.

I headed to my bedroom, looking at the bed where I'd slept with Aurelias, where he'd held me all night but didn't even kiss me. The bed looked so lonely now, too big for a single person. But I undressed and crawled inside, expecting to fall asleep instantly. But I stayed wide awake, needing the comfort only Aurelias could provide.

The next morning, a guard came to my bedroom. "His Majesty requests you join him in the infirmary."

"Did Atticus wake up?"

"That's all the information I have."

I dressed quickly then headed down to the infirmary. When I walked into the bedroom, my parents were there, their eyes bloodshot from the exhaustion. My father looked nearly dead, all the stress and sleep deprivation hardening his features. My mother's face looked strained too, like the pain in her neck still bothered her because it hadn't had time to subside.

But Atticus was awake, sitting up in bed, his eyes heavy like he could sleep for another three days. But color had returned to his face, and when his eyes locked on mine, a little smile formed. "I heard you saved the kingdom."

"I *helped* save the kingdom—as did you." I moved past my parents to embrace him, but I was careful to handle him gently, not to apply too much pressure to his wounds that still needed to heal. "You look better."

"More handsome?" he said. "It's the battle scars."

My heart melted at his good mood, the way he could dismiss a tragedy and make me smile.

"Can't wait to try them out on the girls." He flexed his right arm, where a long scar was forming from an enemy's blade. He made his muscles plump over and over, showing off like he was with the boys.

I rolled my eyes. "I liked it better when you couldn't talk."

He chuckled then turned serious. "You okay?"

"I'm fine." I touched my cheek absent-mindedly, where the bruise was beginning to fade. "That's the worst of it."

Father remained at his bedside, unable to take his eyes off his son, his expression hard but his eyes emotional. "Rolfe blood is powerful." He clapped his son gently on the shoulder. "I'm proud of you, son. You served your kingdom valiantly."

Atticus avoided his gaze, clearly touched by our father's praise but unable to accept it openly. "So… what were those things?"

Now the air in the room changed, the joy sucked out and replaced by a veil of tension.

Mother looked at Father for direction.

His eyes dropped for a moment before he spoke. "We'll discuss it when you're feeling better."

"Wow," Atticus said. "That sounds bad."

"Nothing for you to worry about right now," Father said.

"That means it wasn't a war," Atticus said. "It was just a battle, and we'll be seeing them again. If it weren't for that vampire in our ranks, we would all be dead right now. Father, I don't think we're in any position to wait for me to get better."

Atticus was transported from the infirmary to the castle, where he would be more comfortable. A wheelchair was supplied, and one of the guards rolled him around where he needed to go—even though it made him furious.

The guard placed him at the table with us, the cooks in the kitchen preparing our lunch even though none of us were hungry. At least I wasn't…because I was about to say something to my father that he wouldn't like. "I think Aurelias should join us." I looked across the table at my mother, who had gauze secured around her neck, medicinal herbs and ointment constantly reapplied every hour.

My father's stare pierced the side of my face, white-hot. "That vampire will never sit at my table."

I finally had the courage to meet his gaze. "His name is Aurelias—"

"*I don't care what his name is.*" He kept his voice quiet, but his tone was furious.

"*He saved us.*" I slammed my closed hand down on the table.

He quickly looked away, like I'd just said the wrong thing.

"Father, this is ridiculous—"

"Don't tell me what's ridiculous." His eyes moved back to me. "The fact that you feel any affection for him after what he did—"

"Let it go." Now it was my mother who spoke. "Huntley."

He slowly turned to regard her.

"This is not you," she said calmly.

He wouldn't look at her. Wouldn't look at me.

"Harlow. Atticus." My mother stared at my father. "I need to speak with your father alone."

FOURTEEN
AURELIAS

I went into the wild to feed on animal blood, forcing myself to enjoy the taste rather than despise it. There was no other option. Human blood would make me far stronger, and I was certain I could find someone to give it to me willingly, but a man like King Rolfe would never understand that. However long I would remain here, this was how I would feed.

When I returned to the cottage, a guard was posted outside.

I was treated like a criminal...again.

"King Rolfe wishes to speak with you in his study."

I stilled, expecting a very different message. "Alright."

"I'll take you there now."

I followed him to the castle, entering it for the second time after I'd spent the night with Harlow in her bed, and I moved down the hallway until I approached a room with double doors, both of them wide open to allow me entry.

The guard extended his open palm to me. "Your sword."

My hand rested on the hilt, but I didn't dare withdraw it.

"It's fine, Baron."

My eyes moved to the study inside, seeing King Rolfe sitting behind his desk, dressed in his heavy armor, his closed fingers resting against his hard mouth. His crystal-blue eyes were on mine, hostile as always.

I stepped inside and approached one of the armchairs that faced him.

"Close the door," Huntley instructed. "And do not disturb us."

The guard shut the door.

The silence was so loud I couldn't even hear my own breathing. I sat in the armchair, feeling his stare burn through me like a fire through skin. The hatred emanating from him was as hot as the blazing sun. The man couldn't stand to be in my presence—not even after I saved his wife.

"And I thought I was stubborn..."

He dropped his hand, took a slow breath, and kept his gaze focused on me even though it physically hurt him. "I should be thanking you for what you did for my family, but that's hard for me to do because of what you did to Harlow."

"I understand." His emotions ran rampant the way Harlow's did. Most men didn't feel a lot, only in times of intensity, but King Rolfe had a spectrum of emotions that always burned. He was passionate. Whenever he spoke of his daughter, I could actually *feel* his love for her, feel its intensity, feel that unconditional dedication that not all parents felt toward their children. Truth be told, there were times when I wasn't sure if my own father cared whether Kingsnake lived or died.

"Until you're a father yourself, you'll never understand..." His eyes shifted away, looking at the cold fireplace behind me. "I'm a very stubborn man. It's hard for me to see the good when I only want to see the bad."

"I understand that as well...since I'm also very stubborn."

His eyes came back to me as he straightened in his chair. "This is hard for me to say...in ways you couldn't possibly understand..." He hesitated, his eyes shifting away momentarily before he had the strength to look at me again. "Thank you for saving my wife... and my daughter...and the kingdom that's mine to protect."

I felt the sincerity mixed with anguish, the self-loathing, the guilt. "You resent me for being the one to save them. I understand that. I understand how much you love your family and how shitty it feels that someone else saved them and not you—especially me, who caused you so much pain."

His stare remained hard, but there was a flash of something I couldn't discern.

"I hope you forgive yourself...someday."

He hadn't moved, hadn't spoken. Instead of a jolt of anger, there was nothing there at all. "Harlow tells me you didn't return with your kin. You've chosen to stay here…and fight with us."

Fight for her, actually. "My brothers will ask our father to send our armies to your cause. I can't promise they'll come, but since I asked, I think he'll oblige. I've made my desire to stay very clear, and he knows there's no other way to get me back unless he sails to these lands himself."

An invisible pain moved through him, unexplainable. "What are your intentions with my daughter?" His voice came out quiet, pained, like it took all his strength to ask the question he didn't want to ask.

It was a heavy question, a question with an answer so complicated I couldn't explain it. "May I speak candidly?"

He inhaled a slow breath, like he wanted anything but that. But he gave a nod, regardless.

"You have no chance against these beings. If my brothers and I hadn't been here, your kingdom would have fallen. If I leave these shores, Harlow will be killed…or worse."

A surge of terror exploded inside him, invisible under his rough exterior.

"I can't let that happen to her. From the moment I met her, I respected her, and that respect has only grown deeper in her company." The way she fought me. Her refusal to give up, even when the match isn't fair. Her refusal to look weak in front of anyone…except me. "My intentions toward your daughter are to protect her with my life."

Huntley looked away, trying to process that declaration as calmly as possible. He already knew humans would perish against these enemies, but it probably hurt to hear it. And it probably hurt to know that he needed someone other than himself. "You're a vampire…and she's human." He still wouldn't look at me, like this was unbearable. "How will that work?" His eyes remained on the fire.

"It won't."

His eyes shifted back to mine instantly.

"It's temporary."

"And she knows this?"

I nodded. "Yes."

He straightened in his chair again. "Why risk your life, along with the lives of your people, for a woman who's temporary?" His eyes narrowed in suspicion. "I don't mean to accuse you of deceit, but that simply makes no sense."

"It's...complicated."

"I'm a smart man, Aurelias."

It was the first time he'd called me by my name, so I knew our standing had improved. "Vampires are immortal."

His eyes remained sharp.

"Unless we're killed in battle, we live forever."

"So you're risking even more for her."

"I guess you could say that." Now my actions felt even heavier. I risked not only my life, but my afterlife as well. Because after this...there was nothing. I could return home and live ten thousand more years...or I could risk it in battle for humans.

He was quiet for a long time, pain brewing in his heart. "If she were a vampire, would that change anything?"

Another heavy question. "If she were already a vampire, everything would be different." There would be no barrier between us, no reason for restraint. "But she's not...so it doesn't matter."

"Unless you turned her into one..." He didn't ask the question, like he was scared of my answer.

"I can sire her, but even if she asked, I wouldn't do it."

"Why?" His question was unleashed with the quickness of his blade.

I wouldn't tell him the real reason. It was none of his business. "Once you become a vampire, you forsake your soul, so when you die...you just die. There's nothing afterward. No afterlife. I would never take that from her."

Huntley's expression was so tight, it was as if he was about to snap a cord in his neck. There was terror in his heart, rampant and uncontrollable, slowly poisoning his veins. "Are you an honorable man, Aurelias?"

"Yes."

"Then you keep your word?"

"Always."

"Promise me you'll never allow my daughter to be one of you." Desperation burned in his eyes, a plea from a father.

"You have my word."

When he looked away, he breathed a deep sigh of relief.

"Even if I asked, she would never do it."

He looked at me again.

"I know her heart, and she couldn't bear to live a life where everyone she loves dies, while she lives on. To know she'll never see you and her mother in the afterlife. To know she can't have children. I never have to ask the question when I already know the answer."

"You can't have children?"

I shook my head.

All his emotions stilled, but they changed. Now there was pity, pity so strong it was like a cascading waterfall. "I'm sorry to hear that." Calm sincerity broke through, apparent on his face and in his heart.

"I knew the consequences when I made my choice."

His eyes dropped, the sadness still in his heart.

"I have a request."

His thoughts seemed lost elsewhere, probably thinking about his child-rearing years, an experience I would never have. His eyes found mine again. "I'm listening."

"Let me help you."

His heart sank like a stone.

"We both know how this will end unless you do."

His closed fingers returned to his jawline.

"Put aside your prejudice and embrace me as your ally. I will fight for your daughter's life as hard as you will. Even if my kin don't come to my aid, my sword is still yours. I've fought in many battles and won many wars. My expertise is invaluable. Forgive my transgression—and let me help you."

Huntley looked away, his silence starting as seconds but turning into minutes. An array of emotions swept through him as he sat in consternation. "I don't want my daughter to get hurt."

"I've made it very clear that I'll be leaving once this war is over. I didn't tell her the specifics because she doesn't need to know the reasons, but the expectations have been set. She's smart and strong…she'll be fine." It was hard to imagine that moment, when I stepped onto the ship and sailed away forever, back to my previous life that would feel stale and empty after the heat of her flames and the brightness of her mind. "I'm the one who won't be…"

FIFTEEN
IVORY

I removed the gauze that had been secured around my neck, the ointment and herbs absorbed into the fabric. Pieces of skin were still coming off, slowly dying and withering away. I stared into the mirror at my vanity and saw the mark of flames across my skin, the distant outline of the monster's closed fist. No healer could remove it. The scar was permanent, an ugly reminder of the tragedy that had struck my home.

I refused to pity myself, not when I'd escaped with my life and so many good men didn't. The piles of bodies on the battlefield were some of the biggest I'd ever seen. Our army had been decimated by half.

Huntley entered our bedchambers, dressed for battle, not for bedtime.

I sucked in a deep breath and dropped my sadness, knowing I had to hide my grief from him most of all.

He set his blade against the wall, close to the bed and easy for him to grab in the middle of the night. Then he started to undress, pulling his armor apart piece by piece, his eyes on nothing in particular—and definitely not on me.

"How'd it go?"

Huntley took a long time to answer. "We settled our differences."

"Good."

"He'll join us in the morning."

"I think that's wise." I preferred my daughter to want a man who was human, who served the Kingdoms honorably and came from a good family. But she seemed to want a vampire...and I had to accept that.

He removed his shirt, showcasing a powerful body with endless muscles. His arms were boulders, his chest like the stone that built this castle. An insatiable appetite and a dedication to strength had preserved him in his youth, making him the most desirable man to most people.

I was already his inferior, but now with these ugly scars…I was even more inferior.

He sat on the edge of the bed, his back to me.

My heart pained at his actions, knowing he was doing everything he possibly could not to look at me.

I didn't want to look at myself either.

I inhaled a slow breath, dissipating the tears before they had a chance to form. "What did you discuss?"

Huntley said nothing for a long time. "He'd pledged his sword to Harlow. Pledged his life…"

"A very strong declaration of love." I stared at his back in the mirror, watching the way he breathed.

"Since he's a vampire, there's no future for them. When the war is over, he'll leave these shores, never to return. She's aware of this."

"He's willing to risk his life for an unsustainable relationship?" I asked incredulously.

After a pause, he spoke. "Yes."

"That's senseless."

"That's what he said, and I believe him."

"While I'd rather she be with a human, I don't see why being different species should keep them apart. Look at Elora and Bastian. Or Ian and Avice—"

"Vampires are immortal. He could make her a vampire, but that would require her to forsake her soul, and then there would be no afterlife if she were to be killed."

I inhaled a slow breath, my teeth clenched in terror.

"He promised me he would never do that…and I believe him."

The breath I held came out slow, unsteady. "He's even more honorable than I realized."

Huntley was quiet. "Yes…I suppose he is."

I left the vanity and moved to his side of the bed, taking the seat beside him.

He stared at the wall ahead of him, his eyes dead and empty.

I waited for him to look at me.

His forearms rested on his thighs as his hands came together, his muscular thighs exposed in his shorts.

"Huntley."

His eyes remained fixated.

"You need to look at me."

He inhaled a deep breath, the kind that made his chest rise several inches. His hands automatically balled into fists, the tendons popping from the strain.

"It's better than being dead."

"You don't understand..."

"You can't be everywhere at once—"

"But I should be at your side always."

"Your duty to our people comes before us—"

"*No.*" His nostrils flared as he released a hard breath. "I once believed that was true, but I couldn't lead if I lost you. If I lost Atticus or Harlow. You are first—always. Every time I look at those scars, I'm reminded that I failed as a husband." He closed his eyes briefly, like he was on the verge of tears. "I'm unworthy of your love."

My hand cupped his cheek to turn him toward me, but he fought it, refusing my pull. "Huntley..." I turned his head again, and this time, he allowed me. Our eyes locked, his blue eyes drowning in pain. "I've never needed you to protect me. When your mother handed me to the Teeth, did I need you to rescue me?"

He was silent.

"No—because I rescued myself."

He started to turn away.

My fingers forced him back to me. "It's hard to look at these scars in the mirror, to see my beautiful skin destroyed by fire that still burns my flesh. But it's much harder to watch your husband avoid you, avoid your stare, pretend you don't exist...when you need his love more than ever."

He closed his eyes in shame.

"I need you to accept the way I look. I need you to look at me the way you used to, like any time we're in the room together, you can't keep your eyes off me. If I didn't have these scars, you would have taken me to bed the second you came home. But now...it's like you don't want me anymore."

His eyes remained closed. "You know that's not how I feel—"

"But that's how it seems. That monster destroyed my flesh...but don't let him destroy us."

When he opened his eyes, it was accompanied by a heavy breath. "Nothing could ever destroy us, baby. It's just hard to look at the injuries I failed to prevent. You don't understand how sick it makes me to know that someone did this to you...that someone hurt my wife."

My hand squeezed his. "I know."

His fingers squeezed mine back before he brought my palm to his lips and kissed it.

"Now make love to me." I missed the way he made me feel desirable, like women half my age still couldn't compete with me, the way he expressed his love with his touches and kisses. I'd feared he wouldn't return to me when he left for HeartHolme, and I'd nearly died in his absence, so all I wanted to do was unite our bodies and let our souls touch.

He stared into my eyes for a while, searching for the strength to carry on from the heaviness of this conversation, from the reality of our war-torn lives. In times of peace, our lives felt like a fairy tale, but now they felt like a nightmare.

He brought his forehead to mine and moved his big fingers into my hair, the heat from his body like the surface of the sun. His nose rubbed against mine before he kissed me, a gentle touch between our lips, but it was enough to make my stomach warm. He turned his head and kissed me again, and once our mouths felt each other, everything else fell into place. He gripped me like he didn't want to let go. He breathed into my mouth with desperation. He desired me the way I wanted to be desired.

He laid me back on the bed as he continued to kiss me, his hand yanking up my dress so his fingers could slide into my panties. His fingers found my nub and rubbed it hard as his tongue slipped into my mouth. Then he inserted his fingers, feeling the wetness that he caused.

His mouth left mine, and he stood upright, dropping his boxers to show his raging hard dick. Possession burned in his eyes, his jawline tense from the way he clenched his mouth. He grabbed my hips and yanked me down to the edge before he pulled my underwear over my ass and dropped them to the floor. Then his big hands scooped me up, and he moved inside me, invading me slowly, coated by my arousal.

I moaned when I felt him, when I felt the reunion I'd wanted since the moment he was home. My hands gripped his wrists as he held me at the edge of the bed, my body stuffed with his thickness.

Then he thrust into me over and over, eyes locked firmly on my face, taking me like there was no other woman in the world he wanted more than me.

SIXTEEN
AURELIAS

I felt her mind before she reached the front door.

It had its own signature, its own color, its own power. I could recognize it in a crowded room full of angry people. It pressed against my mind in a distinct way, like the warmth of the sun...when I used to enjoy it.

Then she knocked.

I was on the couch in front of the fire, using it for light in the dark living room. I'd cleared out all the personal belongings of the previous owner when I first moved in, put everything in the basement along with his dead body. It didn't make the house feel more like a home—just empty.

In my boxers, I walked to the front door and let her inside.

The second her eyes were on me, there was a flush of emotion, like a flash of lightning across the sky, striking the earth and setting the surface on fire. White-hot and burning, her flames exuded from her presence in an infinite diameter. It was more than just desire, rather profound longing. It was hard to believe a woman so fucking perfect could desire me so deeply, a man who thrived on human blood, a man haunted by endless demons.

If only she could feel the way I desired her.

She said nothing as she stared at me, like she expected me to speak first or forgot what she was going to say. "How did it go with my father?" She entered the cottage, not wearing her uniform and armor this time. She was in a short-sleeved dress, her dark hair long down her back.

I shut the door and followed her to the living room. "We're on good terms now."

"What was said?" She grabbed my glass of scotch from the coffee table and took a drink.

"That's between him and me."

Her eyes were locked on mine as she drank, licking her lips when she was done, enticing me whether it was intentional or not. "I'm glad he's accepted you. We have a war to win, and that should be our focus." The flames highlighted her features in a beautiful glow, the kind that made her pale skin rosy. Blood pumped through her veins, made the artery at her neck twitch, but I desired only her flesh.

I didn't crave her taste whatsoever. "I agree."

Her eyes stared at my face but slowly moved down, taking in my nearly naked appearance, climbing over the hardness of my bare flesh. But she didn't step toward me, didn't make a move, even though she clearly wanted to. "When the fuck are you going to kiss me?" Her voice was quiet and sultry, sexy in a way most women couldn't pull off. She tried to be stern and unflinching, her walls unbreakable, so when she did show her vulnerable side... Fuck.

The heat rushed through me at her request, the weakness in my knees, the painful throb of my heart that wouldn't stop. A magnetism existed between us, impossible to overcome, the strength rivaling mountains. I fought it as long as I could until I finally gave in.

I moved close to her, watching the way she sucked in a breath when I drew near. The firelight continued to blanket her in warm color. My hand slipped into her hair, and I cradled her head, my stare on her lips, her perfect little nose, on the beautiful blue eyes that reminded me of the summer sky.

Her fingers immediately grasped my wrist, squeezed it as she turned into my palm to kiss my flesh.

My arm snaked around her body and brought her close, the two of us standing in the light of the fire, eyes glued to one another like they were locked in place. I wanted to kiss her, wanted to do all sorts of things to her, but I also just wanted to look at her.

My thumb brushed the corner of her mouth, and her eyes closed at the touch, like every little move I made was intoxicating. We were two bits of metal connected by a surge of electricity, a transfer of heat so powerful it happened instantaneously.

I dipped my head and pressed my lips against hers, landing on pillows made of clouds, absorbed by her desperate desire. My lips parted hers before I took her bottom lip, feeling its plumpness, tasting its goodness. Her kiss was immediate and anxious, her head tilting to kiss me hard, to give me her tongue. Her desperation was so profound that she needed more of me, quickly.

It was a rush from that point onward, clothes on the floor, her tits in my big hands, her tongue in my mouth. My spine was on fire and frozen solid all at once. I felt her pull me to the couch before she pushed me against the cushions.

I sat against the back of the couch and watched her climb on top of me, scooting close to my chest so her tits were right in my face, perky with hard nipples. She grabbed my base and pointed me inside her, not even moistening my length because her pussy was wet enough for the both of us. She sank on my dick with a moan of satisfaction. "Aurelias…"

When she said my name, I was fucking done. "Baby…" My hands gripped her ass, and I kissed the valley between her tits, sucked on her nipples and tasted her delicious flesh. I could feel her heartbeat, feel the pounding of blood through her body, but I still didn't crave it.

She moved up and down, rocking her hips and catching my dick, moaning every time she took me balls deep.

I was lost in the rush of emotion between us, my fingers kneading her ass as I guided her up and down, wanting her harder and faster. My dick parted her perfect pussy again and again, the length smeared by the pool of arousal that her body produced just for me. "Fuck," I whispered against her neck, my heavy breaths hitting her skin as she continued to ride me.

Her hand cupped my face, and she tilted my head back to catch my lips, to kiss me as her fingers dug deep into my hair. She paused to moan against my lips when the euphoria became too much, but then she kissed me again, her pussy taking my dick over and over.

By some miracle, I held on, wanting to release inside her the second I felt her. I wasn't the kind of man that had to battle himself to the finish line, but every time I had her, it took all my restraint to focus. It wasn't her tits or her ass or the fact that she was great in bed. It was something more than that, the emotion she provoked in me at the simplest touch, the way it hurt just to look at her sometimes, the way I cared for her when I tried with all my might not to give a shit.

She interrupted our kiss and spoke against my lips. "I'm gonna come…"

My fingers squeezed her ass even harder, my dick desperate to rupture.

She started to drop onto my dick even harder, rock her hips deeper, moan loud enough for the neighbors to figure out exactly what we were doing. Tears exploded from the corners of her eyes and started to streak down her red cheeks.

My dick disobeyed my command and released, my moans matching hers, the both of us coming simultaneously, pulling at each other with desperation. It felt so damn good to come in a pussy that was coming on my dick.

It was a long high, both of us clinging to it like the last light on a winter day. We both finished then came down slowly, like snow falling in the twilight. Her beautiful skin was coated in a sheen of sweat, and I kissed away all the grains of salt on her chest and neck.

Her hands were in my hair again as she kissed me, her tongue diving into my mouth possessively, like our orgasms had been a mere interruption. "Take me to bed," she said against my mouth. "And fuck me the way you did last time."

She was flexible and foldable, so I had her pinned underneath me as I rammed hard into her body, making the headboard clatter against the wall and leave even more marks. I fucked her like a whore I'd paid for the night, and no matter how hard I gave it to her, she still wanted more.

"I'm gonna come again." Her hands were planted against my chest as she heaved with the deep breaths she took. She always told me when she was on the verge, as an invitation to join her.

My lips moved to her ear. "You want my come, baby?"

Her nails clawed down my back instinctively. "Yes."

"*Please.*" I continued to thrust hard as I breathed into her ear.

"Please..." Her voice cracked with tears, and her nails dug in deeper.

"Here it comes," I said, my voice breaking as the desire took me.

She came with a yell, slicing my flesh with her nails, moaning to the ceiling as her body gripped me with the strength of a clenched fist. "Yes..."

I gave my final pumps as I groaned in relief, coming harder than I did last night, dumping my empty seed inside the object of my desire. Our orgasms overlapped the way they had downstairs, and we clung to each other until the final high had passed.

It wasn't until I rolled away that I felt the searing heat from my movements, the sweat coating my skin, the strain in my muscles. I lay on my back, my breathing still elevated, and stared at the ceiling.

She crawled on top of me, her legs straddling my hips, her long hair touching my shoulder.

"Really, baby?"

"This is your fault."

"My fault?" I asked, a smile moving on to my lips.

"If you hadn't kept me waiting for so long…" She moved closer to me, pressing a kiss to my lips.

"Give me a couple minutes."

Her fingers moved to my mouth, tracing my jawline. "Can I see?"

"See what?"

"Your fangs..." She continued to outline my mouth. "I don't feel them when I kiss you."

"They retract when I'm not feeding."

"Show me." Her thumb brushed over my bottom lip.

I would never show her. "They emerge when I feed. I can't do it voluntarily."

She sat back, dropped her sex right on my dick. "Why don't you feed on me...?" A heavy bout of silence filled the air after she spoke, a tension that penetrated deep into my muscles.

I propped myself up on my elbows, my dick hardening when I felt her wet sex. "Because I won't."

"You said it feels good." She moved farther over me, our lips close together. "Really good."

My eyes remained hard in defiance. "I'll never feed on you, baby. Don't ask me again."

"Why not?"

"Because I won't."

"You can bite me where no one can see the mark—"

"The answer is no." I didn't raise my voice, but I felt the way it changed, the way it turned vicious.

Her eyes were on me, guarded in offense, and a tidal wave of disappointment rushed through her. All of her emotions were always at the surface, always intense, always striking, whereas the average person rarely felt things intensely. It was addictive, even when she was pissed off like this.

"Don't ask me again."

She climbed off me and walked away, her perky ass shaking as she strutted with purpose across the room and out the door.

I stayed where I was, not the kind of man to chase a woman.

She grabbed her clothes downstairs and left, making sure to slam the door so I'd know she'd walked out on me.

I sat there for a minute, maybe two, until the discomfort in my chest turned unbearable. A heavy sigh escaped my clenched teeth, and then I was out of bed, doing the one thing I never thought I would do.

Chase a woman.

SEVENTEEN
IAN

I smoothed out the scroll and weighed down the edges to read the letter Huntley sent. "Atticus is awake, and Ivory is okay. Her neck will be forever scarred by the siege, and I ask that you not stare when you see her." I read it out loud for my mother to hear. "Based on what Harlow has described to me, these are the same beings we spotted in the east. The leader came to Delacroix in search of me—but he found Ivory instead." I paused to read, the weight of the situation suddenly heavy. "He grabbed her by the neck and produced fire, fire that charred her flesh as she dangled there. The only reason she got away was because the vampire intervened. He raised his sword and fought five of them at once so Ivory and Harlow could escape. Then his brothers joined him and effectively saved Delacroix.

I've spoken to Aurelias in private, and as offensive as his words were, they were also true—that our kingdom would have fallen if he hadn't been there to save it." I stopped to look at my mother, who kept her composure but looked ill at the same time. "His brothers have returned to their lands to ask for the armies to come to our defense. It's not a short journey, so we may not get an answer for a long time. I'll prepare the Kingdoms for the defense because we have no way to march into their lands and attack with the mountains barring—" I stopped when General Macabre entered the room, dressed in his armor and weapons because he'd been reinstated to his position. If our chances of survival weren't so dire, I'd be angrier at the sight of him.

He hesitated before he approached, keeping a distance between us and avoiding my gaze.

I started over so he could hear the full letter, and then I continued. "There's no way to march into their lands and with the mountain barring our path. Our only option is to be ready for the second battle. There's no doubt we'll need to embrace the vampires if we have any hope of surviving this war. I've accepted Aurelias as an ally and trust his pledge to our cause. I'll send orders when I have them." I finished the letter then removed the weights so the scroll would tighten into a roll once more.

None of us spoke. Not for seconds. Not even minutes.

My mother rested her arms over the back of one of the chairs at the dining table. "This is grave news, indeed."

"Our dragons are useless," I said quietly. "You can't fight fire with fire."

"Unless we use them in a different way," Mother said.

General Macabre looked out the window. "We're preparing the battlefield for war. Hidden trenches primed for collapse. Barbed arrows. We would normally use fire as well, but I realize that's not an option."

"That's not enough..." I said it to myself more than the others.

"Then what are your orders, m'lord?" He still wouldn't look at me.

"We need to identify their weakness. If we don't, we're fucked."

"And how do you suggest we do that—"

"I'll need to return to their lands and figure it out."

"Ian," Mother said. "They'll be expecting you now."

I turned to my mother. "You heard what Huntley said. They can produce fire at will. We have no chance. Maybe if we had more soldiers, but I have no idea how big their army is. If we're outnumbered, I need to know that too."

"And what will we do if we are?" General Macabre asked.

"Flee." I stared at the table as I said it, as I felt the anguish of surrender.

Mother hesitated, horrified by what I'd said. "*Flee?*"

I nodded.

"These are our lands, Ian," Mother said. "They belong to us and no one else—"

"*Mother.*" She was the strongest person I knew, but sheer will wouldn't win this war. "Did you not hear what Huntley said? If the vampires hadn't been there, Delacroix would have fallen. You know what that means? It means men don't stand a chance against these demons. It's not a fair fight, and instead of sending everyone to their deaths, we flee. There's no shame in that."

"And go where?" she demanded.

"I don't know, but the world is a big place—"

"We'll travel to someone else's lands and become slaves," she snapped. "That's what will happen, Ian. You would do that to your own people?"

I closed my eyes in anguish. "What other option do we have?"

"We fight."

Now I snapped. *"We can't fight these things. Do you not understand?"*

She flinched at my hostility. "The vampires may come—"

"But they may not. Why would they make an arduous journey for someone else's battle? I'm not holding my breath on that. And a single vampire isn't enough to defeat their forces. I'm just being practical here."

She looked away, her arms crossed over her chest.

"We can't go to war without a viable plan. Trenches and arrows…it's a fucking joke."

General Macabre stared at the surface of the table.

"I have no other choice but to go."

"Huntley made it very clear he wants you to stay here," Mother said. "As do I."

"Well, that's too bad," I said. "I've been there before. It's better than someone who's unfamiliar with the east. And if I get captured, I'll never talk…and someone else might. The less they know about us, the better."

Mother was furious, her eyes like daggers. "You would defy your king."

"I would defy the fucking gods," I snapped, "if it meant I could protect my family." I slammed my hand on the table and made it shake. "Mother, leave us."

She stilled, shocked by the order.

"Leave us," I repeated.

"You're not the king, Ian," she said coldly.

"I'm as good as," I said as I met her gaze. "Since Huntley appointed me as his successor if he's killed."

"That job belongs to Ivory—"

"In a time of peace, not war. Ivory is strong and brave, but she would be inconsolable if she lost Huntley to our enemies. And neither she nor her children would be able to carry on if that were to transpire. Now leave us—so I can speak to my general in private."

Mother's eyes flashed in hostility, but she didn't speak.

"You may not think I'm worthy of the crown, but your favorite son does."

All her anger disappeared at the insult. Her eyes immediately softened, like those words cut through her. "Ian—"

"*Leave.*" I wouldn't look at her, wanting to be rid of her presence as quickly as possible.

After a pause, she walked out and left us, the guard closing the door after her departure.

I stared at the table for a moment, doing my best to let the rage simmer before I regarded General Macabre beside me. "You've been reinstated to your position due to our current circumstances, because the perseverance of HeartHolme is more important than your transgression. I won't ask you to kneel and plead for my forgiveness. I ask us to fight together to protect the good people of this glorious kingdom, to shed our blood together and let it seep into the soil as we sacrifice our lives for those we love."

He was distinctly guarded as he studied me, but as he heard me speak, that sheathed hostility began to wane. His eyes turned receptive rather than cold. "It would be an honor to fight alongside you, Steward Ian. And to give our lives for those we've sworn to protect."

"Then let's move forward and put aside our differences."

He nodded in agreement.

"However."

The air in the room changed with that single word.

"Avice is my wife—and I will behead you myself in the town square and hang your body outside the castle if you come near her again. If you speak to her. If you so much as fucking look at her. Do we understand each other, General?"

His eyes were guarded once more, the anger deep inside. "Yes, m'lord."

I continued to stare him down, furious that he had the opportunity to sleep beside the woman whose soul was bound to mine. The fact that he got to touch her the way I'd touched her. Kiss her the way I'd kissed her. If we weren't at war, I probably would have handled this situation much differently. "Then let's get to work."

The soldiers gathered Avice's belongings and brought them to the castle, where we would live together in my royal bedchambers. The place had been uncomfortable since she'd left, haunted by her ghost, her smell still lingering even though she'd been gone so long... Or maybe I just imagined it.

Her clothes were hung in the closet, her toiletries in the bathroom, all the elements that I remembered from our time together.

But she was still missing.

She finally came to the castle, in a long sweater dress with black leggings underneath, her dark hair pinned back in an elegant updo. I knew my wife was a beautiful woman, but every time I saw her, I realized my memory had muffled just how stunning she really was.

There was defiance in her eyes, coldness in her tightly pressed lips, but she still showed up to honor our agreement. She walked up to me, her eyes so guarded it seemed as if that passionate night we'd shared had never happened. Her stare was ice-cold, like she hated me, and then she walked off to our bedchambers. Her hostility was paramount, but it still felt like the happiest day of my life.

I followed her into our bedchambers, an expansive part of the castle with several bedrooms and bathrooms, breathtaking views of the city below. These chambers should belong to Huntley, but since he was here so infrequently, he had offered them to me.

She kneeled in front of the fireplace and lit a match, getting the flames to rise and heat the cold room.

The cold never bothered me, and now I remembered how much she hated it, that she preferred to keep our chambers scalding hot because the cold made her shiver.

I would have to accommodate her requests, but that was a small price to pay to have her back in my life. I remained behind her, waiting for her to turn and look at me, but she continued to stare at the fire and ignore me.

I gave her time to stare at the fire and collect her thoughts, but when the minutes passed without a word, I broke the silence. "Avice."

She inhaled a deep breath before she turned around, her arms crossed tightly over her body.

"I honored your requests—and I expect you to honor mine." I'd reinstated General Macabre and spared him the embarrassment of kneeling at my feet. I'd buried the hatchet between us because there were more important things to worry about right now.

"And here I am."

"Begrudgingly."

She looked away. "What do you expect, Ian?"

"I expect you to try."

She still wouldn't look at me.

"Don't pretend you don't love me anymore. Don't pretend your heart doesn't ache for me the way mine does for you. Don't pretend this marriage isn't worth fighting for. You wouldn't have slept with me if those feelings didn't exist."

Her head slowly turned back to mine.

"Forgive me—and try."

"I said I would try, but I said nothing about forgiving you—"

"*Avice.*" I stepped forward, getting closer to her. "We can't rebuild a marriage until you forgive me first. I've been faithful to you, even when you left me. I've been drinking and moping every fucking day since you've been gone. I've been praying to the gods day and night for you to come back to me. Yes, I fucked up, but there's never been a question of how much I love you. You *know* how much I love you."

She still wouldn't meet my gaze. "Ian... I just need time. Changes like this don't happen overnight."

"I can give you all the time you want. But I want there to be effort."

She rubbed her arm through her sweater, like she was cold.

"Truth be told, we may not have the time to put this marriage back together. There may be no future for us anyway. But if this is the end...I want us to be together."

She lifted her chin and looked at me, her eyes filled with pain. "What does that mean?"

I didn't want to scare her, but I didn't want to pretend everything would be alright when it probably wouldn't be. Whether we fought these demons or we fled for safety, our lives would be forever changed. "These enemies are unlike anything we've ever faced."

"But Delacroix defeated them—"

"Only because the vampires were able to slay their leader."

"But they're gone now, Ian. It's over."

I shook my head. "There're a lot more of them, Avice. And one vampire isn't enough to win the war that's bound to come. They're demons with fire in their veins—and they can burn their enemies at will."

Her face drained of all color, like a riverbed that went dry in the heat of summer.

"I don't want to scare you."

"What—what are we going to do?"

"Our vampire ally has called for his people to fight for us. Hopefully, they come. In the meantime, I'm going to search for a weakness."

"What if they don't come?" she asked. "What if you don't find a weakness?"

"My suggestion is we flee."

"Flee where?"

"I don't know."

Her arms tightened over her chest, her breathing now uneven.

"Avice." I came closer to her, my hands moving to her arms. "I will do everything in my power to protect you—"

"I'm worried about our daughter..."

"You know I would give my life for hers."

Her eyes remained on my chest, her face tight with unease. "I want her to know only peace."

"I know."

"I don't want her to see those horrible things. I don't want her to be scared."

"I know, baby." My arms circled her, and I felt the warmth in my chest when she allowed me to hold her. I brought her into me, her face resting against the hard plate of my armor. "Just know that Huntley and I will do everything we can to protect this beautiful world and the people we love."

Her arms moved around me, hugging me even though she embraced my armor instead of my body.

My lips brushed her forehead, pressing a kiss to her hairline. "If these are my last days on earth, I want to spend them with you...like this." My arms tightened on the small of her back, her affection dulling the ache in my chest.

"Me too."

I left my bedchambers and moved down the hallway to leave the castle.

"Steward Ian." My mother's guard appeared. "Lady Rolfe wishes to speak with you."

I wasn't ready to speak with her yet, so I ignored him and continued on my journey. I made it down the stairs and to the main door, ready to enter the city and have a very difficult conversation.

But then her voice sounded behind me. "Ian."

I approached the double doors, but then the guards moved into my way to block them.

I cocked an eyebrow at both of them.

They tightened their pikes, but their eyes showed their terror.

"Mother, we can't afford to lose any good men right now, so I'd rather not kill these guys for standing in my way." I turned around to face her, my eyes heavy with resentment.

She was able to catch up to me quickly, her body lithe despite her age. "I wish to speak to you—in private."

"I don't care what you wish."

"Ian—"

"I have important business in the village. Now's not a good time."

"Is it ever a good time when you're this angry?" She stood in a long dress with her cloak, feathers from crows woven into her hair. Her healer had recommended a cane years ago, but she refused, adjusting her gait to compensate instead.

"Just because you wish to speak with me doesn't mean I wish to speak to you." I turned back to the guards. "*Move*."

They started to obey.

"*Stay.*"

They flinched and held still.

I turned back to my mother.

"You may be the steward of this castle, but I will always be its queen."

I pulled out the sword from my scabbard.

The men darted out of the way in half a second.

"Good choice." I returned my blade to the scabbard and walked through.

Mother followed me. "Ian, please—"

"No."

"Ian—"

I continued to walk, ignoring her.

"You're right—Huntley is my favorite son."

I halted in my tracks, stopped by the omission.

"But that doesn't mean I don't love you so much it hurts..."

I slowly turned back to her.

"It doesn't mean I wouldn't give my life for yours without hesitation."

I stared, my heart injured by her confession.

She came closer to me. "I'm so sorry that I've made you feel inadequate, that my preference is so obvious that you can see it with the naked eye. I failed as a mother, and I'm ashamed of my sin."

I appreciated her honesty, even though it hurt.

"I don't want you to return to the east...because I couldn't bear it if you didn't come home. I wouldn't want you to be king in Huntley's stead...because I want you to live. Just because I prefer him doesn't mean you don't mean the world to me. You only have a single child...so you don't understand the complexities of having two sons."

"Huntley has two children, and he loves them equally."

"He does love them equally, but he connects with one deeper than the other, and we know which one that is."

I refused to admit it, but my niece's face came into my mind.

"The time of peace has come to an end, and it's very hard for me to accept. Instead of being blessed with a long life, I wish I were cursed with an early death, just so I didn't have to see the horrors that will come to pass. I don't want to flee the lands my sons worked so hard to take, but I don't want to watch them die fighting for it either. The reality of your words is hard to swallow…like a tough piece of meat."

It was hard for me to swallow too.

"The fact that you're willing to do what's necessary while I refuse to accept the truth sets us apart, Ian. You're a better steward than I ever was as a queen—and for that, I'm deeply proud." Her soft eyes gripped mine and sucked me in deep. "And your father would be proud of you too—both of you."

I gave a subtle nod in appreciation. "Thank you, Mother."

She pulled me in for a hug, squeezing me as she rested her face against mine.

I held her for a moment before I pulled away.

"What business do you have in the village?" she asked, trying to lighten our emotions.

"Lila."

Her eyes fell, knowing I hadn't spoken to my daughter in a long time. "I wish you the best..."

My daughter lived in a little cottage alone, getting her own place when Avice had left the castle. Even as an adult, Lila had been fine sharing the space with us because we were a close family, but once Avice and I fell apart...she was gone.

I knocked on the door, my heart a lump in my throat, more afraid to face my daughter than the demons that had nearly taken Delacroix.

When she answered the door, she looked exactly as I remembered her, carefree, a smile on her lips. But once she realized I was the one who'd come for a visit, all that joy was sucked out of her face as if with a sponge. "What is it?"

I kept a straight face even though I felt knocked off my feet. She used to be so happy at the sight of me, happy to give me a hug, happy to tell me about her day. But now…I saw indifference. "Lila, I'm your father, and I deserve more respect than that." I didn't want to scold her the second our eyes met, but I was tired of the disrespect, tired of letting her get away with the bullshit.

"That's interesting," she said. "Because I think Mother deserved more respect than she got."

The hardest part about being a parent was shit like this, bottling your anger instead of unleashing it in a firestorm. Because if someone else spoke to me like that, they would be dead. But since it was my daughter, if I got angry, she just hated me more. I had to be the bigger person when she was the smaller person. "I'd like to come in so we can talk."

"To talk about what?"

"Lila."

"Fine." She left the door open and walked inside. "Talk all you want, but that doesn't mean I have to listen." She moved to the couch in front of the fire and pulled the blanket over her legs. She grabbed the book she was reading and picked up where she'd left off, like I wasn't even there.

I sat on the other couch, looking at the cozy cottage she'd made her own. A sweater hung over the back of the couch, and a bottle of wine had been left open on the kitchen counter. My eyes shifted to hers, seeing the same dark hair her mother had. "Your mother and I have decided to give our marriage another chance. She's moved back in to the castle."

Her eyes flicked up at that information. "What?"

"You heard what I said."

"But why would she do that? She's seeing—"

"*That relationship is over.*" My own daughter knew about it and didn't even seem to care that I'd been replaced. "Your mother chose me. We want to be a family again, and I would appreciate it if you also made the effort."

"You cheated on her—"

"*Lila.*"

"If I were married to a guy who cheated, you'd kill him—"

"It is way more complicated than you think."

"Did you or did you not sleep with another woman?"

"Yes, but—"

"It's not that complicated, Father. You betrayed Mother. Period. If this were the other way around, I'd be just as furious with her."

"Really?" That seemed unbelievable, judging by her harshness. "Because I would never want that. No one deserves to watch their daughter hate them for something they don't even understand. No one deserves to lose their daughter. I would never, *ever* want your mother to go through this, no matter what she did."

She stared, the book open on her lap. "I don't hate you."

"You said you did."

"But I didn't mean it."

"It seems like you mean it. You refuse to speak to me. You refuse to see me. We haven't spoken in over a month, and it seems like you're perfectly fine not having a father. Seems like you embraced General Macabre as my replacement just fine." I felt the tears buried deep behind my eyes, but I refused to let them fall. "You must have heard about the attack on Delacroix, but you haven't cared to check on me."

"There was an attack on Delacroix?" she asked blankly.

Maybe she didn't know.

"Father?"

"I didn't come here to talk about that—"

"Is everyone okay? Harlow? Aunt Ivory—"

"They're all fine," I said quickly. "We can talk about that after we finish this discussion."

"You just told me Delacroix was attacked, but we're going to talk about you sleeping around—"

"*I didn't sleep around.*" Now I was really losing my cool. "You don't have the full story. I know you're smart, but you clearly lack the maturity to understand that what happened with your mother is way more complicated than you assume. You chose sides like a child and didn't even give me the chance to explain anything. Nothing that happens between your mother and me should affect our relationship with you."

"Fine. Then tell me what happened." She crossed her arms over her chest.

I dragged my hands down my face, feeling like I was on trial. "Lila, I feel like you're going to judge and vilify me no matter what I say. You've already made up your mind. I'm in unbearable pain as it is, and the last thing I want to do is open my heart to you and be judged for it. I know I'm the parent so I need to be the bigger person here, but Lila, you're a grown-ass adult now. You need to stop acting like a child. Even if I were some unrepentant adulterer, it shouldn't change our relationship. There's no mistake you could ever make, no matter how shameful, that would ever change my love for you. But a mistake was all it took for you to forget I ever existed…" Being a parent was a challenge, and up until my separation from Avice, it'd all been worth it because my daughter was my pride and joy, but now it was the most painful, excruciating thing I'd ever done. There were no words to describe the horror of being the recipient of your child's hatred.

Her eyes dropped as she considered what I said, her arms folded over her body.

Why the fuck had I come here? Did I really think a reunion with her mother would make her forgive me? I'd tried for months and months to get my daughter to say two words to me, but I was done trying. I left the couch and headed to the door. "The Teeth have formed an alliance with enemies to the east of the mountains. They're the ones who attacked us, but there's nothing to worry about because we'll defeat them with our armies and dragons." I wouldn't tell her the truth. I wouldn't scare my daughter if it could be avoided. I opened the door and walked out.

"Father." She was behind me in the doorway.

I looked down the street, feeling the heat from the torch on the back of my neck.

"I'm sorry..."

I didn't look at her. It was too fucking hard. Those tears I battled were breaking through.

"Come inside...let's talk." Her hand moved to the back of my arm and gently pulled, trying to get me to come back inside.

I blinked back the tears that were becoming harder to fight.

She gently pulled me again—and this time, I let her.

Her eyes were no longer harsh, but soft like they used to be, full of light and warmth. But then they saddened, probably seeing the evidence of my tears along my lids. "It's okay, Father." Her arms moved around me, and she hugged me...hugged me.

My arms hooked around her body instantly, and I sucked in a deep breath, squeezing her tightly. "Sweetheart..."

She listened to the tale without interruption.

"It doesn't justify what I did, but...we'd been having problems for a long time with no reconciliation in sight...and I made a mistake."

"I had no idea..."

"Your mother never told you because she didn't want to talk about...you know. She's still not over it, and I suspect she'll never be. That anguish has left a permanent heaviness in her eyes. Her turmoil changed her, made her into a different person I didn't recognize. We were both at fault, but that doesn't matter anymore."

"I'm glad you worked it out."

"We're still working it out. It'll be a while before we're what we used to be."

"What led to this sudden change?" she asked. "She just woke up one morning and forgave you?"

"No. It was..." I didn't know what to say, how to tell my daughter her mother and I had basically hooked up for the night. "We just...found our way back to each other."

Lila didn't pry, like she knew this was a topic she wanted to avoid. "Mother was really hurt."

"I know."

"I don't think you'll ever really know, Father. I was with her...you weren't."

My eyes dropped in shame.

"I was hurt too."

"I know, sweetheart. I'm sorry." I lifted my eyes again, looking at my daughter on the other couch...looking back at me. The hostility had evaporated, replaced by a comfortable familiarity that I experienced with very few people. "How have you been?"

"Good...just working."

"How are you liking the bakery?"

"I get to make pie and bread all day. No complaints."

I smiled.

"Plus, it's warm with the fires going all day."

"Another bonus."

"So...the Teeth betrayed us?"

Now I was back to reality, the cold, hard truth that my world might be over soon. "We should have killed them after the war."

"Why didn't you?"

"Huntley wanted to be a merciful king."

"Would you have done otherwise?"

"Yes." I was the one who had wanted them dead, and Huntley refused to do what was necessary. I respected him as my king, but I didn't respect every decision he made.

"Who's on the other side of the mountains?" she asked. "More men?"

"No. These other beings..."

"Like Necrosis?"

"No."

"Then what are they?"

I didn't know what to do. I didn't want to scare her, but I didn't want to keep her in the dark either. "Creatures...monsters...something we've never encountered before."

The blanket was over her arms and legs as she sat near the fire. Her eyes dilated in the light as the emotion swept through her. "I can't believe they attacked Delacroix."

"They'll be back, I expect."

"But we're prepared, right?"

I nodded, not having the heart to tell her the truth, at least tonight. "If you ever want a position at the castle, let me know. I can find something for you in the treasury."

"It's okay," she said. "I like the bakery. I think it's badass that Harlow is so skilled with the blade and Atticus will be general of the army, but I like what I do."

"Then that's what you should do." She was supposed to take my place as steward upon my death, but if she didn't want it, she didn't have to take it. I'd rather she do whatever made her happy. "It's getting late... I should go." I wanted to stay there forever, to have my daughter look at me the way she used to, but I had so many other things to worry about.

"Okay." She tugged off the blanket and walked with me to the door.

"You can come back to the castle...if you want." Our section of the castle had several bedrooms and living rooms, making it comfortable for all three of us to have our space. It had worked out well before. Maybe we could do it again.

"I actually like my cottage a lot..."

I nodded in understanding. "That's fine." I hid my disappointment as best as I could, reminding myself that she was a grown woman who wanted her privacy, just the way I'd wanted it when I was her age. "Goodnight, sweetheart." I pulled her into me and kissed her on the forehead. "Love you."

She said the words that made me melt into a puddle on the floor. "Love you too, Father."

When I returned to my chambers, Avice was on the couch in front of the fire, staring at the flames instead of reading a book, obviously stressed about everything I'd told her. It took her a moment to realize I was there. "How is she?"

"We're finally in a good place." I couldn't help but smile, treasuring the feel of her in my arms.

"That's great to hear."

I moved to the couch beside her, the flames instantly warm when I drew near.

"Did you tell her...?"

I shook my head. "I didn't want to scare her."

"I'll ask her to join us in the castle."

"I already did. She said no."

"But if she knew the circumstances, perhaps she would give a different answer."

"She's right next to the bakery. It's more convenient for her. And until we explain why we want her closer, it won't make any sense. Let's leave it be for now." Truth be told, it had been a great night, and I wanted to hold on to that...for a day or two. "I told her what happened with us... Hope that's okay."

She was quiet.

"I thought she deserved the whole story."

"I understand."

I sat beside her, several inches of space between us, but there was still a feeling of closeness there, like we were on the same team again. I'd seen my wife and daughter on the same day, so it was the best day of my life. "I'm going to shower." I left the couch and hung up my armor and weapons in the closet before I washed off under the warm water. I stood there for a couple minutes, just to cherish the memory of my daughter's love. I'd been estranged from them both for so long that I couldn't believe that used to be my life, seeing both of them every day.

I returned to the bedroom, and Avice was already under the sheets. I wasn't sure if she'd sleep with me tonight or use one of the spare bedrooms to have her space, but she was there...waiting for me.

I pulled back the covers and got into bed in my boxers, feeling her warmth because she'd been between the sheets for a while. The mattress had never felt so soft.

The room had never felt so warm. My nightstand used to be littered with old glasses with drops of scotch at the bottom, but now there was water instead.

She was on the other side of the bed, turned on her side, facing me.

Our lives could be over very soon, so I wanted to roll on top of my wife and consummate this new marriage. I wanted to feel our bodies connect, our adjoined souls dance. But I also didn't want to rush her, not when I was just happy that she was with me.

EIGHTEEN
AURELIAS

I could track her through the streets, not by her scent or footprints, but by the intensity of her emotions. She moved down the alleyways instead of taking the main road, like she suspected I might follow her and she wanted to make that as difficult as possible.

I emerged behind her, seeing her dress shift in the summer breeze that swept down the alleyways, and I increased my speed while keeping my boots quiet. When I caught up to her, I grabbed her by the arm and turned her toward me.

She spun out of my grasp instantly, then threw a punch on instinct.

I caught her wrist and twisted it down. "You have quick reflexes."

"Not quick enough." She wrenched herself free then kept walking.

"Baby." I followed.

"Goodnight, Aurelias."

I continued to walk behind her. "Harlow."

A surge of anger ruptured through her, like the use of her given name was actually offensive.

I grabbed her again, but this time, I forced her back to the wall. We were in the shadows of the alleyway, everyone asleep in their homes because it was deep in the night. My body pinned her to the wall, and I dipped my head close to her. "Trust me, you don't want my bite."

"Why not?"

"Because the second I do, you become prey. I don't see you that way—nor do I ever want to."

"But you said it's euphoric…intimate—"

"It can be, yes. But it can also be violent. My fangs are sharp, and your flesh is soft. It wouldn't take much to kill you accidentally, and I would never risk your life needlessly. Don't take it personally, baby."

She was still angry, flames in her eyes.

"Take it as a compliment."

"You said it was the greatest pleasure—"

"Fucking you is already the greatest pleasure," I said. "I don't need more, and neither do you."

Her eyes shifted back and forth between mine.

"I'm never going to change my mind, so let it go."

"I trust you not to hurt me—"

"*Stop it.*" The rage was too potent to control. The teases and the taunts were already insufferable, but the misplaced trust was worse. "Bring it up again, and we're done. Do you understand me?"

Another surge of rage moved through her, but she didn't give voice to it, probably because she knew I meant what I said.

"I asked you a question."

She didn't answer out of defiance, and judging by the hardness in her gaze, she never would.

My mouth dipped to hers, and I kissed her, hard like we were alone together in the cottage, demanding her mouth open wide and take mine.

Her lips were immediately eager, not having the same defiance as her eyes. Her hands were on my shoulders, and she hiked her leg for me to take.

I gripped her knee and pressed it against my torso as I continued to kiss her, immediately lost in the flames of desire that sparked out of nowhere. That was how it was anytime I was with her, like a match could ignite without warning and burn everything. "Answer me."

She undid my trousers as her hungry mouth took mine, working to get to my hard dick, anxious, as if we hadn't already fucked all night. She got me free before she yanked up her dress, her mouth still on mine.

I lifted her against the wall until her foot left the ground then lowered her onto my length, my cock sliding perfectly into place.

Her arms wrapped around my shoulders, and she buried her face into my neck, moaning against my skin to stay quiet. "Aurelias..."

"*Answer me.*" I thrust inside her, my lips near her ear, knowing how utterly addicted I was to this woman to be fucking her in a dark alleyway after I'd already fucked her countless times. But somehow, it felt like the first time, the first hit, the first moment.

"Yes…"

The next morning, I entered the castle and was escorted to the dining room. There was a long table there, laden with fresh fruit, breakfast meats, and coffee and tea. I rarely ate human food, because the taste was dull and it didn't satisfy my hunger. Blood was a surge of metal and salt, a burn on my tongue that nothing else could replicate.

When I approached the table, I realized Harlow wasn't there. It was just King Rolfe and his queen.

King Rolfe gestured to the chair on his left.

I took a seat directly across from his wife, her neck a horrible mixture of red and orange.

"Atticus is still recovering in his bedroom," Ivory said. "And Harlow has never been a morning person…"

She definitely wasn't a morning person after last night. She didn't return to her bedroom until at least four in the morning.

"Help yourself," she said. "If you're hungry…"

"I'll just take some coffee." I filled a mug before I placed it in front of me, but I didn't drink any of it.

Ivory continued to stare at me, her emotions quiet but intense. There was an unfulfilled longing inside her. "I never had the chance to thank you for what you did… for saving me."

I avoided her gaze, uncomfortable with the praise. "It was nothing."

"It wasn't nothing," she said gently. "You could have died."

And for a second, I'd thought I was going to. To avoid her gaze, I looked into my mug then took a drink, the taste bland like everything else. The only exception to that was alcohol. It was strong enough to ignite lifeless taste buds.

She seemed to sense my discomfort because she dropped the subject.

King Rolfe sat at the head of the table, digging into an omelet that had to contain at least a dozen eggs. It was stuffed with bacon and cheese.

"I'd like to make a request." *And I'd like to make it before Harlow joined us.*

"I'm listening." King Rolfe continued to eat, perpendicular to me as he sat at the head of the table.

"You won't like it," I said. "But I have to make it."

When he heard that, he set down his fork and pivoted his chair to look at me head on.

"I need to feed—and not on animal blood."

The rage was instantaneous, like he'd expected the request. "I already gave my answer when I released you from prison."

"Animal blood is a poor substitute—"

"You're alive, aren't you?"

"Huntley..." His queen's hand moved to his forearm, sheathing his anger with a single touch.

"Yes, I'm alive," I said calmly. "But I'm weak. It's like not getting enough sleep and not eating for a couple of days. You just aren't the same. I need to be strong for what we're about to face, not emaciated and exhausted."

His stare accompanied his emotions, full of anger. "There's no scenario where I allow you to prey on the people I've vowed to protect."

"I wouldn't kill them. And I would only take volunteers."

"Why would anyone volunteer?" King Rolfe asked blankly.

I didn't give the real reason. "Because I've pledged my life to their protection, and I think it's in their best interest that I succeed. I also saved their kingdom from destruction, so it would be a nice way to show their gratitude."

He released his breath slowly, his nostrils flaring in the process. He crossed his arms over his chest. "If you ever—"

"I would never feed on Harlow. Even if she volunteered, I wouldn't accept." And I hadn't accepted last night, even though she'd begged me to do it.

"Why?" His eyes pierced my flesh, searching for a hint of a lie.

Because I might kill her. "I care for her."

King Rolfe looked at his wife, and a silent conversation passed between them.

"I think it's fine, Huntley."

"What happens when the others come?" he asked. "They feed on all of us?"

"They would bring their own prey," I said. "Keep them on the ships."

"So, you keep prisoners." He stared at me again.

I didn't deny it. "Some are prisoners…some are volunteers."

He turned guarded once again.

"Different vampires have different ideologies." I answered the question he never asked.

"And what ideology do you hold?" he asked.

I wouldn't lie, not for anyone. "When I left my lands, I despised humans and believed their only purpose was to serve us, The Originals. But since I've come to your lands, I've had a drastic change of opinion. My brothers have always held the opposite belief, that we should coexist peacefully with humans."

The king looked at me, his stare cold and hard, analyzing me with his intelligent eyes. "You can accept volunteers. But if you kill a single one, our alliance is broken."

"You don't have to worry about that."

"I better not."

At that moment, Harlow came into the room, her eyes tired and puffy. She'd clearly forced herself out of bed because it didn't look like she wanted to be there. Instead of taking the seat beside me, she sat next to her mother and poured herself a big cup of coffee.

I tried not to stare at her, to appreciate the way she looked first thing in the morning. Whenever we were in the same room together, she sucked in all my focus, making it hard to concentrate on anything else. But I couldn't let my thoughts slip when I was in the presence of her parents, especially her father. "What did you discover during your trip to the east?"

He finished off his omelet with a few more bites, a mountain sitting at the table, making his wife and daughter look even more petite in comparison. "Ian and I infiltrated a labor camp and spoke to one of the prisoners."

Harlow was about to drink from her coffee, but she returned it to the saucer instead. All the sleepiness left her gaze, and there was a flash of unease across her body.

King Rolfe continued. "They described them as demons, coming from a ring of fire in the earth."

"A ring of fire?" I asked.

"Ian and I saw it from the sky," he said. "It's literally a ring of fire, black in the center. It was dark when we flew overhead, so I don't have the details."

"There was an earthquake before they struck," I said. "Perhaps they come from underground."

"But how can something live underground?" Harlow blurted. "I can see something living inside mountains, but straight up in the earth? How would that be possible?"

I didn't have a clue.

King Rolfe stared at his coffee.

Ivory looked past me, out the window to the city beyond.

"You said a labor camp. What kind of labor?" I asked.

"The prisoners were digging in the earth, mining jewels."

"I can't picture these creatures caring about diamonds and rubies." Fire pumped in their veins, and they had brute strength that rivaled mine. I couldn't picture them as traders or merchants, just conquerors.

"Neither can I," he said. "But that's what they were doing. The prisoner said they were from a great city called Palladium. It fell quickly once the demons emerged. Some have escaped but gone into hiding. The rest have become prisoners to their regime."

"Did this happen recently?" I asked.

"We didn't have much time to speak," he said. "Had to bribe him for what little knowledge he would impart. But yes, I get the impression this didn't happen a long time ago, that these beings are fairly recent."

"Why mine for jewels if they already lived underground?" Harlow asked. "They can do this themselves."

"Why do anything yourself when you can have someone else do it for free?" I asked.

Her eyes switched to me, and a flush of heat burned through her body like a strike of lightning. She quickly looked away, like she remembered every scene of our fuck-a-thon from the night before.

I couldn't think about that right now, with her father a foot away from me, when this world was on the verge of domination. It was easier to look at Ivory or her husband, to avoid Harlow's gaze altogether. "Those jewels must be important."

"Ian agrees."

"I doubt the Teeth would have come across the beings while underground," I said. "They must have emerged from the surface before the Teeth arrived. And if they were aboveground when they're normally underground...something must have made them pop up."

King Rolfe looked at me. "A need of some kind."

I nodded. "I think it has something to do with the jewels they're mining."

"But why are they important...?" King Rolfe said it more to himself than to the rest of us.

"They know we've defeated their army by now," I said. "Which means they're going to take us more seriously for the next battle. We need to prepare for war, and the best way to do that is to combine all resources in a single location."

"The only place big enough for that many people is HeartHolme," King Rolfe said. "But we would have to evacuate all the Kingdoms—"

"If you leave them behind, they'll be killed," I said quickly. "You don't have a choice."

"What if they attack the Kingdoms first?" King Rolfe asked.

"Then your cities will fall—but not your people. If my kin come to our aid, it'll be to the bottom of the cliffs anyway. If the demons attack anytime soon, there's no chance my people will get here in time. We need to prepare for that reality." And the reality was that all their soldiers combined probably still wouldn't be enough.

"It's hard to prepare for a battle against foes you've never seen." He looked ahead, down the table of endless chairs, all empty. "All I know is they're full of fire and strength. We need to figure out a way to combat that if we want to save lives. You must know your enemy if you want to defeat them."

"The humans that have gone into hiding would be good allies," I said. "They'll want revenge for their people."

"But how many of them remain?" King Rolfe asked. "Very few, probably."

"But I wouldn't be surprised if they're working to overthrow them anyway. And they may know something we don't."

"And how do you suggest we find them?" King Rolfe asked.

"That...I don't know," I said. "But I think this will require another trip to the east, regardless."

King Rolfe turned quiet for a long time, considering everything we'd just discussed. He turned his attention to Ivory next. "Once Atticus is well, he'll need to evacuate the Kingdoms and usher them to HeartHolme. General Henry will march the Delacroix army on foot. Removing armies from the safety of their walls would normally be stupid, but in this instance, we need every soldier in one place if we're to face these demons."

Instead of refusing to pledge her son, Ivory gave a nod.

"I suspect he'll be safer away from HeartHolme, at least for now," King Rolfe said. "We'll depart by dragon."

My eyes wanted to move to Harlow, but I forced them to remain in the conversation. She would travel to HeartHolme by sky, arriving in just a day, whereas it would take me days, probably a week, to get there on foot. The separation caused a jolt of fear in my heart, knowing that if something happened at HeartHolme, my steel wouldn't protect her throat. My eyes dropped down to the table beneath me in shame, remembering how shitty it felt to care about something more than myself.

"I think Atticus will be ready in three days," King Rolfe said. "Let's plan for then."

"We should notify Ian that HeartHolme will need to accommodate all the Kingdoms," Ivory said. "And we should bring all the food we can carry. Their supplies may not be able to feed everyone."

King Rolfe nodded. "I'll send the letter."

NINETEEN
HARLOW

I sat at my brother's bedside, looking at his weakened body tucked underneath the covers. He was asleep, so I stared at his tanned face, remembering how pale he had been immediately after the battle.

My stare must have burned his face, because his eyes slowly opened and found mine.

"I didn't mean to wake you."

When he spoke, his voice came out strained. "I'm used to people staring at me like that."

"Like what?"

"Like I'm still going to die."

"I don't think that."

"But I bet you're wishing for it." A teasing smile moved on to his lips.

I rolled my eyes playfully, my own smile coming through. "You got me."

He ran his fingers through his hair before he sat up in bed, his chest exposed once the covers dropped. He was thick and muscular like Father, with dark hair on his chest. "I haven't slept like this since I was a kid."

"Enjoy it while you can. Life's about to suck."

"I've never been in a war before. Just had my first battle. So, I'm nervous...but I wonder if Father is more nervous."

"He's always nervous." He was always paranoid about the worst coming to pass, and now that it had, his eyes were perpetually bloodshot. He was tense like a tightrope.

"I love the sleep I'm getting, but I'm anxious to get out of bed."

"Enjoy it while you can, because once you're better, Father is going to have you evacuate all the Kingdoms and bring them to HeartHolme. Aurelias thinks we should combine all our armies into a single location rather than leaving them scattered and vulnerable—at least with an enemy like this."

"The stewards won't like that."

"They won't like being dead more."

He gave a slight nod in agreement. "It's still a big task. It'll take me a while to accomplish it. For all the citizens to pack up their essentials and say goodbye to their homes. They'll all be scared."

"I'm scared."

His eyes shifted back to me.

"Father is too. We all are."

A softness entered his gaze, like he wanted to be a good brother and assure me everything would be alright. But he knew he couldn't say that, so he didn't. "Aurelias...the vampire has a name."

"Father has embraced him as one of our own."

Atticus didn't voice his concerns. He wasn't as stubborn as Father, so if Aurelias was accepted, he wouldn't question it. "While I'm gathering our people, will you travel to HeartHolme?"

"Yes. Father will send a scouting mission to the east to gather information about the demons that oppose us. He's desperate to discover a weakness since our dragons are powerless against their flames."

He nodded in agreement. "It's dangerous, but they already know we're aware of them, so…"

"Yeah."

"And it's not like we have some elaborate plan they could learn if they capture us."

"Yeah."

We sat in silence for a while, both of us thinking about the arduous journey we would each have to take…that we would all have to take.

"Hard to believe that just a month ago, life was easy," Atticus said. "Boring. I trained with soldiers for a battle that would never come. You wore dresses to tea parties and ignored all the advances from your admirers. A very different time."

"Yeah…" It was hard to believe it'd ever been that way.

"Now I wish I'd appreciated it more," he said. "Because it'll never be the same."

Once evening arrived, I left the castle and visited the village, moving down the cobblestone streets to the little cottage tucked behind the alleyways. It was away from the main road, a perfect place for someone who wanted to keep a low profile. I was tired of sneaking down at night then sneaking back in the morning, but I suspected Aurelias wouldn't come to my chambers if I asked. His relationship with my father was different now, and that was a line he probably wouldn't cross.

I knocked on his door and waited for his deep voice to invite me inside, but there was only silence. I knocked again, but there was no answer, no footsteps. When I grabbed the handle, it turned because it was unlocked, so I let myself inside.

A few lamps were on, but the room was still dark, shadows in the corners. The counter had a bottle of scotch with a few drops of amber at the bottom. "Aurelias?" I moved to the foot of the stairs and looked to the second landing, expecting to see him emerge in nothing but his boxers, but he wasn't there.

I was disappointed by his absence and assumed he was at the bar, drinking alone in the corner, thinking about the long road ahead of us. I moved upstairs and approached his unmade bed. A dagger was on his nightstand, red jewels in the hilt. His sword was against the wall, a snake engraved down the black scabbard.

I decided to undress and help myself to his sheets, getting under the covers so he would discover me when he returned. The mattress didn't match the quality of mine at the castle, but it somehow felt infinitely more comfortable. I could smell him on the sheets, smell that scent of snow, smoke from the fireplace, and scotch. I lay on my side and closed my eyes, so comfortable that I felt my mind gently relax.

Sometime later, the front door opened and closed, and the heavy sound of a man's footfalls made its way up to me.

My eyes opened, and I listened to the sound of a bottle leaving the counter, the booze filling a glass, and then the bottle returning to the counter. I imagined he was drinking the scotch he'd just poured, even though he'd probably had plenty at the bar. Then his footsteps moved to the stairs, up to the second landing, and he emerged in the bedroom, dressed in his regular clothes instead of all the heavy armor that made him twice as big.

He looked at me with his signature intensity, his gaze hot like the sun, not remotely surprised that I was there. "Baby."

A shiver ran down my body, starting with my heart and traveling all the way to my toes. A tingle remained afterward, a numbness in all four extremities. There were bumps on my arms like I was cold, but a flame had burst to life inside my stomach.

He undressed, shedding his shirt and then his trousers, leaving them as a pile on the rug.

I sat up and let the sheet slide down to my stomach, my hard tits suddenly exposed to the cold air. My nipples sharpened, and I felt the tightness across my chest.

His eyes dropped down as his thumbs hooked into his boxers to lower them to the floor. He pulled them down, revealing a rock-hard dick that looked right at me. His knees hit the bed, and he moved up, getting on top of me in seconds, throwing off the sheets so he could smother my body instead.

He kissed me.

No—he inhaled me.

Demanding and incessant, he took my lips with ownership, his hand hooking into my hair so he could get a firm grip. He possessed me fully, enveloped me in the warmth only he could provide.

It was a connection hard to describe, but all I knew was I'd never had it with anyone else. No other man could hold a candle to Aurelias. There had been fun times, some *really* fun times, but nothing like this.

I tried to roll him over so I could get on top, but he pinned me to the bed and separated my thighs with his knees. He growled against my mouth when I tried to take the lead. Then he adjusted me underneath him, planting one foot against his chest as he folded me to his liking. His dick pushed inside me, pushed past the tightness at my entrance, and slowly sank in.

I moaned against his mouth. "Yes..." There was no better feeling than this, than feeling him enter me with a shove because he was too damn big. He only made it the rest of the way because my inner flesh was so soft and smooth, primed to take his impressive girth.

He supported his body with a single arm, which was flexed and muscular, all the muscle bulging to hold his weight. His other hand fisted my hair, holding it like reins as if I might try to ride off. "You like this dick, baby?"

"Yes."

He thrust into me, hard and fast, tapping the headboard with a distinct pace.

I lay there, pinned in place to the mattress, watching this gorgeous man fuck me when he could be fucking any woman he wanted that night.

"Good," he said, his breaths even despite the way he worked his body. "Because I love this pussy."

His shoulder was my pillow, his body my sheets. I stared down at his muscular chest and looked at my arm as it draped over his hard stomach. When he took a breath, everything lifted, and when the breaths left, everything tightened even further. His perfection was chiseled out of stone.

I wanted to stay there forever, but I had to pee, so I left his arms and walked around the bed to the bathroom down the hallway. His things were on the counter, his toothbrush, his razor, soap. I did my business then returned to the bedroom, my eyes on the floor beneath me. I glanced over at his clothes, ready to look away the second I saw them, but then I stopped when I spotted something red.

On his black shirt, it was hard to notice, the color more of a maroon, but it was there, close to the neckline.

"Something wrong, baby?" Aurelias asked, arms folded behind his head.

"There's blood on your shirt."

He propped himself up on a single arm and looked at me, his hard stare borderline disinterested. "It's probably wine, but even if it's blood, it's probably an old stain that's never come out." He continued his stare, his muscular body tight even when he was propped up like that.

I wasn't sure why I hesitated. Must be intuition.

"Baby?" He continued his piercing stare. "What's the problem?"

Honestly, I didn't know. My father had made it clear he couldn't feed on anyone, and Aurelias didn't strike me as someone to break a promise. But he did look different, his eyes brighter, his muscles plumper, like his weakened body had been invigorated by something. "Did you feed today?"

He held my stare in silence, his hard eyes focused on my face. "Yes."

"On animal blood?"

Silence ensued for a few seconds before he answered. "Yes."

When I heard that answer, I forgot about the clothes and returned to bed. "I want to stay here tonight." I was tired of going back to the castle in the middle of the night. Tired of moving like a ghost through the streets.

Aurelias came close to me, hiking my leg over his hip before his arm squeezed my lower back and dragged me close.

"Is that okay?"

"You think that's wise?"

"I don't want to sneak around."

"Have you slept over in the past?"

"No, but this is different." I spoke before I thought, the words coming out like a river over a waterfall.

His eyes remained locked on mine without a hint of discomfort.

I tried to alter the meaning of my words. "Because we're at war, and everything could be gone tomorrow." I covered it up as best I could, tried to convince myself of that truth as well.

"Your father is aware of our relationship, but I think it's unwise to parade it in front of him."

"I'm a grown-ass woman who he thinks is worthy of the crown," I said. "I can do what I want. And I know Atticus has slept in other beds far more often than he's slept in his own."

His fingers rubbed my back, gently stroking the skin. "You know it's different, baby."

"It shouldn't be different."

"As true as that may be, it doesn't change the fact that I'm a vampire."

My hand rested on his forearm, feeling all the cords underneath my fingertips, the tightness of his muscular body. "If you don't want me to stay, then be a man and tell me."

His eyes brightened noticeably, and a subtle smile moved on to his lips. "Baby, you know I never want you to leave."

My heart clenched again, loving the way he called me baby, loving how good his big hands felt on my body. To feel a beautiful man's possession was the sexiest thing in the world.

"And you damn well know that." He tightened me to him, his lips catching mine for a soft kiss, the kind that made my body melt into the sheets. It was slow and tender, but breathtaking, nevertheless. He grabbed my ass with his big hand before he rolled me onto my back, opening me up so he could take me again. He guided himself inside then sank nice and slow, his eyes locked on mine with that potent possession. "Don't you?"

My nails were deep in his back, our bodies grinding together.

His mouth moved to my ear. "Say it, baby."

Fuck, I was already going to come. "Yes...I know."

"Know what?"

"How much you want me..."

He started to move harder. "Attagirl."

When I opened my eyes, Aurelias was still beside me. We'd separated sometime during the night, but he was still close, close enough that I could hear him breathe. I took him in for a moment, feeling the morning light in the crack between the curtains. A veil of peace swept through me, my body on a cloud and my mind still in the land of dreams.

It was the nicest morning I'd had in a long time.

He opened his eyes a moment later, looking right into my face, his eyes soft from being half asleep. The sheets were at his waistline, his body still hard despite his relaxation. His hand snaked to me across the mattress until he grabbed me and pulled me close, bringing me right up against him. "You look beautiful in the morning."

"Funny," I said. "I thought the same thing about you."

He hiked my leg over his hip and closed his eyes again, his body pressed into mine, our breaths in sync.

I wasn't tired, but I was so relaxed I could fall right back to sleep. It was easy to forget our world was on the brink of collapse when we were wrapped together like this, the morning light bringing a warmth to the room that rivaled a fire.

Our serendipity was destroyed when he let out an annoyed sigh.

"What?"

"You should get dressed."

"Why—"

Knock. Knock. Knock.

"That's why," he said. "Come on."

A guard's voice was heard from downstairs. "Open up. By order of the king."

"Oh fuck." I grabbed my clothes off the floor and dressed as quickly as possible.

Aurelias remained calm, taking his time pulling on his clothes before his fingers moved through his hair.

"I can't believe this."

He said nothing, but his look said it all. *I told you so.*

I rushed downstairs and opened the door. "I'm fine. See?"

There were three guards there, all armed to the teeth. "Princess Harlow, we're here to escort you back to the castle."

"*Escort me?*" I snapped. "I can walk my ass there all by myself—"

"Baby." Aurelias's calm voice appeared behind me. "Go with them."

"This is ridiculous." I walked out, and the guards followed behind me. We walked back to the castle and entered the grand room with the staircase. My mother was there, consternation in her eyes.

"Oh, you're alright," she said, her hands immediately squeezing my arms. "When you didn't come down for breakfast, we were worried. I checked on you in your chambers, but you weren't there… We assumed the worst."

"Mother, I'm fine." I tried to say it as calmly as possible, but the irritation was heavy in my voice. "That was completely unnecessary...and embarrassing."

She pulled her hands away, her look guilty. "I told your father you were probably with Aurelias, but we live in uncertain times right now. It's better to embarrass you than the alternative."

I held my tongue and decided to let it go. Since I'd been taken before, I guessed it was reasonable to fear I'd been taken again. "In the future, if I'm not home in the morning, just assume I'm with Aurelias."

My mother took a deep breath, like she was prepared to venture into uncomfortable territory. "Harlow, we're at war right now. I don't think it's the best time for you to run off whenever you feel like it. If this were a couple months ago, we'd be having a very different conversation."

"What are you saying?" I asked, shocked that my mother, of all people, would say what I thought she was about to say. "That I can't stay over anymore?"

She avoided my gaze for a moment. "I think it's best if we all stay together under one roof."

"Mother—"

"*Harlow.*"

"I know you're the one talking, but I can hear Father's voice."

Her hands came together at her waistline. "Would you rather speak to him about this? Because I can promise you it would be the most uncomfortable conversation for you both."

I looked away, knowing how tense and awkward that would be.

"It's a reasonable request considering the circumstances, considering that you were taken before. Your father wants to keep us safe. That's all."

"And don't you think being with Aurelias is the safest place I can be?"

Her eyes flashed in offense. "Aurelias may have abilities your father lacks, but I have no doubt that your father's intellect triumphs his—*every time*."

"I didn't mean to insult Father—"

"We're your family. He's not." Now her stare was cold. "Your place is here, with us, always. This discussion is over."

I wanted to push back, to seize my independence, but I knew my mother was not a woman to be trifled with when she was like this. She may be the voice of my father, but she clearly shared his opinion. "Alright, then."

I didn't see Aurelias that night. Even though I understood my parents' perspective, I was still frustrated by the situation. I'd been an adult for years, had been selected to inherit the crown over my brother, but I didn't have the full autonomy I craved. Aurelias was a temporary affair, but if that was true and we could all die tomorrow, I wanted to enjoy every moment of our nights together. It was the only time I had with him, when duty and family obligations required me to be in the castle throughout the day.

I sat on the nook at my window and looked out over the horizon, still seeing the scorch marks from the pyres that had burned our people as well as our enemies. The scene looked different now, the blades of grass black from the battle. Summer had been hot, so the heat had dried all the water from the surface.

A knock sounded on the door.

"It's open."

My father opened the door, a king in his armor and weapons, his presence distinctive and formidable. He and Aurelias both had that kind of energy, the kind that could change the tone of a room just by stepping into it. "Atticus is up and about."

"He is?" I turned from the window to look at him. "That's great news." But that also meant we would be leaving soon—and maybe for the last time. I might never see this castle again. Even if we won the war, it might be destroyed by the time we returned. This very castle could be crumbled into a pile of stone.

Father remained by the door. "He said he'll be well tomorrow."

"I don't know...that seems quick."

"Your brother is a strong man."

My father never spoke of me that way. I would always be a soft, delicate flower. Meant to be admired but never touched. The second I was cut from the stem, I withered and died. Atticus was like a weed—impossible to kill.

"Put on your armor. I'd like to train with you."

"Really?" I asked in surprise. "Now?"

"Yes."

"We've trained my whole life. I don't think another session is going to make a difference—"

"Every little thing makes a difference, sweetheart." He turned back to the door. "Get dressed, and I'll meet you outside."

We met on the grounds outside the castle, the sun behind the wall so we were comfortable in the shade. My father unsheathed his blade and came at me, and the second he moved, I knew this was the real deal. He didn't hold back, but he barreled down on me like I really was his enemy.

"Shit." I got out of the way just in time, ducking his blade before I rolled aside.

He came at me hard, his blade flying through the air, his powerful shoulders putting so much effort into his movements, like I was his enemy rather than his daughter.

All I could do was evade.

"Come on, Harlow."

I threw up my blade and blocked his sword, but his strength was overpowering. I sidestepped it and blocked the hit I knew would come. But all I could do was avoid his blows and keep my head. I could do no damage in return.

"Hit me." He swung again.

I rolled out of the way, grabbed a rock along the way, and then threw it at his head.

It hit him right in the temple, drawing blood.

It was enough of a pause for me to strike down my sword onto his armor, hitting it right in the groove as he'd taught me so the piece would pop off.

Now his forearm was exposed, and a small line of blood dripped down his head. But instead of looking pissed off, he looked invigorated. "Attagirl." He came at me again, barreling down on me, facing me with the ferocity of real battle.

It made me realize how easy he'd gone on me in the past.

"Come on, sweetheart. Go for the chest plate."

He continued to chase me down and swing his sword, moving so fast that all my energy went into staying alive and protecting my body from his powerful hits. It went on for a while, and not once did my father slow down or give me a second to breathe.

I blocked hit after hit, waiting for the perfect opportunity to strike, and then the opening came. When his sword was down, I sliced my blade across his shoulder, pushing into the lock perfectly so the second piece came off.

Now his entire arm was exposed.

"Fuck yes..." I said it under my breath, too exhausted to talk any louder.

My father spun his blade around his wrist, his eyes shining with the glow of pride. "Almost there."

"Father, I'm tired—"

"*I don't give a shit.*" He slammed his fist into his chest. "*Come on, Harlow.*"

My father never spoke to me that way. Never cursed in my presence. Now I met the version that Atticus knew, that Uncle Ian knew, that General Henry knew. The hard-ass version that our guards and soldiers knew very well.

He came at me, even more ruthless than before, and slammed his sword down on my arm.

I grimaced at the contact. There would be no wound, but there would definitely be a bruise. When my father hit me, it was always gentle, but now, that mercy was over. The pain made me grit my teeth—and pissed me the fuck off.

I was back on my feet and coming at him, sidestepping one hit and then another, dodging his attacks until I was close enough to do some damage. He swiped down, and that was when I slammed the flat of my blade onto both of his wrists, making him hesitate for a split second.

But it was enough time for me to slam my sword down onto his chest, not once, but twice, hitting him hard enough to make a tiny dent. I kicked him in the stomach to knock him over, but all he did was stumble back a foot or two. But I pressed on, stabbing my blade right into the split of his armor, and then I pushed. The armor cracked and finally popped loose. It was still attached to his body, but now he wasn't as protected.

He stepped back, his eyes more intense than I'd ever seen them. "Keep it up."

I wasn't joking when I said I was tired. I wanted this to end. "Father—"

"We don't stop until you defeat me." He raised his voice. "Do you understand me?"

I wanted to argue, but this wasn't the version of my father that could be argued with. He was maniacal, focused on completing this training until he was fully satisfied. "Yes." I ignored the pain in my arms and shoulders and straightened.

"Attagirl."

When we were finally done, I dropped down onto the grass and sat there. Training had never taken so much out of me, because my father had always given me a tempered version of himself. This one was ruthless, like he really did want my head on a pike.

"Good job, sweetheart." He stood over me, his sword back in its scabbard.

"Yeah...thanks." The sun had set further, so the shadows stretched across the ground. The temperature was dropping, which was welcome after sweating in the heat for the last two hours.

He squatted down so we were level with each other. "You alright?"

"*Am I alright?*" I asked with a laugh. "Gods, I'm exhausted."

His eyes dropped momentarily. "I need you to understand what battle is really like. It's a lesson I hoped I would never have to teach you. But now you know the strength of a man, that there will be few opportunities to attack, so when you do, they need to count."

"I understand."

"I hope you never have to use what I've taught you."

"Me too." My eyes met his, knowing that my skill with the blade was good, but when it came to opponents like him and Aurelias, I really didn't stand much of a chance. And I probably wouldn't stand a chance against the demons.

"I wish my only job was to protect our family. But I have to protect everyone else too."

"Father, I know things look grim right now, but it'll be okay."

He watched me, eyes guarded.

"It'll be okay." He was the one who always comforted me, but I knew in that moment he was the one who needed reassurance. He didn't express fear the way everyone else did, by stating his worries or running from his problems. He did it by working harder and harder to prepare for the worst. He brought me out here because he was scared—scared that he would die and the only person left to protect me...would be myself.

His eyes moved away. "I'm sorry this is happening."

"It's not your fault."

"I feared one of the Kingdoms would stage a coup against me...or the Teeth would attack HeartHolme... or perhaps Necrosis would somehow return... All battles I knew I could win. But I never expected this."

"No one did, Father."

"But I should have been prepared...somehow."

"Not all hope is lost. We have Aurelias. He thinks his kin will answer his call for help. Or perhaps we'll discover their weakness on the scouting mission and not need them at all. There are other possibilities besides defeat."

His eyes remained on the ground.

"It'll be alright," I repeated, wanting to rid his heart of his pain.

His eyes lifted to mine again. "The last war was much easier, because I didn't have as much to lose."

My eyes dropped, knowing he was referring to Atticus and me, the two people he loved most in this world. He didn't have to tell me how much I mattered to him to know exactly how he felt. It was unspoken and constant.

He rose to his feet and extended his hand to me.

"I think I'm just going to sit here for a while."

"I can carry you."

"No, it's okay," I said quickly. "I'll get up when my muscles stop screaming."

He cracked a small smile. "I'll make sure the cook knows to make you an extra portion of pot roast tonight."

"Ugh, I love pot roast. It's my favorite."

His smile faded, but his eyes remained bright. "Mine too." He turned away and walked off, his sword in the scabbard across his back, walking with a rigid posture like our training hadn't exhausted him the way it exhausted me.

I lay back on the grass and looked up at the sky. Everything was sore, from my thighs to the muscles in my forearms. And I knew the place where his sword had struck me would develop into a painful bruise.

The time continued to pass, the shade becoming longer, the temperature becoming cooler. I should return to the castle so I could bathe and put on something clean, but the idea of getting up and moving… sounded terrible.

Then a face came into my view, upside down and smirking, his boots on either side of my head. "Need a hand?"

"What I need is a nap."

He moved to my feet then extended his hand to pull me up.

I placed my palm in his, and he tugged me hard, bringing me to my feet effortlessly, despite the increased weight of my armor.

"You did well."

"You watched?"

He gave a slight nod.

"He's never come at me like that before."

"He's worried."

"Yeah…"

"And you held your own pretty well."

My hand went to my arm, pressing into the armor to feel the sting of the bruise. "I don't know about that."

"I'm not one to issue false compliments."

"Not even if you're trying to get a woman into bed?"

"I wouldn't want to get her into bed if I had to give her false compliments."

A breeze powered through, ruffling my hair as well as his. He squinted slightly as it stung his eyes. It made him scowl, and his scowl was as sexy as his smile.

"I hope you weren't in too much trouble the other night." He didn't pressure me with questions, but his eyes pried into my soul.

"They were just worried is all."

"Then why didn't you come to me last night?"

"Just because their concerns are warranted doesn't mean I like them." I didn't want to live in a world where my safety was always a concern, but unfortunately, that was our reality. And until we defeated our enemy or they defeated us, it would remain that way.

"Want to shower with me?"

"A hot naked guy in the shower...sign me up."

A small smile moved on to his lips before we began our walk.

"I could train you as well—if you'd like."

"I don't know... I'm already pretty tired after having my dad kick my ass."

"With all due respect, he hasn't fought the demons."

"Are they that different from humans?" I asked.

"They're taller. Taller than both your father and I."

Whenever they were mentioned, I was reminded of the horror we were doomed to face. If I were ever cornered by one, my skills might not be enough to keep me alive. "At this point, I don't think there's much that can be done. They could strike tomorrow."

"That's not the attitude I'd expect you to have."

"Just being realistic. My mother is good with the blade, and they treated her like a rag doll."

He turned to me as we walked, his gaze hard and sympathetic at the same time. "I'd never let anything happen to you, baby."

I'd been called that nickname by lovers before, but they never made me melt. They never made me crave to hear it again. But with Aurelias, I wanted to be his baby always. I wanted to be his always. "I know."

We entered his cottage and headed upstairs where his bathroom was located. The shower was a tight fit, but that wasn't a problem for the two of us. The warm water started to fall on our naked bodies, and his powerful chest had rivers running down. He grabbed the soap and rubbed it into my skin, starting at my shoulders then moving down my chest. He was careful to avoid the bruise that had already started to form.

His eyes watched his movements, focused on the soap against my skin, the way the bubbles dripped to the drain below.

"Aurelias."

His eyes hesitated before they came back to me, like they didn't want to leave the sight of my naked body.

"Can I ask you something?"

He never answered, only stared at me.

I couldn't believe I was going to ask the question because it felt ridiculous. "Ca—can you read minds?"

His expression hardened slightly, but he gave no answer. "Why do you ask?"

"You knew the guards were at the door before they knocked."

"I have remarkable hearing."

"When you battled my father, you seemed to know every move before he made it...like you knew it was coming."

My father had grown frustrated and yelled "*How are you doing that?*" Others had also noticed what I noticed. "And you said something a long time ago...that your plans changed when you knew I was attracted to you. But how could you know?"

"You know I'm attracted to you, and you can't read my mind."

"You're evading the question."

"I'm correcting your assumptions."

"Just answer me." The fact that he hadn't made me more suspicious. "You said different vampires have different abilities…is that one yours?"

He let out a heavy sigh, no longer calm under the warm water that drenched us both. "No, I can't read minds."

That wasn't the answer I expected. "Are—are you lying?"

"No."

"Then what is your special ability?"

He didn't answer. "You're prying, and I don't appreciate it." His tone changed, deepening in his anger.

"So let me get this straight. You didn't leave with your brothers so you could stay here and protect me, but you won't be honest with me. I wouldn't need to pry if you didn't keep secrets from me. Why wouldn't you want to share this with me?"

"My business is my own, alright?" He abruptly left the shower, grabbed a towel, and walked out of the bathroom.

Shocked, I remained under the hot water, unsure what to do because I hadn't expected him to react so viciously. I followed him a moment later, seeing him scrub the towel through his hair before he did a quick pat-down of his body. He was so damn sexy, but I didn't have time to appreciate the sight. "What is your problem?"

He threw down the towel. "This isn't a relationship, Harlow. I'm not obligated to share any secret with you."

"Not a relationship...?"

He pulled on a clean pair of boxers. "You should go back to the castle."

"If it's not a relationship, then what is it, exactly?"

"A fuck-a-thon. That's all."

"So do all your fuck-a-thons include you pledging your life to protect mine?" I snapped. "I've had a lot of fuck-a-thons, and I can promise you none of those guys would ever risk their neck for mine. None of them would choose me over returning to their lands. If it's not a relationship, then what is it?"

He was angled toward the window, his muscular back turned to me. "Just go."

I continued to stare at his back, in disbelief that he could promise nothing would happen to me...and then, thirty minutes later, claim this was meaningless. "Alright." With wet hair, I grabbed my clothes off the floor, put the heavy armor back on, and walked out.

I had dinner with my family and tried my best to pretend everything was fine.

Atticus joined us, looking even better than the last time we'd spoken. He took the seat across from me. "When I heard we were having pot roast, I knew I couldn't miss it."

We gathered around the table and sat down, not really talking because there was only one thing to talk about...and no one wanted to talk about it. Once most of the meal was gone, we dipped our bread into the juice to get whatever was left over. It was a meal better suited for the cold climate of HeartHolme, but we still loved it, even on a hot summer day.

"Are you okay, Harlow?" Mother asked.

"Yeah," I said quickly, eyes averted. "I'm fine."

"That bruise on your arm..." She stared at it because I wore a short-sleeved dress. "It looks bad."

Father kept his eyes on his stew, ashamed.

"I wasn't paying attention," I said, taking the blame. "Knocked it right into a tree."

"A tree?" she asked incredulously.

Father gave a sigh. "I trained Harlow today...and took it too far."

Ivory looked at him, and the shame on his face seemed to be enough to sheathe her displeasure.

"I just need her to be prepared," Father said, still not looking at any of us.

"And I don't mind," I said quickly. "I'd rather experience a real fight than an attenuated one."

Mother let it go, turning back to her bread.

After a long stretch of silence, Father spoke. "Atticus, if you're well enough, we should begin our operations tomorrow. If we weren't in such difficult times, I would let you rest longer, but time is a luxury we don't have."

"I understand, Father," Atticus said. "And I'm more than capable of doing this."

Mother looked like she wanted to say something, to keep our family together, but she knew there was no other option.

"Then we'll leave by dragon tomorrow," Father said. "General Henry will march the army to HeartHolme."

I would ask if Aurelias could join us rather than travel by foot, but after our last conversation, I had no desire to speak with him. He could be the most affectionate and loving man I'd ever been with, but he could also be the coldest. The very lips that kissed away my troubles were also the cause of my despair.

"Bring only the things you can't live without," Father said. "Or have General Henry deliver your things by wagon. I'm not sure if this castle will be here once the war is over...or any of the Kingdoms."

I left the windows open so the breeze could sweep through now that the temperature had plummeted. It was comforting on the skin, just cold enough to make bumps form on my arms. Despite my exhaustion from training, I wasn't remotely tired now that I was alone in my bedroom.

I was too sad to be tired.

I sat on the couch with an open book in my lap, but after reading the same sentences several times, I stopped trying. I let it sit there on my thighs, my eyes on a random spot on the floor. It could potentially be my last night in this bedroom, the very bedroom my mother used to occupy when she was my age. It might be a pile of rubble soon after we left. Everything I loved might be a pile of rubble before long.

Then someone climbed into my window, and their boots thudded against the floor.

My chin lifted to see the intruder, and the terror in my heart was quickly replaced by relief when I realized it was Aurelias. But then that was quickly replaced by anger...fiery anger. "What do you want?" I snapped the book closed and lost my place in the pages, but I needed to do something with my hands.

He came toward me, his hard eyes heavy with frustration. He stood over me, looking down at me like he was waiting for me to do something…when he was the one in the doghouse.

I tossed the book aside and got to my feet. "I'm not in the mood for a fuck-a-thon, and since that's all we are, there's no reason for conversation. So you can crawl back down now and leave me the fuck alone." I turned away from him, moving toward the bed even though I was too charged to sleep.

"Baby."

"Baby?" I asked, turning back around. "I'm sorry, do you have me confused with someone else?" I looked around the room, searching for another woman who would deserve the title more than I did. "Because I'm just some bitch you fuck, not your baby—"

He moved fast, grabbing my face and kissing me hard on the mouth.

I didn't fight it, not when I was paralyzed by the desperation of his kiss. His arm squeezed my lower back, and his hand slid deep into my hair, making me feel thoroughly possessed.

He pulled away and looked me in the eye. "I know I fucked up." His hand left my face, but his arm remained around my waist so I couldn't walk away. "I was just angry…and lashing out."

"I prefer an apology over excuses." I pushed his arm away so he would release me.

His eyes shifted away, that annoyance returning.

"You can crawl out the window anytime you want, Aurelias. I'm not keeping you here."

He looked at me again, his annoyance bubbling to barely sheathed anger. "You know I didn't mean what I said—"

"Then apologize."

He sighed as he stepped away, like I was forcing daggers under his fingernails.

"You've never apologized for anything, have you?"

He looked out the window for a moment, standing in his armor and sword, as if he expected to be attacked while he was in my bedroom. "No."

"It shows."

After a moment of silence, he turned back to me. "I'm sorry." He looked me dead in the eye as he spoke, the sincerity in his gaze. "This is just hard for me."

"What?"

"*This.*" He raised his hand, gestured it between us, and then clenched his fingers into a fist.

"Why is it hard, Aurelias?"

He closed his eyes as he released a sigh, and after so much silence passed, I knew there would be no explanation. "You're right. I wouldn't have chosen to stay behind if you weren't important to me...more important than I'd ever want to admit. I wouldn't call you baby if you weren't the only woman I wanted in my bed. You've become the reason for my existence and I fucking hate that."

"Why?" I whispered. "Why do you hate it?"

"Because..." He shook his head, sighed, and pinched the bridge of his nose like this conversation was literally painful. "Because we both know this will end. And we both know it'll hurt."

"Why are you so sure it will end—"

"Because it will."

"Why don't we just let this relationship grow—"

"*Listen to me.*" His hand tightened into a fist again. "There is no scenario in which we end up together. Period."

I didn't expect that to hurt, but it hurt far more than the bruise on my arm. The air was sucked out of my lungs and my stomach. We had established this was temporary, so even though my expectations were managed, it was still fucking painful. "Why won't you just try to give this a chance—"

"Because I will leave you, Harlow. When this is over, I will get on my damn ship and leave you behind. I will sail the fuck away and not look back. I will return to my world and bed an endless line of beautiful women as if this never happened." He didn't raise his voice, but his entire face was clenched in rage. "So I don't want to share every aspect of my life with you. I don't want you to be privy to my secrets. I don't want to make this any harder than it has to be. Our relationship may be meaningful and intense, but it can never be more than what it is right now. I don't want it to grow. I don't want it to change." He took a deep breath. "I need you to accept that, Harlow."

I looked away.

"I know you want more…and I will never give you more."

The disappointment and hurt were potent, and I wished I could just swallow it down like a bite that I hadn't fully chewed. I forced my gaze back to him. "We're very different people, Aurelias. Even if I know how this relationship ends, I want to feel the full depth and intensity that we share. I would rather regret the pain of loss than regret not embracing its fullness while I could. Seems like a waste otherwise."

Now he was the one who looked away.

"I'm sorry that you're scared—"

"*I'm not scared.*" His eyes were back on me.

"You're scared to get hurt—and I'm not."

A smile moved on to his lips, but it was cold and condescending. "The only reason you're not scared is because you've never lost someone. You've never loved someone with all your fucking heart and soul and lost them forever. You're young and naïve, clueless to real pain and suffering, so don't misconstrue your naïveté for courage."

I felt like I'd been slapped, but I focused on what he'd said. "I'm sorry...that you lost someone." He didn't need to give me the specifics to know what had happened, that he'd loved a woman and lost her, either because she'd left him...or she'd died. I was stung with jealousy and pain, knowing someone else had received his love when I would never earn it, but I also felt pity...deep pity.

He looked away and said nothing, his eyes out the window into the darkness.

"What happened—"

"*Don't.*" He clenched his eyes closed as if that would deflect the pain of my words.

Silence passed between us, neither one of us saying anything. His eyes remained out the window, our relationship in a worse state now than when he'd first entered my chambers.

"Aurelias..." I took a breath before I continued, hoping he would look at me.

He didn't.

"I want all of you...for however long I get to have you. We could both be dead tomorrow, so combating our feelings is a waste of our time and our hearts. If you want me, this is how it has to be."

His eyes turned back to me.

"Please…"

He clenched his eyes shut again.

"Aurelias." My hands cupped his face and forced his stare on me.

He opened his eyes and looked at me.

"I'm your baby…" I brought our faces close together. "And I want to feel like your baby every night we're together."

He released a heavy breath as his arms circled me, as they pulled me tight so my body was against his. His lips caught mine, and then his hand was deep in my hair, guiding me back to the bed. "You'll always be my baby."

TWENTY
IAN

I didn't consider myself the spontaneous type. I dwelled on issues, thinking about them until they drove me mad. So when I made my decision to betray my brother's authority, it was intentional.

I had my wife back. I had my daughter back. I was happier than I'd ever been, but also more terrified. I always had something to lose, but now, I *really* had something to lose. Huntley had chosen to wait like sitting ducks for the enemy to come to us, but I had a very different opinion about that strategy.

And since it concerned the safety of my family, I had no issue pursuing it.

Mother finished reading the letter. "They're evacuating the Kingdoms and marching them to Heart-Holme." She read down the scroll, the scroll that I'd already read. "It's the only kingdom large enough to house everyone, and it's the best shelter for war."

I stared out the window.

"That means Huntley is already on the way."

Which was why I had to make this decision before he could stop me. "I'm returning to the east."

Mother lowered the scroll immediately, her eyes narrowing at my words.

"I must protect my family, and waiting for the enemy to slaughter us is a shitty way to do that."

"Ian—"

"We can do that dance if you want, but it's not going to change my decision." There was no argument she could make to alter my stance. These demons were taller and more powerful and immune to the one weapon we had—fire. "I'll take a dragon rider with me, whoever volunteers to join me."

Mother slowly rolled the scroll back into place, her eyes directed elsewhere as she took a beat. "What do you hope to achieve?"

"To discover anything that will help us defeat them."

"And who will you ask?"

"The prisoner told me there are still Palladium survivors. They might know something."

"And how do you intend to find them—"

"I have no idea," I snapped. "Is that what you want me to say?"

"Ian, HeartHolme needs its steward in the absence of its king. Send riders in your stead if this is important to you."

"I'm not the kind of leader to send someone in my stead to protect my neck. I'm not willing to order soldiers to risk their lives if I'm not willing to do the same. And more importantly, I don't trust anyone else to do this better than me."

She dropped her gaze, disappointed.

"I have to do this—for all of us. Don't pretend you aren't scared, Mother. Don't pretend you don't understand how fucked we are. The only reason Delacroix stands is because a vampire defended it. It wasn't our armies or our dragons. It was a being stronger than us."

She kept her gaze down.

"This mission may claim my life. Or I may return with the information that will ensure our survival. You raised us to sacrifice our blood and our lives for our people. That's what I'm doing. Somehow, you lost Father and carried on…but I couldn't do that if it were Avice and Lila. I just…" I couldn't finish the sentence, because that outcome was infinitely worse than my own death.

Her eyes lifted again. "Huntley will be furious."

"I don't care."

"He'll be furious with me for allowing this."

"I'm the steward of HeartHolme—you are not. I have the autonomy to protect this kingdom as I see fit, and this is how to do it. I will not let them be conquered by an unconquerable enemy."

"Huntley said the vampires may come."

"You think I would risk our people for *may*?" I snapped. "They *may* come. Or they may *not* come. Or they may come when we're all already dead. Mother, I know you agree with me, even though you refuse to admit it. If you weren't so blinded by your favoritism, you would know that my decision is the right one."

Her eyes shifted away when she couldn't meet my gaze.

I waited for her to admit it, to say something.

She looked at me once more. "Please be careful, son. Losing your father was devastating, but losing a son... my heart would never heal. I've been fortunate to watch both of you grow into men I'm deeply proud of. I'm fortunate that I haven't watched my sons pass on like other mothers have..."

"I'll do everything I can to return."

She gave a slight nod. "You should hurry. Because once Huntley arrives, you'll lose your chance."

"I know." I stared at her, unsure what to say now that it might be the last time she would ever see me. I might die in the east, my body impossible to retrieve, buried somewhere in the barren dirt, hidden under the snow. "I'll do my best to return to you."

"And your family, Ian. They need you just as much."

I stepped into our chambers, Avice ready for the day in a long-sleeved dress, her beautiful hair down one shoulder. She was still rigid around me, like she hadn't gotten used to my sharing her space again. When she looked at me, her eyes didn't sparkle like diamonds, like she loved me more than words could say. That sentiment was blocked by a cloudiness that had formed with my betrayal. But it was there, slowly coming through like the sun as the clouds parted. "I need to speak to you."

She pivoted her body to face me fully, her eyes guarded.

We slept together side by side every night, and she allowed me to hold her in my arms, to keep her close as we passed the night. I wanted more, but I didn't want to push for it. But now that I might not come back...I wished our nights had been different. "I'm leaving for the east."

Her hesitancy disappeared at my announcement.

"I'm taking another rider with me to discover whatever I can."

"Ian, I don't like this—"

"I have to protect you and Lila. This is the only way I can."

Her eyes softened like wilting rose petals. "It's too dangerous—"

"Not as dangerous as doing nothing."

She turned quiet, her eyes shifting back and forth in devastation.

I didn't want to cause her pain, but it felt good to know she cared. That she still cared as much for me as she did before. That my betrayal would never be enough to stop her from loving me.

She inhaled a slow breath, a painful one. "Ian." She moved into me, her hands seizing my cheeks, her lips on mine. It was a single, hard kiss, one packed with pain and longing. "Please come back to me."

I rested my forehead against hers, my hands so tight on her body that I might never let go. "Nothing will stop me, baby."

"I'm sorry...for everything." She started to cry.

I slowly pulled away so our gazes could meet. "Don't apologize to me—"

"I'm sorry I pushed you away. I'm sorry I didn't think clearly. I'm sorry for accusing you of something so horrible. And I'm sorry that I gave up on us..."

Now I really wanted to stay forever. "Avice, it means so much to hear you say that, but it doesn't excuse what I did." My hands cupped her face. "I'm so sorry that I hurt you, that I threw us away for something that didn't even matter."

Her hands gripped my wrists, and she continued to cry.

"But we're together now, and that's all that matters." The wound in my chest had finally closed and healed. The barriers around her heart were gone. Now she let me in, let me see all of her. Without the war, perhaps she wouldn't be so forgiving, so that was the only silver lining to this horror.

"Have you told Lila?"

The question caused a pain so intense, it nearly crippled me. "No."

"You're not going to..."

"I—I can't." I couldn't say goodbye to her. I couldn't look my daughter in the eye and know that my failure would result in her death. When my mother had told me how devastated she would be if she lost me, I understood exactly how she felt. "Please...give her my love."

I walked to the field, seeing the two dragons there with their saddles and armor.

Jeremiah was there, in his armor and weapons, looking out across the expanse of wilderness.

I approached Nightshade, a black dragon I'd ridden many times. His eyes turned to me, and then he lowered his head so we could regard each other on level ground. My hand went to his cheek, feeling his scales with my bare skin. *You owe me nothing, Nightshade.*

I'm free because of you. I have hatchlings because of you. He looked at me with gray eyes. **It would be my honor to protect you.**

I moved my forehead to his cheek and held it there, my arm sliding across his snout in a gentle hug. *We have too much to live for not to return.* I pulled away then came face-to-face with Elora.

By her expression, it was clear she was pissed. "Huntley's going to kill you."

"Yeah."

"If you actually survive, that is."

"I know."

She came closer to me. "I only outfitted your dragons because I knew you would do it anyway, and I wanted you to be protected." Her arms crossed over her chest, and her solemn eyes regarded me like I was already dead.

"Thank you."

"Are you sure this is a good idea?"

"I never said it was a good idea, Elora. But these are demons, and humankind stands no chance. You're smarter than most—so you know I speak the truth."

Her eyes dropped for a moment. "I've been working on new armor that's invulnerable to fire."

"How's that going?"

"It works, but not as well as I'd like it to."

"Keep trying."

"That's all I've been doing, which is why my eyes are bloodshot. Bastian is helping me, but there's only so much he can do when I'm the expert and he's the novice."

"You'll figure it out."

"You think?"

"You always figure it out."

A faint smile moved on to her lips. "Make it back, Ian. I kinda love you and shit."

I smiled back. "I kinda love you and shit too."

She stepped closer to me and hugged me tightly, gripping me the way Huntley gripped me.

I didn't want to let go for a while, so I didn't. I held her for nearly a minute before I released her. "See you soon…"

"Yeah."

I turned away and approached Jeremiah. "You sure you want to do this?"

He was a decade younger than me, built in the same way as Huntley, but he had far more arrogance than he should. "I wouldn't have volunteered otherwise."

"There's a strong chance we won't return."

"And there's an even stronger chance we're all going to die if we don't figure this out."

I nodded in agreement.

"King Rolfe may be the King of Kingdoms, but Steward Ian is my king—as far as I'm concerned."

All I could do was stare, too touched to react.

"As far as we're all concerned. If you say this is the way, then this is the way."

I still didn't know what to say.

His hand clapped me on the shoulder. "Let's do this."

We left before darkness and, more than likely, just an hour before Huntley arrived in HeartHolme. We flew across the mountains and slowly watched them disappear, fading as the sun set, and brightening again when the moon replaced the sun.

The only sound was the flap of our dragons' wings, making us glide across the quiet sky. The peaks were visible in the moonlight, the rivers that ran between the valleys. The mountains were impenetrable from the west, but they became more hospitable to the east.

I had nothing to pass the time—except my own thoughts. Thoughts of my wife and daughter. Thoughts of Huntley's reaction when my mother had told him what I'd done. The Kingdoms were coming to HeartHolme for protection, but the steward had long left.

We passed the mountains at the very beginning of dawn, when the sky changed from black to midnight blue. We had less than an hour to observe the land without being seen, digesting the terrain in limited light.

We flew past where Huntley and I had landed initially and flew farther east.

The ring of fire was still there, so intense it looked like a thousand pyres combined into one. It looked the same as the last time I saw it, and I began to wonder how those flames were sustained... perhaps they were sustained by magic rather than wood.

The dragons flew hard, trying to cover as much of the land as they could during the small window of opportunity. Most of the world was covered with snow, but farther east, it started to dissipate.

Jeremiah spotted the ruins before I did. "Steward Ian." He pointed down to the earth.

I saw it right away. A massive pile of stone, so much rubble it looked like all the Kingdoms combined together. Not a single structure remained—and it looked like a graveyard for the biggest battle that had ever taken place. "Palladium..."

"What?"

"The sun is coming. We need to land." I turned Nightshade to the right, getting him away from the rubble in case anyone was watching. There was less snow there, so I directed him to the fields that were lined with lots of trees.

He landed as quietly as possible, and then Jeremiah joined me.

We both sat in silence, listening for the sounds of oncoming enemies. We both gazed at the tree line, both regarded our surroundings for hours, listening for the slightest noise.

Jeremiah was the first to leave his dragon. "We're alone."

I left Nightshade and let my boots hit the ground, ground that felt the same as it did back home. When I looked at the soil, I saw that it had a red hue, which was something I hadn't seen before. I kneeled down to grab a handful, feeling the distinct moisture in the dirt.

Nightshade watched me. ***Their earth is different from ours.***

Yes.

"I'll take the first watch," Jeremiah said.

"There will be no watch. We'll walk to the ruins. I want to see it."

Jeremiah turned to me. "Sounds like a risky plan."

"We won't be able to identify anything in the darkness."

Jeremiah gave a slight nod. "We'll move on foot. Once the ruins are in sight, we'll decide what to do then."

We began the journey, the sun moving higher in the sky and searing our clothing with heat. It was a land where snow and heat were close together, even though their climates were not at all similar. We were close to the mountains, and that was the only difference.

In silence, we moved, the dragons staying behind us since they were bigger and bulkier. It took most of the day to get there because the distance was great, even if it didn't feel that way on the back of a dragon.

We arrived, looking at the massive rubble from the tree line. The piles were enormous and stretched far and wide, an entire city destroyed, a legacy erased.

"I'm not sure what we'll discover here."

"This must be Palladium," I said. "The fallen city. Perhaps it'll provide clues where the survivors have gone."

"Unlikely," he said. "If I were to escape, I would flee as far as I could." He looked at the mountains. "Probably in there. But I don't have another suggestion, so…"

"I suspect the demons are nowhere nearby. They wouldn't have destroyed the city like this if they intended to stay."

"I didn't see any kingdoms along the way."

"I'm not sure if their cities are on the ground—or below the ground."

"That ring of fire... What is it?"

I stared at the rubble, waiting for the sun to drop farther so I could explore. "I have no idea."

Jeremiah stared straight ahead, releasing a heavy sigh.

"We'll make our move at sunset."

"Then I'll take the first watch, Steward Ian."

"Ian is fine."

He looked at me.

"I'm not a steward out here. You aren't a soldier. Right now, we're just two men trying to survive."

At sunset, we made our move into the remains of the fallen city. Everywhere I stepped, I hit stone. It was hard to imagine how the city had looked when it was in such disarray. Without a line of men to move stones to uncover what was underneath, it was difficult to distinguish anything.

I kicked away rocks and stone, hoping to find something meaningful somewhere, and all I came across was a skeleton. I stilled when I stared at it, the white bones speckled with dust and grime. I'd seen dead people on the battlefield, seen horrific sights that made me want to vomit, but skeletal remains…that was new.

I kicked away more pieces and saw the dark stains of blood. There was a lot of it, so this person had probably bled out and died, the rubble falling on top of them afterward. "I found something."

Jeremiah crested a hill of rubble then approached me. Right away, he spotted the bones, which were still intact. "This happened a while ago."

"I'm not sure how long it takes for human remains to decompose."

"Neither do I. But at least we know it wasn't in the last few months." He kicked aside more pieces, revealing the skeleton underneath, no sight of skin or flesh. Everything was gone.

Then we heard the sound of stones shifting, like someone was walking nearby.

Jeremiah and I both stilled and looked up.

"Did you hear that?" Jeremiah whispered.

"Yes." I looked at our surroundings, trying not to breathe, just waiting for something to pop out from underneath the rubble.

Jeremiah didn't move.

We stayed that way for what felt like an eternity.

The sound didn't return, but we were both convinced we'd heard it.

"It could have been stones shifting after we passed through," Jeremiah said.

"Maybe..." I wasn't convinced. But I also wasn't convinced that there could be anything living in this graveyard of dead bodies buried under stone.

I hear something.

I turned to where Nightshade stood at the tree line, but I was hardly able to see his dark scales in the thickness of the wilderness. *Voices?* "Nightshade hears something."

Jeremiah stared at me, knowing I was focused on listening to my dragon.

I hear the ground.

My eyebrows furrowed. *What does that mean?*

It's moving…

"Nightshade says the ground is moving."

"Like an earthquake?" Jeremiah asked.

"I don't know."

It's getting louder.

"We've got to move." I tugged on Jeremiah's arm and pulled him off the pile of rubble we stood on. There were no buildings or structures in which to hide, so we had no other choice but to hunch down behind a pile and hope we weren't spotted.

It's stopped.

Stay hidden, Nightshade.

The world was quiet and still, with no sign of danger as the sun continued to dip farther behind the mountains. The crickets became more audible, welcoming the darkness across their lands. Neither Jeremiah nor I moved. But then we heard someone whisper.

"Over here."

I turned my head to look behind me, and about fifty feet away was a woman. She wore steel armor on her lithe body, and her long brown hair flowed in the breeze behind her. Her features were absent because the light didn't hit her in the right way. She started to wave us toward her. "You have, like, ten seconds."

Jeremiah and I looked at each other.

There's a girl here... Is that what you heard?

Not unless she's underground.

She raised her voice a little more. "Get your ass over here."

Jeremiah and I looked at each other again, both of us knowing it was probably a trap.

She threw her arms down. "Then run!" She took off, running behind a pile of rubble and then disappearing.

"Where'd she go?" Jeremiah asked.

I didn't give a shit. "Let's run back to the dragons." We left the rubble and started to run, and that was when the ground directly beneath our feet began to shake, to shake so hard that walking was impossible. I hit the dirt and caught myself with my arms.

Jeremiah's dragon landed beside him, and he was able to pull himself onto the beast.

I pushed myself back to my feet and saw Nightshade fly toward me, flapping his wings hard to reach me.

Behind you!

I looked over my shoulder and almost fell from the shakes, seeing a group of men a foot taller than me approach, their skin dark like ash, their exposed flesh showing veins of fire. They weren't men at all…

Run.

I tried to run, but the ground was so uneven that I shifted from left to right, tripping over my own feet. But the demons walked effortlessly, like they and the ground were the same. They were close behind me, just a few feet away. *Leave me.*

Nightshade flew straight toward me. **No.**

I looked behind me, seeing one of them had a crossbow, and it wasn't aimed at me, but at Nightshade's face, its mark on one of his eyes. I pulled out my blade and turned around, doing my best to handle the sword when standing on an earthquake. I aimed for the crossbow, missing the mark but causing him to turn and miss, hitting Nightshade's armor. *Leave. Tell Huntley what happened.*

One of them sneered, looking at Nightshade like dinner.

It made me sick to my stomach, so I screamed. "*I said leave, Nightshade!*" The men didn't care about me, deflecting my blades without even looking at me, their hungry eyes on the brilliant dragon right before them. I swiped at one, drawing blood from the arm that smoked as it flowed out, and he didn't seem to feel it.

Then they sprinted, ready to jump on Nightshade and force him to the ground.

"*Nightshade!*"

He launched from the ground and into the sky, his powerful wings lifting him high into the air, the arrow from the crossbow bouncing off the steel my sister had outfitted him with. He was a dot quickly, safe from the demons on the ground. ***I will return for you.***

I know.

The ground had stopped shaking, so I ran for it.

I ran faster than I ever had in my life, knowing I had mere seconds as a head start.

I thought of Avice. Lila. Huntley.

Everyone I would never see again.

And then a fucking miracle happened.

The girl from before popped up from beneath the ground, opening a steel hatch right in front of me, like my path was meant to take me straight here. "Jump."

I didn't hesitate before I dropped into the hole, hitting steel as I crumpled to the ground.

"We've got to run." She grabbed my wrist and forced me up. "*Now*."

I was on my feet, surged with adrenaline, and running as fast as I could.

The tremors in the earth returned, and I could feel the steel implode behind us as the tunnel caved in. It was too narrow to run side by side, so I ran behind her, following her into the darkness…having no idea where we would end up.

TWENTY-ONE
HARLOW

Delacroix began to evacuate.

The cobblestone street was lined with carts, everyone taking whatever they could, but it was mostly food to survive the barren lands of HeartHolme. Some farmers and merchants would remain behind, taking on the heroic role of continuing food transport to HeartHolme so everyone wouldn't starve.

I looked across the village, on the verge of tears because I feared I would never see this place again. The sight was traumatizing, to watch our people leave the kingdom that we couldn't protect.

My father came to my side, a behemoth in height and armor, and he took in the same horrific sight. "I'm sorry, sweetheart."

"You have nothing to be sorry for."

"I'm sorry this is your reality—and it's my fault that it is so. I should have offered death rather than mercy to the Teeth. A mistake I'll never repeat."

"Father, you should never apologize for choosing to be good rather than cruel." I turned to look at him. "I love you for that."

His blue eyes softened as he looked at me, and then his hand reached for my shoulder, embracing me the way he did Atticus, gripping me through my armor. "Are you ready to go?"

"Yes. All my things have been packed in the wagon."

He released me and turned away.

"But I do have one request."

He turned back to me, and the softness in his gaze had quickly been replaced by hardness, like he suspected my request had something to do with Aurelias.

And he was right. "I'd like Aurelias to ride Pyre with me."

"It's inappropriate for a vampire to ride a dragon."

"I asked Pyre, and he has no issue with it. Besides, don't you think the men will be uncomfortable traveling with a vampire in their ranks? Some of them hail him as a hero, but I'm sure others will always fear him."

Father stared, his thoughts protected behind that hard gaze.

"I thought you liked him—"

"I don't like anyone, Harlow. *Like* isn't a word in my vocabulary."

"Then I thought you respected him."

"I do."

"And trust him."

"I trust people as often as I like them."

"Father."

He couldn't hold my stare anymore, so his eyes shifted away. "Your relationship makes me uncomfortable—something I have no desire to discuss."

I looked away too, also uncomfortable. "With all due respect, whom I choose to spend my time with is my own business, whether he's a vampire, a human, or one of the Teeth. I'm sorry that it makes you uncomfortable—"

"It makes me uncomfortable because I don't want you to get hurt." He looked out over the kingdom, unable to look at me.

My arms crossed over my chest. "Isn't that a part of life?"

He continued his stare.

"Isn't it an integral and unavoidable part of life?"

He held his silence.

"I'd rather embrace all aspects of life, the good and the bad, rather than tolerate a dull and watered-down version, even if it's less painful. So Aurelias will join me on Pyre because I'm not going to wait a week for him to join us with the army."

He said nothing—the only acceptance I would ever get.

I entered the cottage without knocking, seeing his two bags by the door because he'd already packed. He stood in the kitchen, finishing off the last of his glass before he left it on the counter, probably never to be seen again. His serpent-crested armor fit him so well, hugged his muscular arms and narrow waist. His sword hung at his side, also engraved with the powerful serpent. He walked to me, eyes locked on mine with their usual intensity, and then stopped directly before me. "I'll see you soon."

"I asked my father if you could accompany us by dragon. He agreed."

His stare remained hard.

"And Pyre also agreed."

"Pyre is…?"

"Our dragon."

He gave a slight nod. "I don't mind traveling with the army on horseback. I've ridden horses my entire life, on treks far longer than the one we're about to take. And you know the cold doesn't bother me."

"But the separation bothers me."

A hint of emotion moved into his gaze, sheathed by his restraint.

"So, you're riding a dragon with me. Unless you're scared?"

A small smile crept on to his lips. "Find it thrilling, actually."

"That's a yes, then?"

He paused, staring into my face. "Yes."

I smiled. "Then grab your bags, and let's go."

We approached the field where our dragons waited for us. Bags were secured to the saddles, and Aurelias added his to the ropes. He traveled light like my father, only having a few things he couldn't live without.

My parents were there, saying goodbye to my brother.

My father embraced my brother in a long hug, gripping him tightly like a boy, even though they were the same height. When Father let go, my mother moved in next, squeezing him tightly like she didn't want to let go.

It was hard to accept the fact that it could be the last time I ever saw him. That any moment could be the last time I saw any member of my family. That my brother could die in an attack before he reached HeartHolme.

Atticus turned to me, strong and healthy like he hadn't been cut down in the battle that had almost claimed our lives. He was handsome again, a smile on his face, like this departure wasn't a goodbye. He looked at me, and just like Father, he tried to make me feel better when he was the one about to be alone. "I'll be there before you know it."

"This is such an undertaking…"

"But you know me. I get shit done."

I chuckled but only slightly, because his joke wasn't enough to erase my unease completely. "Be safe, okay?"

"Always." He pulled me in and hugged me, his chin resting on my head.

We hardly ever hugged. It had only happened once or twice in our lifetimes. But now that times had changed, we hugged more than we ever had.

He was the first to pull away. He looked at Aurelias, and a moment passed because he didn't know how to regard him.

Aurelias spoke first, extending his hand to shake my brother's. "Our swords will join in the great battle to come, and I'm honored to fight alongside a strong general—whether we live or die."

Atticus shook his hand before he gave a nod. "You're not required to give your sword, but you offer it anyway. Thank you for your service." They broke apart, and Atticus looked at Father one last time before he nodded and turned away, heading back to the castle where he would meet the soldiers who would accompany him to the Kingdoms.

Mother watched him go before she looked at Father.

Father met her gaze, and they said nothing as they looked at each other, both of them feeling the same raw emotion.

His hand went to her shoulder. "He'll be alright, baby."

Her hand moved to his, and she squeezed it.

After a moment of silence, we stepped over to the dragons that waited for us. They lowered themselves to their bellies to make it as easy as possible for us to climb up.

I pointed at the rope. "I usually grab on to this and hoist myself up—"

Aurelias climbed up easily, without even using the rope, like the dragon was no different from a horse. Then he extended his hand to me.

I rolled my eyes. "Show-off." I ignored his hand and used the rope to climb up, and I dropped into the seat in front of him. "Hold on." I secured the ropes around our legs so we would be strapped down if Pyre made any sudden moves.

One hand grabbed on to the horn in front of me, but his other arm moved around my waist, hugging me to him like he was the one keeping me in a safe position.

"Come on, Pyre," I said. "Show him what you got."

Pyre released a mighty roar before he launched upward, his large wings flapping to lift us from the earth and into the air in just a few seconds. It was always a thrill to move at that speed, to feel your body flatten from the sheer force of the beast's movements. Once we were in the sky just below the clouds, we started to glide, the wind hard in our faces.

Was he impressed?

"Fun, huh?" I looked at him over my shoulder.

It was the first time I saw color in his face, rosiness in his cheeks, and an infectious, boyish grin. "This is…unbelievable."

I looked forward, a grin on my face. *Oh, he's definitely impressed…*

TWENTY-TWO
HUNTLEY

Storm landed in the field outside HeartHolme, and after a long day of riding, I was eager to let my boots hit the earth. The novelty of flight had worn off over the years, becoming no different from riding a horse.

After I got down, I helped Ivory to the ground.

Pyre landed a moment later, and Harlow and Aurelias climbed off.

The soldiers approached and began unloading our belongings to carry them to our chambers in the castle.

I wasn't sure where Aurelias would stay, because he wouldn't be staying in the castle with my daughter, but his accommodations weren't my problem.

We walked in through the open gate and entered HeartHolme. It was cold and merciless, but it felt like home to me. The cloudless skies and warm sunshine in Delacroix were welcome, but I'd always prefer the snow, overcast afternoons, the fire in the hearths, and my naked wife trying to stay warm in a pile of furs.

My mother was there to greet us just past the gate, elegant as always, her blue eyes on fire as usual. "Son." She grasped me in her arms and held me tightly, embracing me the way I'd just embraced my son before I said goodbye. Then she addressed Ivory, blanketing her in affection that was genuine but would never match the affection she had for me. She embraced my daughter then stopped as she regarded Aurelias. "My son has told me all about you." Her time as queen had long passed, but she could still produce the authority that made people listen. "While I have my reservations about a creature with your proclivities, my son has assured me of your honor and integrity—as well as your dedication to our cause. I put my full trust in him, and therefore, I put it in you." She gave a slight bow. "Welcome to HeartHolme, Aurelias, Prince of the Originals."

Aurelias regarded me before he nodded in return. "Thank you for the hospitality, Lady Rolfe. HeartHolme has my sword and my dagger."

She watched him, her intelligent eyes regarding his face as if there were words marked on his skin. "I hope your kin will come to our aid."

"As do I. But I'll remain at your disposal, regardless."

My mother turned to Harlow and winked. "You've got quite the man, Harlow."

Harlow smiled, giving a chuckle at her grandmother's words.

My mother was far more lenient with her grandchildren than she'd ever been with us. Once I'd pledged my heart to Ivory, my mother had sought to destroy it with all means necessary. Time may have made her wiser, made her heart softer, or she was simply more understanding toward girls than she had been of boys.

"You must be cold and hungry," Mother said. "I know HeartHolme always takes some getting used to whenever you return. Let's enter the castle and have lunch."

"Where's Ian?" I felt a sudden dread in my heart, because Ian would be the one to greet us as steward of

HeartHolme, not my mother, who had stepped down from the role decades ago. He should be preparing the defenses, working on the line with the soldiers day and night. For him not to be present...was troubling.

My mother hesitated—and that troubled me more. "Let's go inside and discuss—"

"*Mother.*" I stepped forward, getting directly in front of her, my nostrils flaring in ferocity because I already knew the answer before I asked the question. "Where the fuck is he?"

She kept her head held high, but her eyes flashed in intimidation. "Huntley, I did my best to talk him out of it—"

"*Motherfucker.*" I threw down my arms and marched off, too furious to look her in the eye right now. I paced, furious, ignoring the stares from my family and the guards on duty. "Why did you let him go?" I was back to my mother, ready to rip her apart for allowing this to happen. "I forbade him from returning to the east—"

"With all due respect, King Rolfe. Ian is the steward of HeartHolme, not I, so I have no power to control his actions. I asked him to stay, and he refused."

I forced myself to stay still, to breathe normally, not to scream and shout right in front of my daughter. "When did he leave?"

"This morning."

"Because he knew I was coming." I'd sent that letter, notifying him of my return. Once I was in Heart-Holme, he would never have had another chance to leave it. He'd betrayed me—and chose to betray me at a time when I couldn't stop it.

Mother stared, her eyes sympathetic. "I don't agree with his decision. But I understand his perspective, and you must too, Huntley."

My eyes turned angry again.

"If we don't know our enemy, we can't defeat our enemy. Necrosis was vulnerable to fire, but these demons thrive on it."

"And you think Ian will figure it out?" I asked incredulously.

"I think your brother is determined to protect the ones he loves."

I was still furious. I'd strictly forbidden him from doing this—and he'd shit on my words.

"There's nothing you can do now," Mother said. "Let it go."

"Let it go..." She clearly didn't know me—because I never let anything go.

"Come," Mother said. "Let's continue this conversation in the castle."

"You do that," I said before I walked off. "But I have other shit I need to do."

I sat alone at the table, drinking my ale in peace, the pot roast in front of me just a bowl of juices. The bread was gone because I'd eaten it all, and I sat alone in the bar and stared at the wall instead of my brother's face.

Ivory pulled out the chair and sat across from me. She'd bathed and changed into something more comfortable, a long-sleeved sweater with tight trousers underneath. Her neck was still red and fiery, and I hoped that one day those scars would fade and diminish. It still pissed me off every time I looked at them.

She said nothing, only got the barmaiden's attention to order herself an ale.

I didn't want company right now, not even from my own wife. My eyes were out the window, pretending she wasn't there.

She got her ale and drank it in silence, as if she hadn't come to talk.

She'd come to listen.

One of the many reasons I loved her more than life itself. She knew me like the back of her hand, recognized my moods and how to navigate through them, knew the flames of my temper and how to douse them.

In this instance, the only way to stop these flames was to let them burn out on their own.

We must have sat there for an hour before I said anything. "Ian's a fucking idiot."

She was on her third tankard—because she was a woman who could drink.

"The second he's back, I'm stabbing my dagger through his hand."

She traced her finger around the rim of her glass, her eyes following her movements. It was late now, probably almost midnight. The bar was nearly empty, and the only people remaining were the ones who needed to drink to get to sleep.

I stared at her, looking hard into her face, the woman who had fused her soul with mine. "I love you."

Her eyes lifted instantly, and a small smile moved on to her lips. "I know."

I looked away again.

"Perhaps he'll return with the information we need."

"Perhaps he won't return at all…"

"Let's not speak of such an outcome."

"I've visited the east. It's a strange place." It was a barren land with extreme elements, with slavers and slaves, with fallen kingdoms and demons. "Ian will find nothing there but his own death."

"Let's not say that—"

"It's a fucking suicide mission." And that was why I was furious—because I couldn't win this damn war without him. I couldn't lead my people to victory with a broken heart. I couldn't think straight without my brother next to me. I loved him with the same intensity as I loved my wife and children—unconditionally.

"Ian is selfless and brave—"

"He's impulsive and irrational, and that's exactly how he fucked up his marriage."

"Huntley..."

"I told him not to go."

"I know."

"And he fucking did it anyway."

"I think it's an outcome we would have considered at some point anyway. Since they've already attacked us, they're already fully aware that we're aware of them. We have nothing to lose by showing our hand now. Perhaps they'll march on HeartHolme, and all humankind will be enough to defeat them. Perhaps the vampires will be standing in our ranks, ready to fight for us with their abilities. But perhaps that won't be enough. Perhaps a weakness would be more effective than an additional ten thousand men."

"If I'd decided to pursue that avenue, I would have sent others in our stead, and I would have sent more men. That decision was for me to make—King Rolfe, King of the fucking Kingdoms, not some lowly steward."

"*Huntley*." Her eyes narrowed. "He has the blood of kings as much as you do."

I looked away.

"And he just put his kingdom before himself and his relationship with his brother."

"Because he's an idiot—"

"Because he loves as deeply as you do, Huntley. He loves his family as much as you do. He loves this kingdom as much as you do. His decision was a betrayal, but it's a forgivable one. I know the true cause of your rage—and its fear. It's fear that he won't come back."

TWENTY-THREE
HARLOW

I stepped into my bedchambers, a room that was close to my parents', with a great view of the city and the cold landscape beyond. I preferred to stay with Aurelias, especially since our world could end at literally any moment, but I knew my father's reaction would be unkind. As an adult woman who had earned her crown, I could do whatever I pleased, but with so much stress already on my father's shoulders, I didn't want to add to the pile.

Grandmother came to my side, looking out the window as she folded her hands together in front of her, her spine straight and her presence regal. She'd had this energy since I was a little girl, and nothing had changed now that I was an adult. "That's one fine man you've got."

A grin moved into my cheeks. "He's a snack, isn't he?"

"He's a feast, my dear."

I chuckled at her comment, loving the fact that we could have conversations like this, like friends.

"I can tell your father approves of him as a soldier, but not as a suitor."

"Well…he is a vampire." A creature that fed off others…except me.

"I've granted him a cottage in the village. It's small, but it's close to the castle."

"Thank you."

"I'm not sure how we'll house everyone else who's on their way." She released a heavy sigh. "It's much too cold to camp out on the barren soil."

"Maybe families could combine in homes? Two families per home? That would free up half the houses."

"Not a bad idea."

"And the barracks have cots. It's not comfortable, but at least it's warm."

"True." She continued to look out the window. "All great ideas."

"How are you, Grandmother?"

"Me?" She turned to look at me, a slight smile on her lips. "No one ever asks me that."

"Not even my father?"

She shook her head. "He's too busy barking orders and being grouchy."

I chuckled. "He can be at times. But to be honest, he's the grouchiest at dinner parties."

"He's always been sour company. His entire life has been about survival, so he's never learned to enjoy peace. He's so traumatized by his early hard life that he's always waiting for it to return, like it's right around the corner."

I nodded in understanding, even though I didn't understand at all. My father and mother worked hard so I would never have to.

"He and Ivory could have chosen their relationship over destiny," she said. "Could have chosen a quiet life in HeartHolme, surrounded by Teeth and Necrosis, but they chose to take back the kingdom and give you and Atticus a life they were both denied."

"Yeah."

"And now they're fighting for that again. Your father is dedicated to his people, carries the weight of the world on his shoulders, but I know his children are his true motivation. All he wants is for you to have blue skies full of clouds and dragons."

"I know he does."

We stared out the window again, in silence.

"I know Father is mad when he leaves." He wasn't the kind of man to run from a fight or give up. To remove himself from a situation meant his rage was inconsolable. "He's really upset about Uncle Ian."

"He's *worried* about Uncle Ian."

"Are you?" I asked, scared to hear the answer.

She gave another sigh, the world almost plunged into darkness now that the sun was gone from the horizon. "He's my son. Of course I'm worried. But I also know that my sons are the blood of the crown, and that means they have to spill that blood to protect it. Power can't be maintained without risk." She pivoted toward me, no longer interested in the view. "So. Do you feel deeply for this man?"

I shrugged. "It's complicated..."

"As are all relationships."

"Even with Grandpa?" I asked, asking about a man I'd never met.

"As he was my husband and my king, it was even more complicated."

I considered my words carefully. "Aurelias said he would return to his lands when the war is over."

"Why?"

"I—I don't know. That's just what he's decided. He has a whole life there. Brothers. Sisters. His father. I suppose I understand because I'm not sure I could live far away from my family."

"But for a man to pledge his sword to you is a substantial commitment."

"I know."

She regarded me, looking down at me slightly because she had my father's regal bearing, despite being shorter than him...or my father had her regal bearing. There was a knowing twinkle in her eye, a magic that only a grandmother could possess. "A man either fights for loyalty or love—and he has no loyalty to the Kingdoms."

He opened the door, his eyes intense like he already knew it was me before he looked.

I walked inside the humble cottage. A fire was in the hearth, probably for light rather than warmth, and there was a large bed against the wall with a bathroom in a separate room. It was meant for a single person—so it was a perfect fit for him. "We don't have electricity here."

"I noticed." He'd already ditched his uniform and armor, wearing nothing but his lounge trousers, his powerful chest bare despite the frigid cold that was constant and unbearable.

I preferred the heat of Delacroix, the sunshine through cloudless skies, the smell of jasmine in the breeze. I'd always hated coming here as a child because there wasn't as much to do, but now I appreciated it as a respite from the heat.

"How are things?" He sat on the couch at the foot of the bed, his chiseled body highlighted by the glow from the fire, beautiful skin stretched tight over thick muscles.

"I haven't seen my father."

He stared into the flames.

I took the seat beside him. "Or my mother."

"I understand his frustration."

"I miss our lives before...when everything was easy."

His eyes remained on the fire. "It makes you appreciate better times."

"But I know when peace returns, I'll miss this time even more."

He turned his head to regard me, his intense gaze capturing mine.

My hand went to his shoulder, my fingers tracing the powerful muscles of his arm, all the different segments. His skin was warm to the touch, warmed by the fire directly in front of us. I watched my finger trace his beautiful body, and my mouth went dry at the touch of him, like this was our first night together rather than however many times it was. The thrills he gave me set my skin on fire, made my thighs shake from the tremors of his touch.

My eyes dropped to his crotch, seeing the perfect outline of his rock-hard dick. It wasn't there a second ago, and all it took was a simple touch to make him stiff. Or maybe the sight of me was enough, just the way the sight of him was enough for me.

"Get over here." His hand slid into my hair as he pulled me to his lips, kissing me with a searing passion that made my body warm. He guided me to him, putting me in his lap as he pulled my sweater over my head. My bra was unclasped in quick succession, and then his lips were on my tits, kissing my small boobs like they were the nicest tits he'd ever seen. His big hands were on my body, in my hair, everywhere.

He pulled my leggings over my ass, and to get them fully off my body he guided me onto my back in the corner of the couch, standing up to remove my boots before he got them all the way off. I was in the same position as the first time we'd had sex, and the memory of that made me ache harder than I ever had.

He dropped his bottoms, letting that big-ass dick come free.

I remembered the way he'd gone down on me in my bedroom, when I didn't even have to ask, and his mouth was infinitely better than my fingers.

He moved to his knees on the floor then scooped my ass and thighs in his big arms, cradling me before his hard mouth pressed into my most tender place. As if he knew exactly what I wanted, he gave it to me, the heat of the fire keeping me warm as he made my body twitch and writhe.

My fingers dug into his hair, and I ground my body into his face, moaning so loudly it was like I hadn't gotten laid in months, like I'd never had sex as good as this. "Fuck…" I threw back my head because it was so good, so good my body couldn't handle it. This man did incredible things to me every time he touched me, every time he looked at me.

I was there, sitting on the edge, trying to stop it from coming because I didn't want it to end. I could lie there all night while this man did this, could writhe from the power of his tongue.

I couldn't stop it, and it happened—a fiery explosion between my legs that made my hips buck automatically. I ground right into his face, tears streaming down my cheeks, coming as hard for his mouth as I did for his dick.

Instead of pulling away so he could fuck me, he kept going, his mouth glued to my pussy like it was his honor to be on his knees with his face between my thighs.

I waited for him to stop, but after several minutes, he didn't. He kept going, exhibiting the same enthusiasm, like making me come was a joy rather than an obligation. I closed my eyes and felt lingering tears spill down my cheeks as the buildup started all over again. "You're fucking me in the ass when we're done," I said breathlessly. "You earned it."

I lay beside him in bed, the fire much smaller than it'd been when I first walked in. Candles on the dresser were lit, dimly illuminating the four corners. My head was on his shoulder, and my arm was hooked around his waist, his body and the blankets keeping me nice and warm.

I wanted to lie there forever. He made it easy for me to forget all the things I wanted to forget. My hand moved up his chest, and then I pressed a kiss to his shoulder, a wet one with tongue, the kind that made my bottom lip catch on his skin.

His fingers moved into my hair. "As much as I want you to stay, it's time to go."

"No." I propped myself up on my elbow and felt his chest with my palm. Felt all the hardness. Felt the muscles of all his abs, the rivers between the mountains. "I want to stay like this…forever." I watched my hand worship his body, and when I felt his heated stare on my face, I lifted my gaze.

His intensity was there, a small fire in his eyes, but I also saw something else. Something I couldn't describe. "I don't want your father to come looking for you."

"I'm the last thing my father is worried about right now." My fingers moved to his jawline, the tips stroking the coarse stubble. I could feel the bones in his jaw, feel the cords in his neck when my fingers brushed against it. He was the single most beautiful man I'd ever seen...and I knew I would never look at someone else this way. When another man occupied my bed, I would wish it were him instead. My heart ached in a way it had never ached for anyone else, a pain that hurt so much it felt good. No other man would ever make me hurt this way. Ever.

He shifted his gaze away. "Get dressed."

"I'll leave later. It's still early." If my parents looked for me, they would know exactly where I was. They wouldn't need to send guards to fetch me this time.

"It must be midnight."

"Why do you want me to leave so bad?" I snapped.

He looked away entirely, his jawline tight with annoyance.

"We were fine, and then two seconds later, you're an asshole."

He threw back the covers and moved to the edge of the bed. "I'm always an asshole. You just don't notice it because you're too busy getting fucked." He rose to his feet and retrieved his boxers from the floor.

I stilled at the venom in his words, paralyzed by the harshness that came out of nowhere. "What is your problem?"

He pulled on his trousers, standing in the firelight, his expression ruthless. "Because I want you to leave, and you aren't leaving."

I sat up in bed. "You just said you didn't want me to leave—"

"I was trying to be nice about it," he snapped. "But you can't take a hint."

The man I'd spent the night with had disappeared, and this asshole had taken his place. He'd always been a I-don't-give-a-fuck kind of guy, but he'd never been a straight-up asshole. He'd never treated me this unkindly, not even when he'd kidnapped me and handed me over to the Teeth.

I threw back the sheets and got out of bed. "How about I take your hint and shove it up your ass?" I reached for my clothes and quickly dressed, not looking at him, too furious to meet his gaze.

I threw everything on then stormed out, and the second the cold air hit my face, all the anger left my body. Now all that remained was pain, pain so intense

I felt the moisture build up behind my eyes. I wasn't the kind of woman to cry, especially over a guy, but to feel this deeply for him and for him to care for me so little…it broke me.

As I stood there, all I could think about was how much he meant to me…and all he wanted was for me to leave. I started to walk home, barely putting one foot in front of the other because I wasn't in a hurry to get home, not when it was obvious that I'd shed tears. Even the cold wasn't a strong enough reason to hurry.

My tears practically turned to ice as they slid down my cheeks.

"Baby." Now his voice was cloaked with layers of affection, remorse, self-loathing. All conveyed in a single word.

I kept going, refusing to let him see my face. "Goodnight, Aurelias."

He grabbed me by the arm and tried to pull me back.

I twisted out of his grasp then slapped him across the face. *"Take a hint and fuck off."*

He closed his eyes briefly, swallowing the pain I'd just inflicted.

I turned away again.

He grabbed me once more, this time digging his hands into my hair as he forced me against the wall. "I'm sorry." He cradled my face in his palms as he pressed into me, as he blocked out the cold and kept me warm. "I—I shouldn't have said any of that."

"Why are you here?"

He stilled at the question, clearly having no idea what I was asking.

I pushed his hands down. "Why are you here? Why have you vowed to protect me when I mean so little to you?"

"You don't mean little to me—"

"You just treated me like a fucking whore who was paid for the night. You fucked me in the ass and then kicked me out right after. Practically threw me onto the street."

He clenched his eyes shut as he cringed.

"So, why are you here? What the fuck are you doing—"

"Because you mean the fucking world to me—"

"*Stop lying.* A man doesn't treat a woman like that if he cares for her. You know damn well how I feel about you, but that doesn't mean I'll tolerate this fucking bullshit. You may as well return to wherever the fuck you came from because whatever the fuck this is is now over—"

"That's the problem." His voice came out quiet, defeated, broken.

My eyes shifted back and forth between his, trying to read his meaning on his face because I had no idea what he was saying.

"I told you I'm leaving..." He stepped back slightly, the air dry and cold, his breath escaping as a cloud of vapor. "And I'm not coming back. I meant those words when I said them to you, and I still mean them now."

"I'm sorry...I don't understand."

He looked away, his handsome face tight in consternation.

"There is no scenario where we end up together—"

"You've said this a million times already—"

"*Then why didn't you listen?*" He was angry again, angry like he'd been inside the cottage. "Stop. This."

"Stop what?"

"*This.*" He placed his hand on my chest, right where my heart was settled. His face was harder than it'd ever been, his eyes wide in rage. "What you feel...I will never reciprocate. I *can't* reciprocate." He dropped his hand and stepped back, breathing hard as he looked at anything else but me.

It took me seconds to understand the implication of his words. "I knew it."

He still wouldn't look at me.

"You can read minds..."

He dragged his palm across his hard jaw, his other hand on his hip, uncomfortable like a caged animal that had no route of escape.

I was embarrassed for a moment that Aurelias knew the full depth of my desire, understood my desperation for his mind, body, and soul. He knew every thought that came across my mind, all the secrets I would never tell another person. But then that embarrassment faded...because I wasn't ashamed of my feelings. "I love you—"

"*Don't.*" His eyes found mine again, full of menace. "I told you—"

"Why are you afraid to say it?" I snapped. "You chose to stay behind and risk your life for me, but you don't feel the same way? I don't believe that, Aurelias. Not for one fucking second."

"I meant what I said before. I'm leaving, and I'm not coming back—"

"*Shut up.* I'm so tired of hearing you say that—"

"And I'm tired of saying it."

"Whether you stay or go doesn't change the way we feel. I would rather love you with my whole heart and lose you than pretend you're just some guy I'm fucking. You're not Ethan or all the other guys who don't mean anything to me. You mean *everything* to me."

He turned away entirely, like my words were punches. "I said we aren't doing this—"

"Why—"

"*Because I don't want to hurt you.*" He came back to me. "Because I will fucking leave you, Harlow. I will get on that ship and return to my lands and go back to my life, and you'll move on with yours. Yes, all we are is two people fucking. I am Ethan. That's what I signed up for—and that's all we are. Period." He held up his hand to silence me, even though I hadn't opened my mouth. "I don't want to discuss this ever again. We're but a moment, a very brief moment, a flower that blooms in spring and then dies in the first frost of winter. That's it." He lowered his hand again, his stare furious.

I couldn't read minds, but I could read between the lines, read the hurt written all over his face. I remembered our previous conversations about this, and I hadn't noticed it then...but now I saw it. I saw it as clear as day, as clear as the sun on a cloudless afternoon. "You aren't afraid you'll hurt me..." I felt my eyes water because I understood him for the very first time. "You're afraid I'll hurt you..."

There was no rebuttal to that statement, and the viciousness in his eyes slowly darkened to something deeper, a pain that had no depths, an infinite ocean of agony. He swallowed, his throat shifting with the movement. When the deep breath left his nostrils, it was a trail of mist into the air. His eyes remained on me, the hardness slowly softening, the petals in his eyes withering in decay.

My body was paralyzed by the realization, something I would have noticed long ago if I'd just paid attention. I'd listened to the lies of his words when I should have focused on the truth of his actions. It had been right in front of me this entire time. Looking me dead in the eye.

I stepped toward him, and the second I drew close, he inhaled a deep breath in anticipation, but he didn't step away. He let me come to him, watched me with his guarded eyes. I moved into his chest and cupped his face, rising on my tiptoes to kiss him, to feel our warm lips come together and burn the cold away. "Tell me you love me." I spoke it against his lips, spoke it between our kisses, my fingers tangling in his hair.

He kissed me back, his hand sliding into my hair and cradling the back of my head. His arm circled my waist and squeezed me into his body, smothering me with his passionate kisses. His breath filled my lungs, and his tongue danced with mine. He bit my bottom lip before he kissed me harder. "I love you, baby."

TWENTY-FOUR
HUNTLEY

I watched the shadows move across the ceiling. They started on one side of the room then slowly crawled to the other side as the sun crested the horizon then inched slowly higher. My eyes were tired. Without seeing my reflection, I knew my eyes were bloodshot. Ivory was tucked into my side, dead asleep while I was wide awake.

I couldn't sleep when my brother was probably dead.

Now I understood how Ivory felt when I left her behind to do something dangerous. Powerless, all she could do was sit there and wait. And if she never heard anything…it was because I'd been killed in battle.

Ivory finally woke up, taking a deep breath as she stretched her legs under the sheets. Her eyes opened, and she looked at me, relaxed and sleepy. She watched me, and once she realized I hadn't slept all night, her stare hardened. Her hand moved to my chest, and she gently dragged her fingertips across my skin, comforting me when I couldn't be comforted. Nothing could comfort me—not even a bottle of scotch.

An anxious knock pounded on the door. "King Rolfe? It's urgent."

I was out of bed and on my feet instantly, leaving Ivory behind as I marched to the door in nothing but my shorts. I opened the door, taller than him by nearly a foot, and narrowed my eyes. "What is it?"

"I'm sorry to disturb you—"

"*Speak.*"

"Jeremiah has returned with his dragon and Nightshade...but Steward Ian is not with him."

The agony...it hit me like a pile of stone. It crushed my shoulders and then my spine. "Are you certain?"

"Yes..."

"Tell Jeremiah to come here immediately—"

"He's already on the way. I ran here—"

I shut the door in his face and dressed quicker than I ever had. I didn't just don my uniform, but all my armor and weapons, ready to head to the east the second this conversation concluded.

Ivory quickly got dressed and didn't even brush her hair before we were down the hallway. "Retrieve Harlow and Lady Rolfe."

The guard ran off.

I moved into the deliberations room, where a large table sat with enough chairs to accommodate twenty people. I didn't sit. I chose to stand, to eye the door and wait for Jeremiah to walk through so I could attack him with a million questions.

Mother entered first, dressed impeccably because she was always up before the sun rose. And then Harlow entered, her eyes sleepy like she'd been pulled out of a deep slumber. She was dressed in leggings and a wrinkled sweater, like that was the quickest thing she could find. "What's happened?"

I ignored my daughter, waiting for Jeremiah.

Jeremiah entered a moment later, his eyes bloodshot like mine, terror etched into the hard features of his face.

I intended to fire off a million questions, but now that I saw his expression, I didn't want to know what he had to say.

He walked right up to me. "M'lord—"

"I don't have time for titles and diplomacy," I snapped. "What happened to my brother?"

He didn't bow or fold his hands at his waist. He stood there, slightly out of breath because there hadn't been time to pause on his long journey. "We found ruins of a fallen civilization, farther east away from the snow. We stopped to investigate because Ian believed it could provide clues about Palladium. Nightshade said he heard something, something coming from the ground. A woman appeared out of nowhere and asked us to come with her. Both Ian and I assumed it was a trap, so we remained where we were. Nightshade said the noise was getting louder, and the woman told us to run. Then they appeared, out of nowhere, the demons you'd spotted before. Ian and I tried to run, but I was the only one who made it. Nightshade tried to free him…but Ian ordered him to flee."

Keeping a straight face as I listened to that tale was one of the hardest things I'd ever had to do...almost as hard as when my wife had told me our daughter had been taken. I had to be strong for her, and now I had to be strong for my mother...for everyone else who stood in the room with me. "What happened to him?"

"I—I don't know."

"You could see from the sky. *What happened?*"

"When the demons were momentarily distracted by Nightshade, Ian ran. I took my eyes off him for a second to watch the demons turn and pursue him...but then he was gone."

"What do you mean, gone?"

"I lost track of him."

"How? Were you near the woods?"

"No. It was a barren place."

"Then explain to me how that's possible."

"I—I don't know."

"*Explain it to me.*" I stepped forward, getting in his face like he was a demon himself. "You don't just lose sight of someone. If there are no buildings and no trees, then where the fuck did he go—"

Ivory placed a hand on my arm, and that was all it took to silence me. "Jeremiah, if what you say is true, then how would it be possible to lose track of him from the skies? Are you sure there isn't something you aren't telling us?"

"Steward Ian is an honorable man whom I've had the pleasure to serve," Jeremiah said. "I want to find him as much as you do. But that is the full picture as I know it. I never saw him again, and perhaps that's a good thing, because that means the demons probably didn't either. Perhaps he's still there."

"The woman." Harlow spoke from where she stood next to her mother. "Maybe he went with her."

"Went with her where?" I asked.

"I don't know," Harlow said. "But she came from somewhere, right? She warned them about the demons. She must live there and know how to evade them. Perhaps she saved Uncle Ian."

I stared at my daughter, trying to piece that story together.

"Where's the one place they wouldn't look?" Harlow asked. "Underground…"

"But they're from the earth," I argued.

"*Exactly*," she said. "Which is why they wouldn't look there."

Ivory looked at me. "It's possible."

"And it's possible that Ian tripped and broke his leg, invisible behind a pile of rubble." I didn't want to hope for more and be disappointed.

Avice walked inside at that moment, her face pale like she was already anticipating the horrible news. Her eyes went to Jeremiah, and that was when the tears formed in her eyes. "No…" Her hand cupped her mouth, and she stifled a sob.

Ivory rushed to her and held her tightly before she ushered her out of the room to share the news in private.

I was the King of Kingdoms in the middle of a war that could kill us all, but now my brother had been taken… and all I wanted to do was go to him. I'd promised I would never leave my family again, but Ian was my family too. "Someone fetch Aurelias. I need to speak to him immediately."

Harlow was the one who left.

I stood there as I listened to Avice cry from down the hallway.

When I glanced at my mother, I saw her display the greatest restraint, keeping her face tight so her bottom lip wouldn't tremble. Her eyes were determined, but the rest of her body worked hard to betray the command. She wanted to grieve, but the queen in her refused to allow it.

No one spoke as we waited for Aurelias to join us.

I stood there, staring at the entry to the hallway, thinking about all the duties I needed to execute simultaneously. Now I had to decide where my loyalties lay —with my family or my people.

Ivory returned to the room and escorted Avice to a chair, tissues in her hand.

Pale as a ghost, Avice sat there, blood drained from her face.

General Macabre didn't look at her.

A moment later, Harlow returned, Aurelias entering behind her, dressed the same way I was—like he was ready for war. His eyes locked on mine as he approached, but he said nothing, waiting for an order to be issued.

Ivory returned to my side, knowing decisions were about to be made.

I stared at the vampire, my former enemy turned ally. "There's only one right decision. My duty is to my people above all else. My brother made his choice, against my orders, and he should face the consequences of that decision. I know this fully, but nonetheless, I choose the wrong decision. I must travel to the east and rescue my brother, because I don't trust anyone else has the ability to do this besides me. I choose my blood over my people, and even though I'm full of shame at my selfishness, it doesn't change my decision." This decision meant I would have to leave my family once again, but I couldn't abandon my brother. He would never abandon me. "Ivory is my successor, and while she's capable of running a kingdom without me, this is a war unlike any we've ever seen. I know she would agree with me that Heart-Holme needs a protector in my stead. I'd like that to be you, Aurelias."

His eyes remained on mine for seconds, but they eventually dropped, his jaw hardening as he considered the offer. "I watched Queen Rolfe face her enemy with more courage than the soldiers who served her. I watched her wield a sword against creatures that should have crushed her from the beginning, but she held on longer than anyone would ever expect. I watched her sacrifice her life for her people without a second thought. I decline your offer."

I was too touched by his compliment to care about his rejection. There was only one way to get to my heart, and that was through my wife. I loved my children because she'd given them to me. I respected any man who respected her.

"However, I promise to serve Queen Rolfe fully, to provide whatever she needs to succeed, whether that's my advice or my sword. I will protect your family like it's my own—and I will die for your family like it's my own."

I shoved the essentials into my pack and threw it over my shoulder. The things I couldn't live without were already on my body, my sword, my axe, and my daggers. The armor was specifically designed by my sister for me to wear, and it required more materials than any other set she'd created. It was fire-resistant, and, as a result, it was heavy.

But it would keep me alive.

Ivory hadn't said a word to me. She followed me from room to room, watching me gather my things, pack for a trip I might never return from, all while looking as white as snow. When I had everything, there was nothing else to do but walk out to the field where the dragons and everyone else were waiting.

I stood there, dreading the words about to be spoken. "I'm tired of having this conversation." I turned around to face her.

Her arms were crossed over her chest, and her eyes were dead. "As am I."

I stared at her, waiting for her to look at me.

She didn't.

"I have to do this."

She inhaled a deep breath, her eyes watering slightly. "I know…"

"I promised I would never leave you again—"

"Ian is my brother as much as he's yours." She lifted her chin and looked at me. "I release you from your promise, Huntley. But please..." She closed her eyes, and that made the tears streak. "Don't die."

"I won't." I moved to her, my hands cupping her face because it always killed me to see her cry.

"If he's already lost...no revenge. You come back to me. That's what Ian would have wanted."

I nodded.

"You get revenge here...on the battlefield with us."

"I promise." I pulled her to me, hugging her gently because my armor was hard as stone. It was jagged and rough, could easily cut her if she pressed against me the wrong way. My lips brushed her hairline, and I pressed a kiss to her warm skin.

When she pulled back, she quickly wiped away her tears with the pads of her thumbs.

"Are you comfortable with Aurelias?"

"I am."

"I'm sorry I didn't ask you beforehand—"

"I trust him with my life," she said. "And our daughter's life..." She sniffed. "He may have started as a curse, but he's become a blessing. I'll ask him to stay in the castle with us so he's near."

I nodded in agreement.

Now there was nothing left to do but leave.

She stayed put. "I don't think I can watch you fly off." Her eyes dropped in shame. "I don't want that to be my last memory..."

My hand cupped her face, and in an instant, our entire lives flashed before my eyes, the birth of our children, the days we would sit in the sun and watch our kids play in the fields, the nights when we didn't get any sleep... "This won't be your last memory either."

General Macabre, Mother, Harlow, and Aurelias stood on the field with the dragons, Jeremiah and the other riders ready to join me on our journey to the east. Elora was there too, her confident gaze broken into infinite pieces. The cold was not a factor for me, not in this armor, not when my muscles gave off this much heat to support the weight.

Elora moved to me first. "I want our brother back, but not at this price."

"I'll come back, Elora."

"You don't know that—"

"I do know that." My hand went to her shoulder and gave it a squeeze before I moved to my mother.

She was rigid and strong, but once she was alone, the tears would fall. "I don't want to lose a son. But I couldn't bear it if I lost two."

"I know..."

"Then please come back, even if that means you need to leave him behind."

I nodded then moved to my daughter.

She'd looked dead inside the moment Ian's disappearance had been announced. She said so few words, and now she looked even more defeated because I was leaving. Her eyes were down, barely able to meet my gaze, like she was a child about to get in trouble.

"It'll be alright, sweetheart."

"What if he's already dead—"

"We don't know that."

"And you're going to die too—"

My hand moved to her shoulder. "I'm not going anywhere, sweetheart." I forced her chin up to meet my gaze. "But this is something I have to do. I know your heart, and if this were Atticus, you would do the same."

Her eyes watered before she gave a nod.

I moved to Aurelias next.

He was the only one who possessed no emotion. With a steely gaze, he met my look, tall and proud, young in appearance but wise in the eyes. He extended his hand to take mine. "Godspeed, King Rolfe."

I took his hand. "Huntley."

His hand stilled in mine before he pulled away. Then he gave a slight nod, his eyes harder than they were a moment before.

I turned to Nightshade, choosing to take him and leave Pyre and Storm behind for Ivory and Harlow. "Let's get Ian back, Nightshade." I climbed up his side and entered the saddle, and I strapped my legs into place.

Nightshade released a mighty roar, the kind that shook the earth and rattled the mountains. Then he pushed off the ground and launched into the air, the riders below following suit to join me on our journey across the sky.

TWENTY-FIVE
IAN

I'd never run this fast, this long in my life.

The pipe bent in around us, the metal denting loudly, just feet behind. If I slowed down at all, I would be crushed by the metal.

The woman ahead kept up her pace. "Almost there!"

"Thank the fucking gods…"

Then by a miracle, the pipe went still, the outside forces no longer present.

But we continued to run like our lives depended on it.

She reached a hatch, a large circular door with a wheel in the center. She turned it quickly, going as fast as she could, but it still took several seconds to unlock. I came to her side and helped, spinning the wheel as we both gasped for breath, still afraid that the earthquake would return.

We finally got it unlocked, and she pulled the heavy door open.

I jumped in, stepping into an underground cave with lights strapped to the ceiling by wires fused with hide. I took a few steps forward before I bent at the waist, breathing hard as my hands pressed against the top of my thighs.

The woman shut the door behind her then came to my side. "You alright?"

I nodded, still out of breath. "You?"

"I'm fine."

I righted myself to my full height. "Alright...so who the fuck are you?"

She released a laugh through her deep breaths. "I was about to ask you the same."

Others entered the small cave, jogging through the open door and joining us. It was two men and another woman, and they all looked at me like I was a goat with three heads. They looked at my armor, looked at my weapons, studied my expression like they didn't know what to make of me.

"I'm Ian." They were all tanned, like they spent all their time outdoors, which seemed strange since they were hiding underground. Other than that, they looked as human as I did. "I'm from the west, over the mountains—"

"You have dragons." One of the men stepped forward, and I assumed he was the leader. He didn't wear armor, and neither did the others. Their clothing was simple and unremarkable, like they didn't have the resources to make elaborate clothing.

"Yes."

"Many dragons." His eyes were wide with fascination. "We saw you from the skies."

I guess we weren't as hidden as I thought.

"We rescued you," the man said. "Now you owe us."

The woman who was with me placed her hand on his arm. "I know we haven't interacted with anyone in a while, but let's be diplomatic here." She turned back to me. "I'm Mary." She gestured to the man who had just spoken. "This is Paul." She introduced the other two. "Kyle and Carla."

"Nice to meet you all..." *At least, I hope.* "Thank you for rescuing me."

"That tunnel is irreparable," Paul said. "And now they probably know where to find us. We showed our hand to save your life—and now you owe us."

"What about the other tunnel?" Mary asked.

"It survived," Paul said.

"Good," Mary said. "Then not all is lost."

"You're from Palladium, right?" I asked.

They all stilled as they stared at me.

"How did you know that?" Mary asked.

"I asked one of the prisoners at the labor camp," I explained. "He told me their city had fallen to the demons."

They all looked at each other, a silent conversation happening between them.

Mary looked at me again. "Why are you in these lands? The demons are not enemies you want to trifle with."

"The demons have forged an alliance with our enemies, and they're intent on destroying our kingdoms just as they destroyed yours," I explained. "I traveled here to learn whatever I could about them, because they appear to be invulnerable. Our dragons breathe fire, but add fire to fire and you just get more fire. You said I owe you for saving me?" I looked at all of them. "Well, I'm your ally now. Tell me everything you know about these demons, and let's defeat them together."

They were all silent, not remotely pleased by that little speech.

"What's the problem?" I asked.

Paul crossed his arms over his chest. "It's far more complicated than you realize."

"It doesn't matter how complicated it is," I snapped. "It's us versus them. If we fall, you fall, and this entire continent will be under their dominion. However fucking complicated it is—make it uncomplicated."

"They can't be defeated," Paul said. "Period."

"Some beings are immortal, but none are invincible. Some of their kind attacked one of our kingdoms to the west, and we were victorious. They can be defeated."

Paul shook his head. "That's what you think…"

"What the fuck does that mean?" I snapped.

Mary stepped in. "They are invincible. You may see them perish on the battlefield, but they're reborn underground. The only evidence of their previous lives is the scars they carry. We know this because the ones we've killed always come back. *Always*."

All the air left my lungs. The air left the room too. In silence, I suffocated.

"We don't want your alliance," Paul said. "We want your dragons—so we can leave this land and never return."

They had caves underground, deep inside a mountain, and the passage led outdoors, to a valley between the hills, elevated and impossible to see from the outside. If I were on a dragon, it would still be really difficult to find.

Since it was dark, I remained in the mountain, sat at one of their tables alone...defeated. They brought me bread and ale, neither of which I touched. My arms rested on the table, and I stared at the wood underneath my elbows, the most discouraged I'd ever been in my entire life. I was lower than when Avice had left me.

"We're all going to die." I said it out loud to no one... only to myself. "And there's not a damn thing I can do about it."

Someone took the seat across from me, an ale in their hand.

I looked up to see Mary, her eyes weary like she was ready for bed but unable to sleep. "We have a bed for you...if you're tired."

"I'll sleep when I'm dead...which is any day now."

She regarded me with sympathy, her eyes kind and motherly. She looked to be about my age, maybe a few years younger. "We're unable to build ships without drawing their attention. Otherwise, we would have set sail long ago. But with your dragons, you can usher us to your realm, and then we can board your fleet and sail somewhere safe."

I had the same idea myself. "Somewhere safe? The world is a big place. We could land on the shores of other monsters...and end up prisoners or dead." I grabbed the ale and finally took a drink. It tasted like piss, but I didn't react.

"We could send scouts ahead."

"I don't think we have time for that."

"The fleet could remain at sea until the scouts return—"

"You've obviously never been on a ship before, because the ocean is fucking dangerous. We lose half of our fishing fleet every year due to storms and unexpected tides. The ocean isn't the same in every place. Sometimes it's deep and frigid, and other times it's shallower than it appears, with rocks lurking just beneath the surface to rip your hull in half. There's an island nearby that houses the worst criminals who have been exiled from the Kingdoms. These demons might be unbeatable, but that option isn't much better."

"But at least we have a chance," she said. "Against these demons...there is no chance."

"What about the prisoners in the camps?"

"What about them?"

"You'd abandon them?"

Her gaze hardened as she looked at me, and the wince in her face told me I'd said the wrong thing. "They can't be saved."

"They live in huts made out of mud. All they do is work and sleep—"

"*Stop.*" She closed her eyes, the information too painful.

I turned quiet, quickly realizing the source of her heartbreak. "I'm sorry."

Her eyes remained averted, her face as emotionless as stone. "He would want me to run rather than risk my life to save him...risk the lives of the only survivors we have left."

I knew Avice wouldn't abandon me. Ivory wouldn't abandon Huntley. Even if we both wanted them to. But I kept my opinion to myself.

"We risked our lives and our location to help you." She looked at me again once she regained her composure. "It's only a matter of time before they realize where we are. The least you can do is give us your dragons—"

"Look." I held up my hand to silence her, her words deeply offensive. "The dragons aren't ours to give because they don't belong to us. They're free beings who *choose* to help us. We liberated them from imprisonment and gave them land to occupy in the south. To show their gratitude, they've volunteered to serve with us. They're not required to do anything they don't want to do. They're not like dogs or cats. They have their own minds."

Mary hung on every word. "You can communicate with them."

"Yes. They speak with their minds."

"Fascinating..."

"So, I can't *give* them to you. Even if I personally asked, none of them would oblige because you are strangers, and therefore, they don't trust you. But what I can do is..." Jeremiah and Nightshade had probably nearly crossed the mountains now. It was just a few hours before dawn, and once they landed, Huntley would know that disaster had struck. "My brother will come for me with a fleet of dragon riders. They'll probably be here by this time tomorrow. One dragon can carry many people, so I can ask them to chauffeur you to our lands in the west. Depending on how many people you have, it might take many trips. If we fly above the cloud bank and only at night, the demons may not know what we're doing. Once you're in our lands, you can take a ship wherever you want to go."

Mary processed all of that in silence, her eyes glued to my face. "How do you know your brother is coming with more dragons?"

"Because I just know." My brother should remain in HeartHolme and prepare for war, but he would abandon his duties and obligations for me without hesitation. Even though I'd betrayed him by disobeying his orders, he would still come for me. There was no reason whatsoever that he wouldn't come for me.

"Who are you? You must be important…"

"My brother is the King of Kingdoms, and I'm the steward of HeartHolme, our largest kingdom to the south. But the title isn't what makes me important—it's the blood that we share."

Her hand remained on her glass, and she didn't take a drink. She was too focused on my words. "If that's true, then we need to prepare for his arrival. The last thing we want is for the demons to notice a fleet of dragons.

They may consider us a bigger threat at that point and come to finish the job."

"Nightshade will bring my brother to my last location."

"Who's Nightshade?"

"My dragon."

Her eyebrows rose.

"Not *my* dragon. But he's the dragon I share the greatest bond with."

"Then we'll have someone there waiting for them."

"I need to be there too. Because if I'm not, Huntley will think it's a trap, just the way I did when I first saw you. I'll be able to communicate with Nightshade when he gets closer and tell him where to go."

"Alright. Then we'll get an audience with the king who speaks for all of you."

"He'll honor what I've already offered," I said. "Even if you hadn't saved me, we would still help you, regardless."

"Really?"

"Why is that so hard to believe?"

"Because men are cruel and corrupt. Because they choose to abuse their power rather than wield it responsibly."

"Whom have you met who exhibits those traits?" I asked. "Because as far as I can tell, you're a peaceful people."

She issued a slight laugh. "Our queen was a bit unkind. I'm glad she's dead."

I didn't ask more about their kingdom or their people because it seemed irrelevant now. All those bodies were buried underneath the stone and dirt…never to be seen again.

She grabbed her ale and took a deep drink, appearing to down the entire contents in a single go. "You should get some sleep, Ian. It's been a long day."

Several hours before sunset, Mary and I entered the alternate tunnel and went back to where we'd come from, back to the ruins of Palladium.

"How did you build these without getting caught?" I asked, following her, lights on the ceiling to illuminate our way.

"They were already here. We used to use them for sewage."

"That explains the smell."

She chuckled. "Yep."

"Why were you at the ruins when I arrived?"

"We've spotted your dragons before. At the time, we didn't know that's what they were because they were too far away. We've been on the lookout ever since, hoping you would be the saviors we needed to leave this nightmare."

"I'm your savior…but you're also mine."

We reached the end of the tunnel, a ladder leading up to the hatch at the surface. Mary made herself comfortable on the ground against the wall and pulled out an apple to eat.

I leaned against the wall and crossed my arms over my chest, exhausted because I'd barely gotten any sleep. I stared at a spot on the wall and felt the melancholy wash over me. Huntley was sending all the Kingdoms to HeartHolme for battle, but they would have to turn around and head back so they could leave from the northern port since we didn't have enough ships for everyone in the south.

Hours went by, and we said nothing. I was fine with silence. Preferred it over small talk.

Mary got herself to her feet. "It must be dusk. Let's open the hatch." She climbed to the top, turned the wheel several turns until the door popped open. She climbed out and then I did the same, stepping into the ruins of the fallen kingdom. It was nearly dark, barely any light left in the sky.

They should have been here by now.

I looked at the quiet world, seeing trees in the distance, an occasional bat fly by as a silhouette across the sky.

"You're certain they're coming?" Mary asked quietly. "Because we shouldn't linger if they aren't."

My heart clenched in uncertainty...wondering if Huntley had decided to leave me here. "He'll be here."

She looked at the sky, her arms crossed over her chest.

We said nothing.

And then the world plunged into darkness.

"We should go," she said from beside me, the only light coming from the open hatch.

I feel your mind, Ian.

"Wait." My voice rose in excitement. "They're near." *And I feel yours, Nightshade.*

Mary stared at me.

There was a pause, probably because Nightshade was telling Huntley that I was alive.

Are you alright?

Not a scratch. I need you to fly toward the mountains. When you get closer, you'll see flames that will guide you where to land. How many of you are there?

Five.

"There should be room for all of you."

Huntley has a message for you.

I already knew what it was.

I'm going to kill you when I see you.

I grinned. *Message received.*

Mary and I jogged back through the tunnel to the mountain, climbed out of the hatch, and then left the mountain for the valley they occupied, where they grew their crops and used the river to drink and bathe.

The dragons were much faster than Mary and I were, so by the time I arrived, they had already landed.

Paul spoke to Huntley, who looked like a twig in comparison to my brother's height and size, especially in all that intimidating armor.

I approached my brother, walking across the grass toward him while all the torches illuminated the clearing.

His eyes shifted to me.

Time stood still.

Despite the fury in his face, his eyes were full of relief, the kind that he couldn't hide, no matter how hard he tried.

I stopped in front of him, feeling his rage like flames from a lit pyre. His eyes shifted back and forth between mine, unspoken words transferring from his frozen lips to my mind. I'd known the consequences of my actions before I'd made them, and I'd taken those actions, nonetheless. "I'm sorry—"

He moved into me and gripped me tightly, his hand on the back of my head.

My armor pressed into his, metal on metal. My arm circled him, and I held him, giving him a clap on the back.

He pulled away and gripped my shoulder. "You're alive. That's all I care about."

I held his gaze, seeing Father in his face, a man I would have forgotten completely if I didn't have my brother to remember him. "I knew you would come."

He gripped me before he let go. "Always."

Nightshade stepped forward, releasing an irritated breath from his big nostrils. *I feared for your life as well.*

"I know you did." I moved toward him as he lowered his snout, my hand moving to his cheek.

He closed his eyes. *I chose the path of a coward and left you.*

You did exactly what I wanted, Nightshade. They would have taken you if you got too close. And I wouldn't have been able to live with that.

He kept his eyes closed as I rubbed him.

You're here now.

He moved his face into my body, rubbing me and nearly knocking me over.

I chuckled then patted him on the head before I turned away. "How's Avice?"

"Distraught. Inconsolable. Broken."

That was like a sword in my heart. "Then we should hurry back."

Huntley drew close. "I guess you were right about these people. They were here all this time—and you found them." There was a note of pride in his voice. "Perhaps this is exactly what we need to win this war."

I almost didn't have the heart to tell him the truth. "Let's go inside... We have a lot to talk about."

We entered the mountain and gathered at one of their tables. Ale was passed around, along with baskets of bread.

Huntley moved for the ale, and I subtly touched his arm and shook my head.

"Poison?" he whispered while barely moving his lips.

"No. Piss."

He did his best to suppress the smirk on his face as he went for a piece of bread instead.

I spoke first. "The remaining free people of Palladium wish for us to bring them to our lands across the mountains. Since there's no way for them to travel without being caught, the dragons are their only option. Since they saved me, this is a reasonable request."

Huntley had barely swallowed his bread before he reacted, his eyebrows arching high up his face. A cloud of confusion was there, reaching every feature. "I don't understand."

Now came the hard part. "They've informed me that the demons are not only immortal...but invincible."

"That's incorrect," Huntley said. "Because we killed thousands of them—"

"They'll come back," I said hopelessly. "They're reborn underground, looking identical to how they were before...but with more scars. Palladium has seen the same demon many times, a demon they'd killed more than once."

Huntley didn't have a comeback or a question. All he did was stare at me—and through me.

"Yeah...I took the news hard too."

He slowly turned to Paul across the table. "How is that possible?"

"Magic," Paul said.

"Magic?" Huntley said blankly. "And where does this magic come from?"

"From the little information we've been able to gather," Mary said, "it's from crystals. Crystals underground. But let us be clear—this is a guess. We aren't completely certain."

An image of the labor camp came into my mind, that night we'd snuck into the mud hut to ask our questions, one of the demons on guard in full armor. "That's why they have the labor camps..." I said it more to myself than the others. "Because they're digging for more crystal."

"We suspect their supplies are running low," Mary said. "And that's why they've appeared aboveground."

Huntley was silent, clearly still in shock. I'd had a full day to process the horrible news, whereas he'd only had seconds—as well as an audience.

"That leaves us with one option," I said. "To usher Palladium to our lands and then all of us leave by boat to new shores to start over elsewhere." It was a dreadful option, but the only one with any chance of success.

"That's not the only option," Huntley said.

I looked at my brother.

"If they need the crystals to maintain their invulnerability, then all we need to do is destroy the crystals." Huntley said it matter-of-factly, like that was no issue at all. He looked at the others at the table, a man too big for his chair. "We destroy the crystals—we destroy them."

"But those crystals are underground," Mary said. "We would have to go down there—"

"Then we go down there," Huntley said. "I'm not abandoning my kingdom. My home. The place where my ancestors have lived for thousands of years because these assholes decided to move in."

I continued to stare at my brother. "Huntley—"

"If we sail to the wrong lands, we end up working in a labor camp ourselves. We end up prisoners when we were born to be kings. I'm not vacating my lands when there's a chance I can save it."

"We can sail to Aurelias's lands—"

"And submit to a vampire king?" Huntley asked incredulously. "*Never.*"

"Huntley, you aren't thinking clearly—"

"Do you know of a path underground?" Huntley ignored me now. "Do you know of a way to enter their cave system?"

Mary looked at Paul then back at Huntley. "We do know a way. But I can't emphasize this enough...*it's suicide*. We want no part of that—"

"If you want to leave these lands, I can't stop you," Huntley said. "I'm not your king. I will give you a ship so you can sail away if you'd like. But in return, I'd like to know everything possible to make this mission a success, because I'm not leaving. I was born in these lands—and I'll die in these lands."

I didn't argue anymore, not when it was crystal clear that Huntley had his mind made up.

"But I urge you not to leave," Huntley said. "Because your people are working their hands bloody for these monsters, and they'll do that for the remainder of their miserable lives unless you help them. Your entire kingdom, with the exception of the few of you, have become enslaved by these monsters. If you have a chance to save them, your duty obligates you to try."

They were all quiet, letting Huntley's words seep into their flesh and bones.

I admired my brother for his spine and integrity, for his ability to change opinions with the power of his words. The odds of success were minuscule, but somehow, he motivated me to gamble on those odds.

"If we agree..." Mary exchanged another look with Paul. "What's your plan?"

"The plan is simple," Huntley said. "We destroy the crystals before they destroy us."

TWENTY-SIX
AURELIAS

I grabbed my belongings and entered the castle. General Macabre led me to a vacant bedchamber, a major upgrade from the cottage I'd had before, with its stunning views of the city. It was a great vantage point to spot an oncoming attack.

"What are you doing?"

I stood at the bed with my bags on top, about to pull out my things and get settled in. But I turned at the sound of her voice and faced her.

She stood in the open doorway, her dark hair in a braid, her blue eyes wounded from her father's departure. "Come on." She gestured for me to follow her. "You're staying with me."

"General Macabre escorted me here—"

"*I don't care*," she snapped. "I'm the princess, and I'm telling you to come with me."

I sighed as I walked toward her, the most irresistible woman I'd ever met. She made her demands without apology. Didn't mince her words with diplomacy and bullshit. She was straight to the point—and I loved that about her. "I think that arrangement will be uncomfortable for your father once he returns—"

"I'm a grown-ass woman, and I can do what I want. I can sleep with whomever I want. Now get your shit, and don't make me ask again."

Her fire sent flames down my spine.

"We could all die tomorrow." She came closer to me, her long hair in a beautiful braid, her chest exposed in a low-cut nightdress that highlighted the plumpness of her tits. "And I'm not spending my last night on this earth alone when I could have spent it with you."

I couldn't just see the power in her stare, but I could *feel* it. I could feel her desperation for me. Her need. The kind of need that would never die until she got what she wanted. I gave a sigh before I grabbed my bags off the bed and followed her to her bedchambers.

They were on the other side of the castle, far too big for a single person. There was a four-poster king-size bed against the wall on the rug, curtains pulled open over the windows, a sitting room that faced the window and the balcony, and a hallway that led to a bathroom.

I placed my things on one of the dressers and looked out the window, seeing that it was nearly dark. The sky still had a hint of blue in it. The fireplace had a fire, and small candles had been lit around the room.

She sat on the couch in her nightdress, the glow of the fire licking her soft skin. The dress stopped just above her knees, but when she sat down, it rose a few more inches, revealing thighs that I'd kissed many times.

I joined her on the couch, seeing the way her braid fell down her shoulder, the way her beauty intensified in the firelight, and I knew I wouldn't be able to leave, even if King Rolfe asked me to. I'd never had a full night with her, always had to watch her leave in the middle of the night or rush out when the guards came knocking. To have her all to myself...it was a fantasy.

A rush of sadness filled her, a crash after a high, and her eyes glazed over in despair.

I loved feeling her desire, the way she wanted me, even the way she loved me. But I hated feeling this. "He'll return."

She turned to look at me, the fire crackling in the background.

"With your uncle."

"How do you know?" she asked quietly.

"I just do."

"I've said goodbye to my father more times in the last few months than I have in my entire life."

I knew the pain of losing a parent, and I never wanted her to feel that.

"I just want it to end."

"I know."

"But I also don't..." Her eyes deepened as she looked at me, full of sorrow, full of want.

I knew exactly what she meant. I wanted this war to end so she would be safe, but the second it was over, so were we.

Her eyes dropped, like she couldn't look at me when she spoke. "Why...? Why does it have to end?"

It was the conversation I never wanted to have, but I'd forfeited the right to forgo it when I'd told her I loved her. Now I was saddled with obligation. Now I carried the weight of a commitment that I'd tried so hard to avoid.

"Is it because your father and brothers live so far away?" Her eyes were still down. "Because I can understand that. It would be really hard to leave my family. But maybe...maybe, we can go back and forth every six months or something..."

This was painful. Fucking painful. "It's one of the reasons...but not the only reason."

Her eyes lifted to mine.

"There are things you don't know about me, baby. Things I've never told you."

She inhaled a slow breath, her eyes bracing for a punch to the face.

"I'm immortal. And at this moment in time, I've lived one thousand five hundred and twenty-five years. My birthday was last week..."

Now her breaths quickened as her eyes flashed. Inside her body, there was a surge of shock, a stone that disturbed the water.

"Since I never age, and you do…our time together would be very brief."

"What if I were immortal too…?" She wasn't the fiery woman she'd been just a few moments ago. Now she was submissive…and scared.

I shook my head, anticipating those very words. "No."

"No, what?"

"That's not an option."

"Why? We could be together—"

"Immortality comes at an immense cost—the ability to have children and to keep your soul. I've forsaken both to live forever. I know your heart and your mind, and I know that those are things you can't live without. Without your soul, you'll never join your family in the afterlife. You'll never see your parents again after they pass on. And you'll never have children of your own."

She was stunned into silence. Her eyes dropped, and then she rubbed her arm like she was suddenly cold despite the blazing fire beside us. She took a moment to process that information, a darkness in her chest from her despair.

"I'm sorry..." It pained me to say this to her, to crush her spirit. I'd felt her love for me grow every single day, felt mine do the same, as much as I tried to pretend it wasn't real, so this was agony.

Her darkness increased, the blackness stretching from her chest to her limbs, invading her flesh and bone. Her chest rose and fell at a quicker rate, the despair grasping her throat tighter. Then it came...the tears.

I closed my eyes because I couldn't bear it.

Two tears streaked down her cheeks before she clenched her eyes as tightly as she could, as if sheer force would stop more from coming. Her eyes stayed closed as her breathing remained hard. She sniffled and swallowed, doing her best to subdue the reaction that was a hurricane inside her chest.

My eyes remained closed, but I could visualize all of this just from her emotions. I opened my eyes because there was no respite from the horror, no way to shield myself from this unbearable pain.

"You're the man I want...and I can't have you."

I should wipe her tears away with the pads of my thumbs, cradle her face in my hands, kiss her temple to soothe her despair with my affection. But it hurt too much to do that.

"It's not fair…" She sniffled then inhaled a deep breath, her eyes focused on the fire, doing everything she could to stop the tears. She was quiet for a while, bringing her breaths back to normal, restoring a sense of calm. "It's not fucking fair."

"I know…"

As if I wasn't there beside her, she stared at the fire, her cheeks still wet from the tears she'd shed. Now her face looked like stone—and her entire body felt like stone. She was defeated, dead inside.

That was somehow worse.

But then I saw a single flame, a candle that was rekindled after the storm. "My aunt used to be Necrosis…" She turned to look at me. "So was my uncle Bastian. The Bone Witch was able to reverse the magic and make them mortal."

Now I was the one to avert my gaze.

"We can find her and ask her—"

"Baby."

Her words died in her throat, and she seemed to fully understand what I would say next.

"That's a sacrifice I'm not willing to make—and I would never let you make a sacrifice if I'm not willing to do the same." I couldn't look at her as I said it, to tell her that I would rather live forever than have one mortal life with her. "I knew how this would end before it began…and I did my best to protect us both… I failed."

She was quiet.

I didn't want to face her look. I didn't want to see her disappointment. Her hatred.

"It's okay…" Her voice was soft, like flower petals in spring.

My eyes lifted to meet hers.

"I understand."

That somehow hurt more.

The silence was so heavy, it was hard to breathe. Like smoke had filled the room and polluted our lungs. Every breath was more difficult than the last.

Her despair was so distinct, so deep it had no bottom.

"Baby." My hand cupped her soft cheek and directed her stare to me, my thumb in the corner of her mouth. "We still have this time together—so let's enjoy it like it's never going to end. Let's pretend...this is going to last forever." I'd never expected to love another woman again, and I certainly hadn't expected it to happen here, in this forsaken land, with the woman I was supposed to betray. But now my heart was in my throat and my body was numb whenever she was in my presence. Now I cared for someone so deeply that I had something to lose.

Her hand moved over mine, and she turned her cheek to kiss the inside of my palm. "Okay...let's pretend."

Don't miss the dramatic conclusion in **Clash of Kingdoms**.

Printed in Great Britain
by Amazon